Chesapeake Beach, MD

(Present Day) Trinity was tucked in the shadows waiting on Daniels to arrive. She had been preparing for this moment for two years. To Trinity, her life had been on hold, waiting for this moment. Her training with Joshua, honing herself into a lethal weapon. She had been following Daniels for the past week, making sure she understood his movements, patterns and making sure no one was with him. She was now confident that Daniels was alone, living in this two-bedroom flat on the edge of town off Old Colony Cove Rd. There is complete visibility to potential combatants, easy regress routes, and two nondescript vehicles: one in front of the flat and one in the rear.

As Daniels walked from his driveway to the house, he paused as if sensing something was amiss. When he didn't see any danger, he finally moved on with one last glance in the dark alleyway. Joshua had said, "Never underestimate special forces/covert operatives. The most experienced means they have developed a sort of sixth sense that alerts them of impending danger. It is how they survive. Those who do not develop this skill die young." Trinity recognized that that is what caused Daniels to pause. As Daniels resumed his walk toward the flat, Trinity slowly moved out of the shadows behind the old tree and eased into a steady pace following Daniels.

Daniels immediately spotted Trinity. Instead of going to his flat, he led Trinity to an area beside his flat, recognizing another professional. This wasn't a chance meeting. He wanted to have plenty of space to deal with whomever it was. Listening to the person's cadence, he quickly discerned two things:

1) this professional was a woman

2) this woman flowed with a grace that denoted this person has martial arts training.

Daniels learned a long time ago the folly of believing a woman can't be as dangerous as a man. Many men have been killed making that foolish assumption.

As Daniels entered the clearing, he immediately scanned the area looking to see if this woman had any other partners in hiding. Not spotting any, Daniels turned around to confront the mysterious person.

"So, who do I have the honor of meeting? Do you think you're good enough to put me down where so many others have failed finally?" Trinity didn't respond. Instead, she pulled back her hood and removed her hat. Daniels just stared at Trinity, not believing that the gods had finally answered his prayers. The only person he had failed to eliminate was standing before him. Daniels smiled, knowing that his name and reputation as the Grimm Reaper would be intact again. Trinity inwardly smiled. Joshua had told her, let the other person be overly confident.

Don't let them taunt you into making a mistake. Look through them as if they don't matter. Keep an expansive view. Take everything in.

"Finally, bitch! It's time for you to join your dead son. For this honor, I will not even use a weapon. I want to watch the life slip out of you while I strangle you with my bare hands." With that, Daniels removed his shoulder holster, which contained his Glock and two knives hidden in sheaths behind his back, then promptly launched himself at Trinity.

Outer loop Baltimore Beltway, MD

(2 years in the past) Trinity slowly opened her eyes. Her combat medical training five years earlier kicked into motion. Assess the situation; is the environment secure; if secure, slowly evaluate your body for injuries from head to toe before you start moving. As Trinity was going through the checks, the shock of what happened came crashing down on her. She screamed, "Oh my God." The car was flipped upside down in an embankment. Her mind replayed the accident. A black SUV had blindsided her out of nowhere. All she remembered was the Airbags deploying then waking up upside down. "Robbie!" she screamed, suddenly realizing he was in the vehicle with her. Trinity managed to unbuckle her seatbelt, landing awkwardly on her shoulder. She

finally manages to crawl into the backseat, where she sees Robbie's lifeless eyes staring at her. There was a pole protruding from Robbie's chest. Trinity sat there in shock. Unable to move. Unable to cry. She was staring at Robbie in disbelief.

Grimm sat in his black SUV parked down the road like so many other vehicles that had pulled over to see if they could help the victims in the car wreck. Grimm was fuming. Just as he was getting out of the car to ensure his target was dead, he saw a car coming down the road. *Damnit, I've never failed to kill my target, and I'm not going to fail now. I will have to finish her off at the hospital*, thought Grimm. He could do nothing now; too many eyewitnesses had gathered and were assisting his target. Grimm heard an ambulance approaching with sirens blazing. Just as he was pulling away, he noted the name & vehicle number of the ambulance and would have the directorate track which hospital he would need to visit to finish the job.

Sean was not expecting the gruesome scene when he and his partner Pete arrived. Dealing with adults at gruesome accident scenes was a regular occurrence, but seeing a dead kid with a pole protruding from his chest was a different matter. Sean was thinking, *just another reason why I have to find a new job. I can't take this shit anymore.*

4

"Sean, snap out of it man!" Pete yelled. "We got a lady pretty beat up here. Let's hustle and see if we can save at least one of them."

Sean and Pete were with Ladder Co. 51 out of Woodhaven. They were part of the rescue squad. It's a good thing that we were the team dispatched, thought Pete. "Only the Jaws of Life will help us reach this poor lady in time to save her life."

Trinity arrived at Mercy Medical Center, immobilized. She remembered how efficient the doctors were discussing her condition. Trinity had a fractured right femur and a broken arm. She had several cracked ribs from being tossed around the vehicle as it rolled. One of the ribs had punctured and deflated her right lung. The paramedics had stated, had she not been wearing her seat belt, she would have been killed instantly. The driver's side roof was crushed down to the door handle by a boulder. The doctors say she was fortunate to be alive.

After the anesthesia wore off, Trinity awoke in the ICU of Mercy General. She immediately noticed the cast immobilizing parts of her body. When Trinity took a breath, she realized her ribs were broken or cracked. The nurse at the ICU duty station noticed Trinity's monitor flashing, indicating she had awakened. As Nurse Carol made her way over to Trinity's bed, she had another dose of sedatives prepared to sedate Trinity. The doctor on call had provided Carol with a specific regiment to make sure Trinity was not in too much pain.

"Good evening Ms. Winters. How are you feeling?" asked Carol. "Truthfully, I feel like shit. Like someone dropped a piano on me and at the same time ripped my heart out. The pain is bearable, but the thought of losing my son is just too much to bear." At that point, Trinity started crying uncontrollably. Nurse Carol immediately injected the syringe into Trinity's IV bag. A few minutes later, Trinity's crying subsided as she drifted back to sleep. Nurse Carol could only shake her head at the agony she knew Ms. Winters was experiencing, to lose a child at such an early age and in such a tragic way. She had seen so much working in the Mercy General ICU. She knew this tragedy would forever haunt Ms. Winters. So, for now, Nurse Carol's only thought, keep Trinity sedated to give her wounds time to heal and her mind a break from reality.

Down the hall, Grimm was waiting in a supply closet. He had just stolen a nurse's uniform, preparing to finish the job he started. Grimm had never missed a target before in his life, and he was not about to start now. Grimm had his syringe ready, stored in his pocket. Grimm would have preferred just to cut his target's throat to end her life, but his orders were to make the death appear natural; hence, the botched car accident. A simple 50 caliber round through the skull was Grimm's preferred method of eliminating targets. While Grimm was an expert in almost every weapon made and virtually a master in Aikido and Krav Maga, he chose not to take any chances. Why leave it to chance with an up-close encounter? Grimm had long since given up on the notion that there was glory in looking someone in the eyes as they died. It's a job. The only thing that matter was that the target was dead. The best way to accomplish this was with a 50-caliber round between the eyes. *Hell*, Grimm thought. *A 50 caliber round anywhere would virtually destroy the target.* As a matter of professionalism, Grimm preferred a single bullet to the skull.

Grimm's thoughts came back to the job at hand. *While not the fastest way to kill someone, air bubbles in her veins would produce the desired effect*, thought Grimm. Injecting air in her veins will form bubbles like putting air in water. However, bubbles in your veins have nowhere to go but toward your heart/lungs. There, they will circulate to other organs via the arteries causing an air embolism. These bubbles can cause obstructions at some of the small arteries causing heart attacks and strokes. *With all of the other injuries his target sustained, death was all but certain*, thought Grimm. That's why doctors and nurses flick the needle to remove the air bubble. *In my case, my target will get 50cc of air to finish her off finally.*

The nurses had just changed shifts. Grimm observed that the new nurse was not as thorough as the previous one. He had already fallen asleep twice in the past hour, the last episode lasting 15 minutes. It was now 3:00 AM. Grimm had made his way over to his target's bed. Grimm had removed the IV and had placed the syringe into his target's arm. Grimm sent the "Go Code" to the Directorate. He waited for the final "Go" on his mission.

Approximately 350 miles away at the Directorate Headquarters, Colonel Carl Myers watched the Threat Board. After updating the Committee, as "they" were called, the mysterious nine individuals approved all actions of the Directorate. Myers never saw the faces of the individuals who gave him orders. During his in-briefing, it was explained that their faces would always be grayed out for operational security. Myers did know there were six men and three women, which made up the Committee. The Committee had given Myers full latitude on how to deal with Winters. With the death of her child, they felt she was no longer a threat to operational security, but if Myers felt the need to eliminate her, it was approved. Myers continued to watch the Threat Board. With 12 active engagements on the board, Myers felt Winters was the least of his worries. He finally gave the code to the analyst, indicating the mission was no longer necessary.

As Grimm reattached the IV, he was not happy. He felt betrayed. The opportunity to keep his record intact slipped through his fingers. While Grimm was upset, he in no way was going to cross the Directorate. That was paramount to suicide. Grimm looked down at this target. "Let sleeping dogs lie, my dear. You might have survived this day, but if you ever cross the line again, I will be there waiting for you." Grimm quickly turned and departed just as silently as he came in.

Trinity was very sedated, but through the fog, she heard a man talking to her. As she opened her eyes, she caught a glimpse of a man that looked to be in his late 30's. She couldn't make out much of his features because of drugs, but she did see a distinctive scar that ran from his left cheek to his chin. With that image, Trinity drifted off again.

Anacostia, Southeast Washington, D.C

Another session with the agency's shrink. HLSORD (Homeland Security Operational Response Division), sometimes just called ORD for short, had a strict mental readiness policy before allowing agents to return to work. Dr. Ann Brussels didn't believe Trinity was ready to assume her duties at HLSORD. She wrote in Trinity's medical file. *Patient is in denial about the death of her son, Robbie. After the funeral, I believe Trinity suffered a mild psychotic break from reality, in my medical opinion. In Trinity's case, her symptoms were being manifested through her depression. While not dangerous and, to be honest, perfectly natural, based on our operational guidelines, I recommend another 3 months of therapy sessions to ensure she is mentally stable to return to the rigors of her job.*

As an analyst for ORD, Dr. Brussels continued, *too much sensitive information is processed, and momentary lapses in concentration could mean the difference between a successful terrorist attack vs. a thwarted attempt.* When Dr. Brussels was asked to join ORD, it was described to her as being the tip of the spear designed to deal with threats which required, in some cases, to act first and question the right of the action later. While protecting the constitutional rights of U.S. citizens was a priority, ORD believed that granting those rights to non-US citizens was not only foolish but downright criminal, especially when given to a suspected terrorist. As Dr. Brussels closed Trinity's files and thought, *I agree with ORD's philosophy, or I never would have joined. Now I'm responsible for upholding those governing regulations for ORD's agents.*

Dr. Brussels mused, *if only I believed what I wrote. In truth, I'm not sure if Trinity will ever recover, but I have to give her the benefit of the doubt. After failing to become a Field Operative and now her son's death, one more failure could be the tipping point for Trinity. The last thing I want to do was to put Trinity on suicide watch. That would be the end of her career and a massive loss for the agency.*

Trinity was sitting in a chair staring blankly at the T.V. She watched some mindless reality show about surviving global catastrophes. She was holding her fifth glass of gin and tonic. Feeling numb, Trinity thought she could finally face the truth again. She thought, Truthfully, I just don't care anymore. Does it really matter if I live or not? Who will miss me? My life is in shambles. Robbie is dead. I just buried my son less than 2 months ago. My right side still hurts from my broken ribs. Although I should be thankful that my other injuries have healed, it just doesn't matter. Phillip, Robbie's father, continuously calls me and blames me for killing our son. While we were married, he was an SOB, and everyone would be happy to know that hasn't changed. What an ass! Trinity could no longer avoid the truth somewhere deep inside. She felt responsible for Robbie's death. She hated Phillip for being an asshole and knew his accusations were the only thing that kept her from just ending it now.

Trinity continued to finish off her gin. She thought about her life and her career. One failed marriage, one dead child, and one stalled career. To be honest, why are they even keeping me on at ORD? …. Dr. Brussels, Trinity thought. I like Dr.

Brussels. She genuinely cares, but she can't help me. I am doomed, and she knows it too. She just doesn't want to pull the trigger yet and permanently end my career. It just doesn't matter though. My job doesn't matter because my life doesn't matter anymore. I couldn't even pass the selection process for being a field agent. I'm a lowly analyst because some bureaucrats probably thought I looked good and needed to fill a quota. As the gin started to numb her thoughts, a nagging thought kept playing at the corner of her mind. Something wasn't right.

In the past, Trinity had always trusted the feeling because, more times than not, it had served her well. Trinity called this feeling her sixth sense. Trinity was proud that she trusted her intuition. Most people did not. She felt she had developed hers into almost a tool that gave her a decisive advantage, but she tried to ignore it, but the "something's not right" itch just wouldn't go away. Her mind kept analyzing the events of the past month, mainly the half-dream of the man in her hospital room walking away while she was heavily medicated. She couldn't shake the feeling that somehow that stranger held her life in the balance.

It had been 3 months since Dr. Brussels cleared Trinity to start working again. Trinity knew she wasn't ready, but she felt a kindred spirit with her. Somehow, she felt Dr. Brussels sympathized with her situation and instinctively knew working was the one thing that would keep her from becoming suicidal. As Trinity was drinking her morning tea at her desk, she mused just how close she came to ending it all after the tragedy of her son. She silently thanked Dr. Brussels for giving her another chance at life. Trinity thought while she knew the immediate danger was over, she still had a long way to go to recover. To that thought, she had been looking for something to feel that void. At first, she thought it would be in finding another relationship. She went through the motions of joining dating sites and trying the dating scene. All her dates ended the same way… miserable failures. What is it with guys these days? They think just because they take you to dinner a few times, they can charm their way into your pants. After the last guy, Trinity had deactivated her profiles. She had thought the last guy might be ok, so after the fifth date, Trinity started opening up to Andy.

Trinity just sat at her desk, staring at her search results, thinking that Andy's immediate solution to her opening up was to have sex. He said sex would solve her problems. Give her something to get over Robbie because he was awesome in bed, and since she hadn't had sex since Robbie's father, she had forgotten how good it could be. Trinity remembered her response, "Really Andy? Is that what you think? I just told you I feel responsible for my son's death, and all you can say is you're so good in bed that I will forget about my life being a fucking mess. Get the fuck out of my house!!!!" Trinity went so far as to pick up the phone and dial 911 before Andy understood she was serious and that his charm wouldn't work on her.

Trinity looked back at her internet search results. She had been looking unsuccessfully for the past week since the Andy incident. She had been coming into work early as a means to escape reality. Today, she tried a new sequence of words in the search engine: suicide, stress, rebirth, life-changing, finding a new path to life. Finding a new path to life led her to a website about this guy, Joshua, who taught Martial Arts, more specifically Tai Chi. His site discussed concepts about changing one's life by reconnecting with the universe. Today, the body is out of balance because society doesn't give us the tools necessary to cope with modern-day stress. As she kept reading, Trinity started to connect with his philosophies on life. She then clicked on the about me menu to understand who Joshua was a little better. She was surprised at how much Joshua had been through in his life. He had been accepted into the hardest college in the U.S., The United States Military Academy at West Point. He served with distinction in both the 1st Gulf War and the Somalia Conflict, plus two hot spots in Egypt/Israel and Honduras/El Salvador/Nicaragua. He served as a Special Forces Officer, including Airborne, Air Assault, Sniper, Pathfinder,

Sapper, and SERE (Survival, Evasion, Resistance, & Escape) Schools. Joshua discussed how he did the typical thing upon getting out of the military. These paths lead to a successful corporate career, filled with stress that eventually nearly killed him. He discussed this journey of getting back in balance mentally, physically, & spiritually. He used Tai Chi to initially find his path that eventually led to, what he called, the "Universal Path." Joshua discussed 3 focal points of Tai Chi: Health, Meditation, and Martial Arts. Joshua stated, he had trained in other styles of Martial Arts, the study of Kung Fu has been the most rewarding. It fully addressed the issues that were going on in his life, not just the physical workout that he was craving, but a process to focus on learning to balance the mental and spiritual demands of life. Joshua wrote, in detail, about his journey of discovery as he dabbled in Buddhism, Taoism, and finally, what lead him to what he calls the Universal Path. The more Trinity read the more she was convinced that she should try Tai Chi. While she was skeptical about Tai Chi because of the stereotype associated with it being for old people, she still felt compelled to try it. Little did Trinity know, her life would forever be changed through this interaction with Joshua.

Anacostia, Southeast Washington, D.C

Trinity sat at her computer, going over the audit log. It was the first time she had conducted this required task since her return. A lot had happened in the past six months. It had been three months since her training had begun with Joshua. While she wasn't back to her usual self, she at least felt like living again. So far, training had focused on learning the basics of Tai Chi, from relearning how to walk to techniques like "Wave Hands Like Cloud." Occasionally Joshua would discuss concepts about living a balanced life. Trinity reflected on her first meeting with Joshua. It had gone quite differently than planned.

"Come in," Joshua said. "Have a seat and tell me how I can help you." Trinity took a seat in Joshua's office and immediately noticed the ambiance of the office. Joshua was playing what sounded like some new-age music. It was so soothing that I started the meeting by asking, "What is that music?" Joshua smiled and said, "You like? So do I. The song is "Afternoon Ceremony" by La Vita." "Thank You," replied Trinity.

"So, I take it your name is Trinity Winters," stated Joshua as he got up to shake Trinity's hand. "It's my pleasure to me you." "No, Joshua, the pleasure is mine." Sitting back down, Joshua said, "So once again, how can I help you?" Trinity had

decided she had nothing to lose. She was at her wits' end.
Nothing else had worked so far. Her research gave her hope that
maybe Joshua could help her. The testimonies on his website
gave her hope. He describes the "Universal Path" or the
"Universal Way" as an approach to life that seemed to ring true.
The one thing the testimonials all said was to be truthful with
Joshua upfront. Even if you were not, somehow, he figured out
the truth. One testimonial quoted Joshua "Through movement, I
can discern a lot about the problems in your life." So what do
I have to lose? I'm already lost. "Well, to be truthful,
Joshua, I don't know where to begin. I'm at my wits' end. I'm
hopelessly lost. My life is in shambles. My son recently died.
My ex-husband blames me for his death. I'm barely hanging on to
my job. To top it off, I'm developing a drinking problem, and I
fight every day not to end my life."

Trinity remembered the look in Joshua's eyes as he sat back
and just stared. He didn't say anything for the longest time.
It was almost as if he was looking not just at me but through
me, seeing inside my soul. As if he were assessing some inner
quality to see if I was worthy of his help. It was the most
uncomfortable feeling. Thinking back, it felt akin to being
naked, exposed…truly exposed for the first time in her life.
Finally, Joshua broke eye contact and said, "I will take you on
as a student, but I don't just take on anyone. When I take on a

student, there has to be something in it for me also. When I teach, I also learn. I learn just as much, if not more, from this shared journey. Make no mistake, Trinity; you have problems, real problems. You didn't get broken overnight, so don't expect to be healed overnight. I will start off giving you what you want until one day; you will be ready to accept what you need." Joshua then sat back and said, "So Trinity, what are you looking for from me?" At first, the question caught her off guard, but the answer was simple as she thought about it. "I want peace Joshua, true lasting peace so I can feel balance again in my life." "Good answer. Now let's begin. After our first session is over today, we will come back to the office and discuss financials. Make no mistake; you can't afford what I am going to do for you. You can't put a value on someone's life. At some point, the price you are paying me will become immaterial, but for now, I will work with you to come up with a rate that you can both afford and compensates me for my time. So, remove your shoes and put them on the floor, and let's begin by stretching."

That memory snapped Trinity back to the task at hand, the computer audit. Since training with Joshua, she now felt more energized. While not entirely better, at least the thoughts of ending it all were now at bay. There were moments when she could almost discern a pattern to the training Joshua was putting her through. Unlike other martial art schools, Joshua believed training, if done correctly, became an individual journey. He said that as I progressed, my training would become more customized.

Joshua designed each phase to bring out a specific response that would enhance a student's development. She recalled how Joshua said that the body has everything within itself to heal itself. We have to shut down the active brain to allow us to access the universal knowledge source to begin this journey of healing. These slow movements of Tai Chi were starting to have an effect. As frustrating as it was, Trinity learned to shut down the active brain even while hearing Joshua constantly say, breathe, relax. Of late, the process of thinking through problems felt more natural. The goal of feeling balanced no longer seemed impossible. Joshua said there would be moments of clarity when everything seemed almost to make sense. When this happens, don't be fooled into thinking all is okay. For now, these moments will be fleeting. We still have a long journey, but that is the beauty of it all. It is not about the destination but the journey. While balance will be the result of your dedication and hard work, enjoy the moments of discovery. There is no rush to an end state.

Sitting with her earbuds in, listening to a playlist that Joshua had created for her, what started as a tedious process to catch up on ten months of work started taking on a different feel. "Enjoy the moment," she heard Joshua saying. "Breathe and relax. You will be amazed at what happens when you embrace this simple process." Closing her eyes for a moment and just sitting there breathing, "Afternoon Ceremony" started playing again.

A smile slowly began to form. Trinity opened her eyes, the task of performing the audit started in earnest. Her fingers just flowed, crunching through volumes of data. A month's worth of work that someone else in the agency should have done but didn't. That didn't matter anymore. The battle had begun. Joshua made everything about doing battle. He said the battle is everything, and at the same time when you become a Peaceful Warrior, the battle becomes meaningless. One of his favorite quotes is, "When you change the way you look at things, the things you look at will change in response" - Wayne Dyer.

It was at that moment that an anomaly in the logs showed up. It might be nothing, but what did it hurt to explore it. Now that the battle had begun, Joshua counseled to embrace it. Fight with everything you have. Use your anger to fuel decisive action, more meaningful action. Joshua said that fear stops us, paralyzes us because society has taught us it is wrong to show anger. So in trying to live by society's laws, we suppress a very powerful part of our persona, the Hulk, as he calls it. We no longer live a balanced life because society frowns upon anyone that shows anger. We introduce schizophrenia in our lives without knowing it. We should be one person, but many of us have a business face and a personal face. Joshua believes that when properly utilized, that anger makes us very powerful. Allowing us to take on challenges we usually would shy away from, to have meaningful actions versus living in fear of the unknown.

While not overpowering, Trinity was still kind of pissed that she was being held accountable to complete ten months' worth of computer audits. If the audits were necessary, they would have been done long before now. Oh well. Embracing the battle, Trinity dug into the bad sectors on her hard drive.

20 minutes later, Trinity was convinced someone had deliberately altered the files on her computer. Perplexed, she just sat there trying to figure out why. What was even more troubling was that the bad sectors showed up the day after her accident. That made no sense because her computer should not have been in use. Trinity accessed the backup server to see if she could recover the bad sector. An hour later proved to Trinity that whoever had tapered her hard drive had at least render all recovery efforts fruitless unless she sent the hard drive out for recovery. Considering the MIL Standard deletion

programs employed by the agency, sending out the hard drive would probably be useless.

"Time to conduct a forensic analysis of what I was working on before the accident," thought Trinity. Combing through emails and audit logs, Trinity was pretty sure she had narrowed down her activities to an email she had intercepted from an anonymous, untraceable source into the office of the Vice President of the United States. Trinity recalled that the email had so far been traced through 300 servers across the globe before the trace just ended. As far as she knew, only the NSA had the level of technology necessary to stop a trace program dead in its tracks. When she had sent a coded inquiry through the official channels, the request was returned coded NIWF (No Information Will Follow), which meant it was either a hands-off matter or, as usually is the case, they didn't know. This anomaly was getting more and more troubling.

How to proceed? *Follow protocol*; the thought came to Trinity.

Gaithersburg, Maryland

Joshua just stared at Trinity. Finally, he said, "I can't take it any longer. What is wrong with you? Sit down." So, in the middle of the floor, both Joshua and Trinity sat cross-legged. "Don't say anything; listen to me, Trinity. You came in here six months ago seeking help. While you appear less stressed out on the surface, inside, you're still out of balance."

"Up until now, I haven't pried. I figured you would eventually open up. Well, I can see that's not the case. So, you need to listen. Your aura is so screwed up right now, and it's stressing me out. Your energy is so erratic; I can only imagine what's going on in your head.

Joshua started to tell Trinity a little about his life and how he got to this point in his life. "Trinity, from the beginning, my life has had tragedies. My mother had four kids. Who knows what happened and where my father was? I vaguely remember my mom living from one situation to another. I distinctly remember living with one man in particular. His name was Charles. I remember he had this very cool and elaborate train set in the attic of his house. The only problem with the train set is that we played with it together after he had beat my brother or me with an extension cord. My mother's situation was complicated within the family. One day, my Great Aunt and Uncle sent for my brother and me to live with them. I still remember that day clearly because I cried all day when the plane landed, and my aunt picked us up. It wasn't that my aunt and uncle were mean; they just weren't my mom. I remembered that they did everything in their power to keep me from crying, but nothing worked. My brother seemed okay, but whereas my pain was outward, he kept his internal. His life, I will save for another day, another situation on what happens when you suppress.

At the end of that day, I finally stopped crying. For a five-year-old, I was pretty weird, for lack of a better word, very unique in my views of the world. I processed information differently from other kids, even adults. At this point, I knew living in TN was now my life. I just had to accept that these people were now my life, my family. They loved me, so while I wasn't with my mom, I was better off than so many other kids. Another weird thing happened that day; I picked up a permanent resident, a voice in my head. Most kids have imaginary friends; well, once again, here is where I differ. My friend actually took an active role in raising me. It gave me advice. It told me when I was doing things right or wrong. It even disciplined me from time to time.

I know you might find this hard to believe, so let me show you a scar. I was doing something terrible, and it told me to stop. I wouldn't stop, so after the 3rd warning, it disciplined me by hitting me one time across the leg, literally. I now have a permanents black line across the inside of my left thigh. I remembered crying out, and my aunt came rushing into the room and asked, "What is wrong?" I told her that something spanked me. She said no one is in the room and that I must have just imagined it. I then showed her my scar, and she wrote it off as an injury I sustained while playing.

I'm sure by now you're wondering what the fuck. Where is this going? That you're training with a crazy man. The point of this whole story is to tell you in my head; I felt this entity was real. It taught me not to crave materialist things as a child because the "want" of things would hurt my aunt and Uncle because they couldn't afford it. They were both older and retired. They lived in rural TN, where great jobs were not aplenty, so retirement consisted of a monthly social security check. When my guardian angel, or resident passenger in my head, finally got me to understand the difference between a need and a want, things weren't as bad. When I had my first birthday party in TN, my guardian angel told me to tell my aunt and uncle that I didn't want another party again. They were perplexed by my strange behavior but didn't question it. I secretly believe they were conflicted because while they wanted to give us everything, they just couldn't. Even during Christmas, I had only two things I ever asked for as a child: a small portable TV and a telescope, which they got for me using a layaway plan. My guardian angel worked hard, in the beginning, to help me understand that these things were not significant. Once again, you're asking why the story? My guardian angel told me my mission was to train to become a warrior, the last of a dying breed.

From the moment I was told I was in training to be a warrior as defined by my resident passenger: a scholar, a gentleman, and a fighter, my entire life has been developed to that purpose. It trained me early and put me on a path that led to my acceptance to the United States Military Academy at West Point. I also completed some of the military's most demanding training: Airborne School, Pathfinder School, S.E.R.E., Sapper School, Jungle Warfare, Desert Warfare, Artic Warfare, Ranger School, & Special Forces Training. I served in two wars and two hot spots. My training is still classified to this day. When I leave this country for overseas travel and come back, I am flagged. Whereas an average person can go through customs without issues, it usually takes 1 to 2 hours. I am passed from customs agent to a supervisor and, finally, the head customs officer because they don't know how to deal with my special designation. Finally, because of the head customs officer's clearance, they clear me back into the country. One of my previous bosses didn't believe me until he finally flew with me on an overseas trip.

I have been married and divorced. I have been morbidly obese. I suffered for years because I couldn't take being a warrior any longer. I got tired of the responsibility of helping people, leading people, so I retreated from life. While married to my wife, I lived in the spare guest room for most of the ten years. I maybe had sex with her a few times a year. There were days that I would work up to 20 hours a day. I averaged working 16 hours. I would wake up with my heart fluctuating wildly in anticipation of my stressful workday.

The one thing the military taught me well was how to survive. Not live, but to survive, and I did that well. Survival comes with a price, and I paid for it dearly, almost with my life.

By running away from my destiny, my resident passenger in my head punished me. Let me explain. When we are born, the universe laid out an infinite set of possibilities/paths by which we could live our lives. However, there is only one optimal path to live. When we grow up, society starts teaching us all these rules we are supposed to live by: from the government to schools, with its incomplete history, or should I say, one-sided narrative to the dogma of religion. All these rules and laws are a system of control designed to keep individuals from reaching their full potential. To coin a movie, we live in the Matrix. We start living a life that society tells us is right for us: go to college, work, get married, have two kids, buy a house, save for retirement, and so

forth.   We have forgotten how to live.   We have become robots.
We learn to become complacent as to fit in with everyone else.

Most people have issues with this existence but develop
various coping mechanisms from drinking to exercising to
religion, drugs, and a periodic vacation.   When we hit a crisis
point, and our very soul tells us that our life is wrong, we
turn to one of these coping mechanisms. 80% of the population
will live this way, finding a delicate balance between living by
societies' laws and managing their reactions to each crisis
point.   10% of the population will self-destruct because they
can no longer cope with society.   They become drug addicts, sex
addicts, alcoholics, murders, or they will simply commit suicide
and end it all.   The other 10% will seek a different path, the
path of enlightenment.

Enlightenment doesn't mean this mystical stuff that everyone
attaches to it.   Enlightenment means seeking knowledge
elsewhere.   As Morpheus would say, take the red pill and see how
far down the matrix goes.   Unfortunately, it usually takes some
dramatic event in our lives to push us to this point where we
question our existence.   The drama is generally so severe that
the tools for coping will not work.   For a time, the person
might even follow the path of destruction, seeking an escape.

When I hit this point, it was right after 9-11.   I was
supposed to be in the city working around Liberty Plaza.   I

could have been killed that day, like so many others. After the event, I finally had to ask myself, "What am I doing with my life?" My friend, an ex-military man also, told me about this Kung Fu master, who was the real deal. He begged me to train with him. So, one day, six months later, I finally went to his martial arts school. This school changed my life forever. I am still striving to get back to my optimal path, but I no longer live in the Matrix.

When we become complacent, we make what we think are the right decisions, but in reality, we are making what the universe says are the easier wrong choices in life. These decisions cause our lives to continue in a loop where we are doomed to repeat constantly, if not the same, similar activities/makes in our lives. It is like Ground Hog Day with Bill Murray. We can't seem to move forward. We feel like we are stuck in time. We are always dating the same type of people, and the relationships all end the same way. We end up with the same kind of job, constantly frustrated. We can't seem to get ahead no matter what we do. Our lives are in a constant circle.

I call this the "Cycle of Crisis." When we finally make what seems like the more challenging right choice versus the easier wrong choice that has put our lives in this cycle, meaningful things start happening. Our lives start changing. Initially, it will feel like a salmon swimming upstream because we are doing things outside of our comfort zone, so we instinctively want to go back to the old way of doing things. However, the more we stick with this path, the easier decisions become. It will no longer feel like we are making the harder right choice. It will become the only choice. Our lives become more straightforward as we start to live the optimal path.

I now live a life that leads me toward my optimal path. People say, "Joshua, you're the luckiest man I know." I look at them and just smile. It only seems lucky, but breaking away, unplugging from the Matrix, takes courage, a commitment to oneself to stop betraying life. We have one life to live. We can either waste it or be true to the values that the universe has laid out before us and live the life we want to live. To embrace a set of principles that allow reason to dictate the course of our lives by becoming a person that thinks versus blindly following what society tells us we should be doing.

Trinity, you are at a nexus point in your life. You have to make a decision right here, right now, about the direction your life will go. I don't know what that decision is. That, you have to make, but make it you must, or we might as well stop training now. The conflict I feel from you is so great that I'm getting a vibe that we have to resolve this conflict, or our future training together will be time wasted.

At this point, Joshua stopped talking and just stared at Trinity. Trinity thought about what Joshua had said. She felt better than she had in a long time since training with Joshua, and she didn't want it to end. However, she was conflicted because working for Homeland Security's Operational Response Division was classified beyond Top Secret. To even mention its existence would result in jail time. This act would be classified as treason against the United States. Treason in this country is still punishable by death. Only a handful of people in the government knew about ORD. Even the POTUS is buffered between the decisions made by ORD, plausible denial. ORD's job was to stop a terrorist attack from ever happening. Basically, the United States would never suffer another 9-11 if ORD did its job, even if it meant violating the constitutional rights of individuals who were citizens of the United States. ORD's job was to make sure the country of the United States survived, even if it meant making terrorists, citizens, or government officials disappear. No one was above the law except the operatives of Homeland Security's Operational Response Division.

While creating ORD's mandate, the President had issued blank Presidential Pardons for future crimes for its operatives. Trinity quickly assessed the actual problem. If ORD had unlimited power, then the group she was tracking was without bounds. They were more powerful than the mandate that created ORD. This scared Trinity, and if she brought Joshua into the mix, what would be next. Mentioning what was going on to Joshua could not only put her in jail but him also.

Tears stood in her eyes as Joshua continued to stare at her. Ending things with Joshua was frankly unthinkable. This man has helped me where everyone else has failed. He single-handedly brought me back from the abyss. "I feel alive again around him," she thought. I don't feel the weight of the world anymore. I feel his energy when he is near. It's like a physical presence that precedes him when he walks in the room and when he touches me, I feel an electric jolt running through my body. "What else can this man teach me? It didn't hurt either that he was a handsome man." Well built, solid, not a weightlifter, but all muscles. His training kept him in incredible shape.

She finally looked up and said, "Joshua, I've made up my mind. I want to live the life I was meant to live." Trinity then proceeded to tell Joshua everything that had happened. Joshua sat there. He nodded periodically and occasionally asked questions. When she finally finished, Joshua asked, "So, what did Sam say when you followed protocol?" "He said the inquiry is over. Cease further investigation." Trinity recalled the conversation she had yesterday. "Sam, that's stupid! I'm close to finally putting meaning to the death of my son possibly, and you are telling me to drop it." "Yes." "Why? There is a connection Sam. If you just let me investigate further, I can prove it." "Trinity, you are grasping for straws. There is no connection.

Furthermore, I read your psych eval. While you finally passed, I understand you are still borderline depressed, and Dr. Brussels has given you a standing prescription for Zoloft. There is no connection between your accident and the so-called anomaly on your computer. Do I make myself clear?"

"Trinity, I sent your computer off to the lab to see if they could pull the information from the bad sector, and guess what? You were correct. There was a bad sector on your hard drive. The problem was, you were so focused on this one sector and trying to ascribe meaning to it, you ignored all the other bad sectors. Simply put, you had a corrupt hard drive. That's why you have a new computer." I say their thinking I'm crazy. I am getting stone walled. I stumbled onto something, something big to make the Director cower. Trinity recalled a lesson from Joshua when he quoted one of his favorite authors. "Sometimes knowing when not to fight is just as important as knowing how to fight." -Terry Goodkind. Joshua went on to say, "You need to understand how to deny the enemy the battle." Up until then, Trinity had thought of Sam as a friend and supporter. Now she categorized Sam as an enemy. "You're right, Sam," Trinity had said. "I've been working hard lately catching up, to be truthful. I'm due for a follow-up visit to see Dr. Brussels. I am approaching the first anniversary of Robbie's death, and it is affecting me. I don't want his death to be meaningless, just a freak accident". "Who does Trinity?" "Thanks for doing as much as you did, Sam. I appreciate you going through the process to address my concerns, not just as my boss, but as my friend."

Joshua said, "So do you believe him?" "No," was all she said. "Now I know what I saw in your aura earlier. I know what the conflict was. Thank you, Trinity, for sharing and being honest with me." All of a sudden, Trinity stopped talking and recalled the incident in the hospital with the man in black. She remembered seeing him before drifting off from the pain medication.

Joshua looked at her and said, "What was that just now? What just happened? What were you thinking?" Trinity told Joshua what she had just been thinking about the incident in the hospital. "Trinity, there is no such thing as coincidence. These seemingly unrelated events will come together to answer us when we are prepared to hear the answer. This is the universe's way of revealing something significant. In this case, it has to do with what happened that day you were hit and wrecked your car. The day Robbie died. Why now, Trinity? Why would I challenge you today to make a decision, or our training would

cease? Why did you get into an argument with Sam yesterday?
Why think of the incident that happened at the hospital? The
way Joshua described things all made sense. There was a pattern.
You have to shut down the active mind, and the truth will reveal
itself. "So what now, Joshua?" "To be honest, I don't know. It
depends on how much you truly want to find the answers to what
happened that day. "I will tell you, Trinity, I saw some things
while I was in Special Forces that didn't make any sense. Some
of our orders seemed like they caused more harm than good. I did
my best to be a patriot, but each deployment made me question
why I am here. I was out of balance with myself and the
universe. I finally had to admit that the military lifestyle
was no longer meant for me." When we fought in the 2nd war in
Iraq, it was about keeping balance in that region so no one
power would gain too much control over the world's oil. So we
fought Iraq. The funny thing, we helped train Iraqi's and
equipped them to keep Iran at bay. "While that is the game, it
was my last mission objectives that finally broke my fighting
spirit. My team was deployed with rebels waiting to stop the
slaughter of tens of thousands of innocent civilians caught in
the middle of a sectarian civil war. We were tasked to take out
several faction leaders. We were set to go in that very night
and eliminate the most brutal faction leader, Abu Hafez Al-
Sheik. We were positioned to move when a group of rebels in

technicals ran down a group of women and children. I had my team aim, and I had just called in for final authority to engage. Only it wasn't given. My finger was on the trigger, yet I couldn't fire. Not 10 meters in front of me, I watched helplessly as a boy probably eight years old die while a bullet pierced the back of his head and exploded out the front." Trinity saw the tears openly rolling down Joshua's cheeks as he told this story. The emotions were still raw.

At the time, I couldn't understand why the go-ahead was never given. I found out later through an old CIA buddy that Abu Hafez Al-Sheik had just promised Axion Corporation Int'l unrestricted access and protection to a potential uranium mine. When the dust settled, it turned out the mine was worthless. So instead of stopping one of the most brutal warlords in Iraqi in the wake of Saddam Hussein's fall, we allowed Abu Hafez Al-Sheik to slaughter, torture, and rape tens of thousands of innocent people. I will never forgive myself to this day and probably for the rest of my life because I still see that boy's head exploding right in front of me, and I know I could have stopped it. I will forever blame myself for not pulling that trigger and taking out the gunner, but I was a good soldier following orders.

Well never again. That's when I resigned from my commission. I'm sorry, Trinity. I guess I still have a ways to go to make peace with myself and the universe." Joshua wiped the remaining tears without a trace of self-consciousness. "After hearing your story, now my story makes more sense." "I always thought the decisions that our government makes are not always in the best interest of our country. Well, that's maybe because our government is not making some of the decisions being made." "You heard all of the conspiracy nut jobs out there talking about shadow governments. I guess they were not too far off."

"Trinity, if what I believe is happening, then you need to make a decision, and it's not the one I thought you needed to make when I first started speaking with you earlier. I truly believe your life is in danger. I believe your son's death was not an accident. You being alive is the accident. They fucked-up Trinity. Only through the intervention of higher-level forces are you still alive. The car accident. The visitation in the hospital. Now you tell me they confiscated your computer. You need to make a decision. Either you drop this immediately, or you need to be prepared to take this fight wherever it might lead." "We are finished for the day. Let's reconnect tomorrow and see where your head's at after a night's sleep."

Anacostia, Southeast Washington, DC

"Expect nothing but be prepared for everything" – Terry Goodkind. Joshua had said this quote many times. She was doing her best to act normal and have the same routine. This was a difficult skill to master because Trinity knew she was being watched. While it was nothing overt, she was sure her new workstation ran slower than her previous workstation. She thought this was illogical.

1. The new machine was more powerful, had more RAM and a faster processor.

2. When she was performing audit logs, she kept noticing ghosts in the machine, for lack of a better word. At first, she thought nothing of it. In her conversations with her colleagues and after a few visits from IT, which turned up nothing, she started getting the itch that something wasn't right. Joshua had told her to learn to trust her senses and stop relying on what man has taught her. Get out of your mind, he would say. Our brain is a marvelous tool when used correctly. Still, the problem is we have to deprogram ourselves from all the bullshit that caused us to have limited thinking capacity. When you come to your senses, you will be less compliant with man's laws and start following the universal path.

After the last few months of training with Joshua, Trinity was sure that someone was monitoring her activities. While alarming, Trinity still went about her day looking for possible terrorist activities. However, her research included areas of industrial activities that she previously wouldn't have paid any attention to. Trinity began to cast a net to review international conglomerates that spanned weapons manufacturing to pharmaceutical manufacturing. It was getting difficult to keep track of the connections, but she was starting to see a common thread. Joshua told Trinity to keep all of her information over his place because he was sure her place was being monitored electronically. Joshua had dedicated his "Oh Shit, the world is being overrun by Zombie's room" to her. This room was accessed through a hidden compartment through Joshua's basement. Joshua had built it with the help of one of his military engineer buddies. It was lined with 2" of lead, 2" of steel, and 1' of reinforced concrete. The outer surface of the room also functioned as a Faraday cage, shielding the electronic components from electromagnetic pulses or as commonly known as EMP. The room was 25' x 25'. It had its own backup generator kept in a soundproof section of the room with an exhaust system. The room could be powered by the solar array that Joshua had installed on his home's roof. The walled-off section of the room also contained its own water purification system. While disgusting, it recycled urine and water from the shower unit. It also had the ability to capture rainwater. Joshua stated the room was designed to operate with no outside air for up to 3

Trinity - The Awakening 2nd Addition

months with built-in CO2 scrubbers. That was a failsafe Joshua had said. Based on all the modifications, Joshua made sure he could live comfortably for 6 months to a year without any outside resupplies.

Joshua had a well-stocked supply of MRE's; can food: soups, vegetables, fruits & meats; flour; various oils; beef jerky; nuts; & water. In addition to the twin bed in the corner of the room, he installed a 37" flat-screen TV with a Blu-ray DVD player with a wide selection of DVDs. Joshua also had a fully stocked armory with more than two thousand rounds of ordnance with various weapons from handguns to assault rifles to a 50-caliber sniper rifle. Joshua had a Mk 19 grenade launcher with 500 rounds of 40mm rounds of multiple types of ammunition. This armory also included a 40mm revolving grenade launcher. Joshua said no arsenal would be complete with an assault shotgun with shredder ammunition. Joshua had smiled with that last proclamation.

What impressed Trinity the most was Joshua's communication center. He had two powerful custom-built workstations. Both ran Apple's OS because of all the security flaws in the Microsoft Operating System. Joshua had said Apple ran its kernel on the backbone of UNIX, a very secure platform. These machines were behind a very impressive firewall in a self-contained network. Joshua had over 10 teraflops of data store.

Joshua described how his network operated. A wiz kid named Kenny Tahir designed it. Kenny was a natural-born hacker. He was also about as unassuming as they came. Nothing about him stood out. At 5' 7", thin frame, glasses, dark hair, and dark eyes, he could be in a room full of people and not be noticed. His grandparents were from Egypt. However, both parents were born in the US. His father was born in Maine, and his mother was from New York. While he had a nice permanent tan, he could easily pass for Italian because of his mother's heritage or Middle Eastern because of his father. More importantly, he knew his way around computers better than the geeks at MIT. For shits and giggles, he routinely hacked into the FBI, CIA, and NSA's mainframes. And to top it off, he has never been caught. Joshua described Kenny's most significant achievement as the "Internet 5.0." Kenny had created one of the most advanced offline Internet functional retrieval systems that Trinity had ever seen. Once a week, Kenny would bring over an external hard drive to upload and replace the data on Joshua's system. Kenny had created specially designed WebCrawlers or Bots that searched out new content and compared it with its every growing index to retrieve new information only. So, in essence, Joshua could view just about anything going on in the world without ever exposing his network to hackers. To top things off, Kenny had built a custom standalone laptop that could connect to the

41

Internet. Not in the way one would think, though. His system connected to the outside via three unassuming satellite dishes positioned around the house. Only the cable company knew Joshua didn't use Satellite dishes for his cable and residential Internet service. The system that Kenny designed actually used a portion of the dedicated bandwidth from satellite TVs reserved for viewing to surf the Internet. Joshua tried to describe the science as explained by Kenny. Eventually, he gave up after realizing he was hopelessly speaking French when he should be speaking Russian. The bit that Trinity was able to understand had to do with the fact the mechanism for watching TV was the same as surfing the Web. With a modified Internet router and changes to the port setting, surfing the Internet was a snap. While theoretically possible, Trinity was still in awe of what Kenny had accomplished. Joshua went on to tell Trinity, "While the system is virtually untraceable, it is still better to have the system isolated." Kenny said with this setup, he could hack into just about every network on the planet, from the US military to China's military.

Trinity had asked Joshua why she hadn't heard of Kenny before? It was her job to track all potential cyber-terrorists/hackers that could be exploited by an enemy of the US.

Instead of answering the question directly, Joshua said, "Trinity, did you ever wonder why I don't compete? Some of the best martial artists never compete because they have nothing to prove. They are content with passing their knowledge on to a few deserving individuals. Those are the masters that truly understand why they train. For me, it is about self-perfection. The betterment of oneself and, ultimately, the willingness and knowledge to sacrifice oneself for the right reasons. Kenny is no different. He has nothing to prove. The knowledge of the fact that he can do it is enough for him."

Trinity thought of the command center that she had set up in Joshua's Zombie Room. Zombie Room, that name still made her laugh. She had articles, notes, pictures, and newspaper clippings posted on the wall from all over the world. When things seem related, she used a string to connect the link. While tedious, a pattern was starting to form between two companies. One of them was Axion Corporation Int'l, and the other was Prometheus Unrestricted. Both were diverse corporations that dealt in just about everything. Trinity also realized that a venture capitalist company called Helixon Venture Funds financed both organizations. She now had 3 connection points. Using Joshua's system, she discovered that the Vice President of the United States, Bill Sartingson, has shares in all three companies. Not only did he have stock, but he also sat on the board of Prometheus before giving up the seat to assume the office of the Vice President.

Further research revealed several prominent Senators and CEOs of various companies were connected. The first lesson they taught you at ORD was to follow the money. Since all these organizations were public, they had to file their quarterly SEC filings. Six months into her hunt, Trinity now had a list of impressive individuals who possibly ran or, if nothing else, were a part of this corruption.

Trinity also tracked assassinations, terrorist attacks, civil unrest, toppled governments, and general regional wars. So far, she had been unsuccessful at connecting anything or trying to find patterns in the madness. She knew she needed help to make these connections. These people were just that good.

Enough for the day, thought Trinity.

As Trinity was packing up for the day, Sam, her boss, asked her to drop by his office. Expect nothing… As Trinity entered Sam's office, Sam said, "Have a seat, Trinity. I know you've been through a lot over the past year. I've been monitoring your activity log, and I'm concerned that you are chasing a ghost. I know we have said follow the money, but you are currently researching 3 of the Fortune 100 companies. Do you really think they are connected with domestic or international terrorism?" Before Trinity could answer, Sam continued. "I've been patient with you because of the trauma you experienced, but at some point, I need the old Trinity back. Monday, I'm going to formally counsel you about your performance. I will be putting a letter in your permanent file. This is a serious situation, Trinity. You are one step away from being an ex-ORD employee."

"I want you to seriously think about whether you want to continue to work here because at this rate, that is not going to happen. So come back Monday, and let's talk again, first thing. I'm trying to help you here, Trinity. I've always liked you both professionally and personally. It pains me to have to do this right now. Dammit, Trinity, maybe if you would let me in and stop putting up all those walls, I might be able to help you. I know you're lonely. Maybe we could just hang out and have dinner or catch a movie from time to time, but you're just so fucking guard these days. I just want to help you. Maybe if you had something or someone to occupy your time outside of work, then your work wouldn't suffer as much."

Trinity saw red. Trinity thought, That fucking bastard. I can't believe he just told me to keep my job that I have to fuck him. Calm down, Trinity. She could hear Joshua in her head. Calm down and take a deep breath. Don't let your emotions cause you to make a stupid mistake. Use them instead to have meaningful action. Trinity calmed down and started breathing deeply. Active meditation is what Joshua called it. Now think of the solution, not the problem. She needed this job, so calling Sam a bastard was out of the question.

"That's very kind of you, Sam. My life is getting better. I thought I was doing a good job, and I was making progress on tracking the money. While these companies might not be terrorists, some of their divisions make a lot of money during the chaos created by their so-called humanitarian efforts in these Middle Eastern countries. And what they are doing is African is downright criminal, but I guess you are right. Maybe this is better suited for the FBI to handle. I will close up my research next week and start investigating other activities on my list. And, Sam, while I truly appreciate you wanting to help me get my life moving in a better direction, I'm just not ready to open up again. I hope you understand. I like you, but the memories are still too painful. To top things off, I still have Robbie's father harassing me every month or so that Robbie's death was my fault and how unfit I was to ever be his mom. So for now, thank you, but no."

"I will come in on Monday and have an answer for you. I will think about all you said today, but I'm telling you now that I want this job, Sam. I not only want it, but I need it. Thank you again, Sam. Have a great weekend." Sam replied, "You too, Trinity."

As Trinity exited Sam's office, Sam breathed a sigh of relief. He felt confident she would refocus her efforts on other purses. Sam removed a second cell phone from his jacket pocket and dialed the only number capable of reaching that phone.

A receptionist answered, "Good afternoon, Man Source Temp Agency. How may I help you?" Sam's response, "Good afternoon, my name is James West. I am looking for a fishing job in Alaska. Can you connect me to your wildlife recruiter?" "May I ask how old you are?" asked the Operator. Sam replied, "Miss, is that really an appropriate question, but if you insist, I'm 38."

Sam had just passed the challenge and support code phase that gained him access into the Directorate Operations Center. At that exact moment, Col. Myers was sipping from his mug on his 3rd cup of coffee for the day, reviewing the threat assessment board. Sam's ID and picture were immediately flashed on one of Col. Myers' three monitors when the call came. Col. Myers quickly read the summary notes and realized Sam was their agent planted at Homeland Security's Operational Division. He was also the agent keeping tabs on Trinity Winters.

"How can I help you, Sam?" answered Col. Myers. Sam replied, "Sir, I just called to let you know I have successfully diverted Trinity off her current line of investigation. I informed her she has not been the same since the accident and that her

47

performance is reflective of that. Chasing ghost was the term that I used. On Monday, I will have her sign a formal write-up letting her know if her performance has not improved in the next 6 months, I would be forced to terminate her." Col. Myers' grunted an acknowledgment then asked if she posed a threat. Sams responds, "No, Sir. If she keeps down this path, I will fire her, and my actions won't raise any suspicions by the review board." Col Myers confirmed hearing Sam by saying, "Ok, Sam. Keep monitoring her activities and let me know if anything appears out of the ordinary." With that, Col. Myers quickly hung up the phone without giving Sam a chance to acknowledge the order. While I don't regret letting Trinity live, she is becoming more trouble than she is worth. I just don't have time to deal with something as trivial as a grieving mom, who might have seen something, thought Col. Myers.

Col. Myers' attention was focused on another part of the world in China. Where he had given Grimm an order to eliminate China's Minister of Trade and Industry.

Hebei Province, China

Grimm was lying concealed in his sniper's ghillie suit on a hillside in the Hebei Province. He was hidden from this position among the high grass and weeds. Even his .50 caliber rifle of choice, the Barrett XM500, intended to be a lighter, more compact alternative to the M82, was camouflaged to eliminate any glare from exposed metal. For the past month, he was in the People's Republic of China trailing Chin Hu, the Minister of Trade and Industry. Making sure he understood his habits and to pick the perfect location for the hit. Killing Hu was easy. Grimm flashed back to his sniper training at Fort Benning, GA. The middle-aged sniper instructor said, "Almost anyone can be an assassin. You can even kill the President of the United States. You just have to have the will and be willing to trade your life for the kill. What we do here is so much more. We teach you to be snipers so that you can live another day to ensure all enemies of the United States are eliminated with lethal intent. Your job is not to ask why they need to die. Your job is to kill them and let God sort them out."

Grimm aimed his cross-hairs on Hu and had slowed his breathing the way he was trained. Always fire on the exhale to minimize movement. When you squeeze the trigger, it should almost be a surprise, Grimm recounted from his training. Grimm slowly squeezed the trigger until 2.5lbs of pressure was applied. At that point, the .50 caliber round leaped from the XM500, traveling 1,800 meters or 1.1 miles to its intended target. While Grimm sighted the cross-hairs of his scope on the left eye of Hu. The reality is he could have aimed virtually anywhere and still kill his target. The reason a .50 cal round can tear a man in half is a process called cavitation. It's like throwing a rock into the water. The ripple made by the rock as it hits the water increases in size due to the rock's mass. The same happens with a body. The .50 cal is a large bullet with incredible kinetic energy (mass times speed, all that good stuff). It's just pure physics. While possible to still kill your target, why take a chance. We do not waste bullets. Our motto is "One-shot, one-kill." We are training you to be snipers, not some common rifleman. Two seconds after Grimm squeezed the trigger, Hu's head disappeared in an explosion of bone and brain matter. As simple as that, Hu was eliminated. Hu's bodyguards, while good, had ultimately failed because they could not protect Hu from an invisible enemy 1 mile away.

Satisfied that he had successfully completed his mission, Grimm glanced down at the picture of Trinity that he carried now, always. She was the only target that ever lived, and that was unacceptable. While Col. Myers had allowed Trinity to live, the deed was not settled in Grimm's mind. With permission or not, Trinity was a member of the walking dead. She just didn't know it yet. With that thought, Grimm started breaking down his XM500 sniper rifle to begin his 5-mile hike back to the extraction point.

Gaithersburg, Maryland

Trinity had been training nonstop for the past 3 months. Joshua taught her not to be afraid of her opponent, then he trained her to hit with deadly intent. To always attack vital areas of the body. "With your size Trinity, you always have to make sure your hits deliver an impact because you might not get a second chance." Joshua was not teaching Trinity to fight like a man but to use her female size and gracefulness to her advantage. "Always move off the line of attack, Trinity. Strike at angles, so you do not have to deal with an opponent's full arsenal of weapons. Use their body against them." Trinity recounted Joshua saying, "You will never be able to match strength with an opponent like me, so don't try. Instead, use their strength against them. Let them think they have the advantage because of their size."

It was during one of the intense training sessions that Trinity had injured her wrist. She went to block a blow by Joshua. Typically Joshua was careful when attacking, but she noticed an intensity that she had never experienced before this time. The hit came at her as countless others before, but when his forearm made contact, it was like a bomb had exploded at the precise point of contact. Trinity went down in pain. She was in tears, having never felt anything like that. Joshua quickly grabbed her wrist and apologized. Trinity had missed the following week of training because she was attending physical therapy. When she finally showed up again for training, Trinity told Joshua that her doctor told her she couldn't train again for 3 weeks. She would have to attend physical therapy.

Trinity asked Joshua with anger and confusion, "What were you thinking, Joshua? Why did you try and break my wrist? What the fuck did you do because you hit me in a way I have never been hit before?"

"Trinity, let me explain." Before Joshua could say another word, Trinity reached up and slapped Joshua with her uninjured right hand. At that moment, everything seemed to converge in on itself. All her helplessness over Robby. The fact that she still was nowhere nearer to identifying his killer. The fact that her career was a sham. Her boss (and supposed friend) was lying to her. More importantly, the person who had been training her had just shown her just how unprepared she was for the coming battle. All these months of training for what? Trinity looked at Joshua again through teary eyes and struck him again.

Joshua had sensed the change in energy from Trinity. He had anticipated the attack. This is what Joshua had been waiting on, for Trinity to break. To finally start grieving and ask herself the hard questions. While Joshua could have easily blocked Trinity's blows, instead, he chose to let her get out her frustrations. In fact, Joshua had created the environment by which this would happen.

As Trinity was swinging her hand again to slap Joshua, he gently grabbed her wrist. "Trinity, are you going to let me explain, or do you wish to continue slapping me?" Trinity stared at Joshua for another minute before she snatched her hand away and said, "Whatever. So tell me."

"Trinity, you are carrying darkness inside of you. That if not excised it will get you killed. The journey you embarked upon is full of dangerous enemies. Any one of them could kill you before you get to your target. You have got to find another reason to live instead of living only to seek revenge for Robbie. Robbie is dead, and there is nothing you can do to bring him back."

Trinity screamed, "How can you say that? At least if I kill those bastards, his spirit will rest in peace. Who cares if I die in the process? I will avenge him so I can rest in peace." Joshua gently said, "Trinity, when you find peace, then Robbie will be at peace. I am teaching you to be a warrior for a higher purpose. In war, I saw some terrible things. I committed some terrible acts in my so-called vengeance for the death of my fellow brothers in arms. To this day, I carry those memories with me. I'm encouraging you to learn from my failures, learn to be a peaceful warrior, and fight for the right reasons. That is why I am teaching you everything that I know in hopes that you will wage peace, not vengeance. Find a reason to live instead of a headlong rush to death. While you are a formidable opponent, you still have so much more to learn."

Joshua's tone was finally calming Trinity down. Trinity had been looking down with tears dripping from her eyes. She finally looked up and said, "Joshua, how did you do that? It felt like a point impact explosion when you made contact with me." Joshua replied, "Energy, Trinity. I am trying to teach you to do the unexpected. Most people are unaware that they possess energy and forget about harnessing it and using it to their advantage. To answer your question, I focused my Chi or "energy" into a single point of contact which I then transferred to you. Chi can be used to maintain health or to allow you to move beyond the so-called normal limits when you learn to harness it. That same energy can allow you to maintain your core temperature when you are outside in freezing weather. Those who practice developing this energy can also heal others by sharing their energy. While most use this energy for self-maintenance and healing, you can also use this energy to inflict damage on your opponent. That is what I did to you."

Joshua sensed that Trinity had a hard time believing what Joshua said. "Sit down, Trinity, start meditating the way I taught you. I will use my Chi to heal your left wrist. It is nothing miraculous, simply a sharing of energy. I will use my energy to assist your body with healing itself."

As Trinity sat down and crossed her legs, Joshua got up to change the music. The music was one of Joshua's favorites when he wanted to have a profound experience during meditation. Joshua played music from the album "Healing Waves" by Parijat. As Joshua settled in beside Trinity, he spoke softly. "Slow down your breathing Trinity. Remember the 5 principles of the breath: Long, Slow, Smooth, Deep, & Even. As you breathe deeply expanding your belly to open up your diaphragm. Take the air in deeply throughout your lungs, then slowly release it. Focus on nothing else but the breath." Joshua continued to give instructions, slowly taking Trinity to a place of calm. "Release your stress with each exhale. Starting with the top of your head, then slowly work your way down."

After about 5 minutes, Joshua put one hand on top of Trinity's wrist and the other hand below her wrist, forming a circle to complete a connection. Joshua started to slowly sink into himself. With each breathe going deeper and deeper. Once Joshua was satisfied that he channeled energy properly through his chakras, he expanded his Chi through his hands to Trinity's wrist. While Joshua successfully attempted to heal some of his student's minor injuries, it wasn't an exact science yet to him. He remembered what one of his instructors taught him.

"Imitation is the best form of flattery. Keep practicing until one day you become like your breath; without thought, you will master the Chi inside of your body." Joshua was fond of his old Sifu. Sifu Jia Peng had passed away years ago. Still, his lessons over the years seem to always be there just below the surface when Joshua needed them. Sifu Jia Peng said, "It takes a tremendous amount of energy to heal. The human body cannot contain that much energy, which is why you must be centered and in the proper mindset before you attempt to heal someone. Energy is always around you. You must draw it in initially through your 1st Chakra, your base foundation. This grounds you to the earth. Once completed, pull that energy up through your 1st Chakra to your 2nd Chakra or your sexual Chakra. Be cautious though, it is this Chakra that causes people to get addicted to meditation. This is your natural Viagra. Putting energy here will sexually charge you but don't give in to those urges, but instead harness this energy and pull it up to your 3rd Chakra or your power Chakra. This is located at what most martial arts call your diaphragm. This is where they say your power comes from when you punch, kick, etc., but they never tell you how to energize it properly. Don't linger once you feel strong enough; take this Chi and move it up to your 4th Chakra or heart Chakra. This is where your compassion comes from. This is where healing becomes possible. It is through your love and empathy for your fellow human beings that you can take on their suffering and give back peace."

Joshua had followed Sifu Jia Peng's instructions and now was ready to attempt healing Trinity's wrist. Joshua visualized taking in the pain and injury from Trinity's wrist with each inhale. On the exhale, Joshua visualized his Chi being pushed into Trinity's wrist. This technique is called "Bone Marrow, Skin Breathing." Sifu had said appropriately done; it would feel like your skin was breathing with each inhale and exhale. That was energy passing through your skin. Joshua could feel his hands heating up as he continued his attempt to heal Trinity's wrist. Perhaps 40 minutes had passed before Joshua thought he had assisted Trinity's own Chi enough to accomplish what was required to finish healing her wrist.

At this point, Joshua decided to do something he had never attempted before. Joshua wanted to try and give Trinity some of his energy to heal her heart. Joshua first started the process of pushing energy into her base chakra. After about 15 minutes, Joshua assisted Trinity's Chi to move up toward her sexual Chakra. Joshua continued to move Trinity's energy up until he finally reached her heart Chakra. At least, that was what he thought he was doing. It was at that moment that both Joshua and Trinity simultaneously opened their eyes at the same time. Trinity stared at Joshua without saying anything. Joshua thought, Oh shit, what have I done? Joshua felt the disturbance in Trinity's Chi flow. It was like a ripple in the pond, but stronger. Trinity pulled her hand back, got up to leave and turned to Joshua, and said, " I have to go."

Joshua said, "Trinity, wait. Let's talk a bit." Trinity quickly replied, "No, I have to go. Thank you. I will see you later." With that, she turned and left the studio. Joshua just sat there and wondered if he had made a mistake. Oh well, nothing to do about it now. Joshua started training to take his mind off Trinity. Of late, all he could do was think about Trinity. It made no sense to him, but he could not get her off his mind. Trinity had invaded Joshua's mind. Her name kept pounding in his skull like a jackhammer. While Trinity was attractive, Joshua had no sexual thoughts about Trinity. He sincerely just wanted to help her. She was a lost soul in the darkness of night. He wanted to be that light for her. To guide her out of the darkness back into the light so she could be whole yet once again. As Joshua started doing the 48 Combination Tai Chi set, he joined his mind with the new resident presence of Trinity. Trying to fight it was fruitless, so he used the principles of Tai Chi to blend with it and bend like the wind. Sifu said, stop using force against force. Flexibility and softness will always beat rigidity and strength.

After years of his 70-year-old instructor putting Joshua on the mat, those lessons finally sunk home.

Stop fighting her. Accept her presence in your head and use it. Joshua started to lose himself in his movements. The joy of just being. No stress, no problems. Just the joy of movement. To move like the wind, bending like a reed in the wind. "Tai Chi is the Grand Ultimate," Sifu said. Properly mastered, there is nothing you can't accomplish or anyone you can't defeat.

Driving home, Trinity started to feel different. When she left the school, she was uncharacteristically warm, then things started getting noticeably strange. At first, it started off as a slight tingling that radiated from her stomach then began to spread all over her body. By the time Trinity pulled into her driveway, the tingling had turned into pin picks as if your foot had fallen asleep and when you stand to walk on it when the blood returned. The sensation was only getting more intense as each minute passed. "Damn," Trinity said out loud as she was getting out of the car. "What the hell did Joshua do to me?"

By the time Trinity had gotten out of her workout clothes to take a shower, the sensation was maddening. The needle pricks felt like there were a thousand upon thousands sticking in her at the same time. Trinity managed to turn the shower on, thinking a warm shower might relieve these overwhelming

59

sensations. As Trinity stepped into the shower, she was not prepared for the warm stream of water touching her. The feeling was immediate. Trinity went down on the shower floor because the sensitivity of the water touching her skin took her breath away. The best description is the feeling of being "super charged." All her senses were on overload. The feel was so overwhelming that Trinity cried out and started crying. As tears streamed down her face, Trinity was assaulted by feelings she thought were gone forever. Lying on the shower floor curled up in a ball, all she could think about was Joshua. Without a doubt, Trinity understood what was happening. She wanted Joshua in a way that was primitive, raw. Trinity stopped crying as she sat up. She felt focused. What she wanted had nothing to do with gentle lovemaking. She needed to feel Joshua touch her, grab her and fulfill a need she didn't know she possessed.

Trinity stood up and grabbed the soap to lather herself. The touch of her hand against her skin was beyond incredible. Trinity started lathering her hands, then moved up her arms. Trinity lingered on her neck, enjoying the feel of her fingers curled around her neck, massaging, caressing. Trinity then ran the soap between her breasts. As Trinity cupped her breast working her way around her nipples, her eyes rolled back with the feeling. Trinity's eyes dilated. She was no longer in the shower. She was in another world with just her and Joshua, imagining that it was his hands on her. Without thinking, her fingers slowly started working their way downward. When they reached the desired spot, she slowly massaged herself. Trinity then brought the showerhead down to aid in her efforts. The feeling of the powerful jet stream was beyond ecstasy. In minutes, Trinity climaxed. The orgasm was so powerful that Trinity fell down to her knees, screaming, "Oh, God! Oh, God!"

It wasn't until the water turned cold that Trinity realized how long she had been in the shower masturbating. While the past 30 minutes in the shower relieved some of the sensations Trinity was feeling, deep inside, she knew there was only one person who could truly satisfy her.

Trinity laid in bed, trying to sleep. At 3am, she stopped trying to sleep and just wished for 6:30 to come, so she could see Joshua again. Trinity quickly got dressed and went downstairs to watch TV to distract herself from Joshua's constant thoughts. It what felt like hours, it was finally time to drive to training. On the ride there, Trinity's emotions went from one extreme to another. She went from wanting to run into Joshua's arms and kiss him to hating him for reawakening this desire.

Joshua did not sleep well either. He was unaccustomed to not being in control of his feelings. While he could finally start sleeping these past few days again, it was only through extreme

force of will. Admittedly sleep had eluded him, occasionally.
He just shook his head, thinking about the only word that
overrode all thoughts…. "TRINITY." Never had a word been so
powerful, so overwhelming. No other thoughts: sexual, love,
desire. Just "Trinity."

Joshua arrived at the school about an hour before Trinity
with the hopes of being able to bring balance back into his
psyche before Trinity arrived. The last thing he needed was to
have her see him this way. Training so far had been haphazard.
Joshua kept forgetting the sequence of forms he had done so many
times, he lost count. Just as he was starting another form, he
saw Trinity parking her car.

When Trinity entered the school, she was unprepared for the
sudden anger that swept over her. Upon seeing Joshua standing
there, she finally found a source to blame for these feelings.
He had caused this.

Trinity shouted, "You did this, Joshua, and you will fix
this." Joshua was confused. "What are you talking about,
Trinity?" "You know what you did. That energy shit, and now
you will take this shit away."

Trinity closed the distance between her and Joshua until he
could feel her breath on him. Joshua backed away. As he did,
Trinity closed the space again. "You will feel this!" Trinity
said through clenched teeth.

Joshua wasn't prepared for this. His first instinct was to go into attack mode. Joshua immediately pushed out his energy field to combat what he was feeling from Trinity. What he did was instinctive and not out of malice. Joshua quickly realized this was not the right move, so he did exactly as Trinity said, feel her energy. Joshua pulled his aura back in and allowed Trinity's aura to encompass him. Trinity had also invaded Joshua's personal space being just mere inches from him. Trinity just stared up into his eyes with tears flowing down. After a few moments, Joshua started to vibrate, feeling Trinity's energy. At that moment, Joshua realized what happened. He gave her too much energy when he was healing her. Trinity's past caused that energy to get stuck in her second Chakra. Joshua also quickly realized until Trinity dealt with her past, she would never be whole.

Trinity just stood there staring at Joshua. No personal space. Trinity was lost in the moment. Nothing else mattered but Joshua and how she was feeling. What Trinity felt was closer to primal versus what one would call sexual. At that moment, Trinity looked into Joshua's eyes and said, "I want to just throw you on the floor and rip your closes off." Joshua stared back at Trinity, totally unprepared for this turn of events. While attracted to Trinity, Joshua realized this was not the time to take Trinity up on her offer. Something was

63

going on beyond just having a sexual escapade. "No, Trinity. That is not something we will do." Instead, Joshua reached out and embraced Trinity and just held her. Trinity embraced Joshua back, desperately seeking refuge in his embrace. Her arms came through his and wrapped around his shoulders. They clung together, not understanding what was happening.

Joshua knew this was dangerous territory. One wrong move and all chances of helping Trinity would be lost, and the trust he had gained would be forever lost. While the thought of being with Trinity sexually was something any man would jump at the opportunity to do, helping her was more important. Joshua tightened his embrace and tried to help absorb some of the excess energy he had given her.

Trinity was at a loss. Joshua had not reacted the way she wanted. To be truthful, she really didn't know what to expect. She was angry, confused, and frustrated with her life. She had suppressed all of her personal needs in exchange for the chance to find her son's killer. So after her recovery from depression, there had only been training, work, & therapy.

Trinity had shutoff herself off from the world. No social life. No friends to confide in. Only Joshua. Joshua quickly surmised what was going on. In his effort to heal Trinity, he had also shared little of his energy with her, hoping that it might give her some comfort. His goal was to push energy into her heart Chakra. Unfortunately, if a person is out of balance, things don't always go as planned. Trinity's never received the energy as intended; it got blocked at her second Chakra. Or more commonly known as the sexual charka. This was the only explanation for Trinity's behavior. In focusing on only one goal in life, she had shut herself off from everything else. It also didn't help that her natural energy state was overloaded by the additional energy.

Knowing now what happened, Joshua embraced Trinity again to try and bleed off the excess energy. "Trinity, I know you don't want to hear this right now, but you have got to find balance in your life. While I understand what is driving you, giving you this supreme focus. That is not enough. You are setting yourself up for a suicide mission. In Special Forces, they taught us that we can always kill a target. The trick is to always come back from your mission."

"You have got to find balance, Trinity. Something beyond the hurt. The hate. The anger. While those things fuel you, it is not enough to sustain you. You have just proven that today. I am sorry for what I did to you. It was not my intention to throw you out of balance. Now that I understand what is happening, we will change our training to help you achieve a different perspective in life."

Trinity looked at Joshua and said, "Joshua, I don't understand everything that is happening or most of your explanation. However, I do know that I need something more than my need for revenge. I don't know what this is between us, but I never want it to end. For now, I will continue to trust in your wisdom and training." With that, Trinity disengaged from Joshua's embrace and turned and left the school.

Zombie Room - Bookes Ave, Gaithersburg, Maryland

Trinity sat in the Zombie room, going over additional data that she had uncovered about the mysterious man in her hospital room. With the help of Joshua's techno-geek friend, they were making some progress with some facial recognition software that Kenny had developed. Trinity had focused her search on the hospital surveillance videos. While this had produced a person, it never generated a face. Her attacker was too clever to ever expose his face to the security cameras. Kenny, on the other hand, decided to expand his search. In one of the videos that Trinity was examining, Kenny noticed a unique tattoo on his hand. So instead of trying to run facial recognition on his face, he instead changed the search parameters to look for this particular tattoo. Kenny's system had virtual access to about every CCTV through his back door network feed. While not real-time, Kenny's bots could read the information stored on a company's server. 3 weeks after Kenny initiated the search for the tattoo, it came back with a hit halfway across the country in Denver. With the tattoo match, they now had a face to examine of all places an ATM's security camera while someone was withdrawing cash. While the software had matched the tattoo, the mysterious man had avoided any images taken of his face.

Now that they had a face, all three just stared at it when a match was founded in the DoD's database. The face belonged to someone who shouldn't be walking around today. His name was Nathan Daniels. An E8, Master Sergeant in the US Army. Daniels was a real American hero. Numerous decorations include 3 Silver Stars, 4 Bronze Stars, and a Purple Heart. Daniels had served in the 2nd Ranger Battalion before qualifying to become a member of Special Forces. He was later selected to serve with the ultra-secret Delta Force. Daniels was qualified: Air Assault, Airborne, Pathfinder, SERE, Ranger, Special Forces, HALO, HAHO, Scuba, & Sniper. He had served 4 tours in Iraq and 6 in Afghanistan. In his last mission in Afghanistan, Daniels was supposedly wounded then medevac to Germany for treatment. It was reported that Daniels died of wounds sustained in combat. Daniels had no surviving family members. Kenny went on to say that Daniels had been dead now for a little over 1 year.

Based on this new information, Joshua asked Kenny to run a fresh profile search. "Everyone has a preferred technique when it comes to killing. Using Daniel's military records of confirmed kills, we can produce a profile of our target. We can then use this profile to see if we can establish a pattern to known assassinations since he was supposedly killed.

While Kenny was compiling the data request for Joshua, Trinity was on the other Mac feeding information into it from her research at ORD. Trinity had been following the money and wanted to play out a hunch based on Joshua's statement. Why was Axion Corporation allowed so much freedom in Iraq? As Trinity started digging deeper, something became apparent very quickly. Axion was a lot older than initially noted. Through Trinity's research, she traced Axion's roots back to a German company founded by the Thule Society to support an archeologist, Herr Byron Schmitt. Schmitt was initially hired by the head of Thule Society, Rudolf Von Sebottendorf. Schmitt was tasked with one purpose. Helping to uncover artifacts throughout the world. Von Sebottendorf was a German occultist. Von Sebottendorf's intent for Schmitt was to find artifacts that would support his belief that there was real magic or power in this world. Von Sebottendorf was obsessed with the idea that older, more advanced beings had visited this earth before. When Hitler came into power, he saw a way to promote his agenda through the Thule

Society, which he later renamed Nazi's. Von Sebottendorf believed that the Thule Society were direct descendants of these advanced beings, he dubbed "The Ancients." Von Sebottendorf built his belief on the works of Friedrich Wilhelm Nietzsche and the concept of Superman. Von Sebottendorf later claimed that he first intended the Thule Society to promote his own occultist theories. It was Hitler that pressed him to emphasize political, nationalist, and anti-Semitic themes. Since this claim was made while the Nazis were in power and Von Sebottendorf had little to gain by denying anti-Semitism. While there was this belief that Hitler was obsessed with created a supreme race, most historians believe Hitler's true agenda was something else. It may well be true Hitler didn't think the myths were simply myths; he thought they were clues to uncovering vast secrets left by The Ancients. History depicted Hitler as obsessed and crazy. The more Trinity discovered, the deeper the mystery became. While fascinating, Trinity closed the research and got back to uploading her data on Axion. As Trinity was closing down her search following her hunch, she made a mental note that there was something else going on with Axion and why they were in Iraq. She couldn't justify spending any more time on this hunch, but this wasn't over.

Directorate Headquarters - Undisclosed Location Outside of Roanoke, Virginia

Col. Myers was standing at attention in front of 9 monitors with figures from around the globe. The faces were darkened to hide their identity. Their voices were also digitized to further mask who they were. The people arrayed before Myers, who called themselves the Committee, gave Myers his operational mandate. They were currently meeting to discuss the operations that Myers had going on around the world. They complimented Myers on the flawless execution in China. They voiced concern about the Columbian Drug Lord, who was now expanding operations in Europe outside the territory he was given. The situation was getting out of control. Raúl Chávez had met a mysterious government figure one night that proposed a joint venture. The proposal was to act on their behalf to smuggle individuals into the US from time to time. In return, they would help him resurrect the Medellín Cartel and turn it into one of the most powerful cartels in South America. It had taken 5 years for Raúl to vault the Medellín Cartel to international prominence with the help of this shadow organization. However, in the past year, Raúl started going off the reservation. It was time to send him a message. The figure from Germany stated, "We created Raúl, and we can create another. Myers, make sure the message is loud and clear when you send Melina's head to him in a gift box." "We are too close to get the assets in place for that idiot to fuck up now. We need that pipeline secure. We still need to get Jürgen Schneider into control. This is just too critical. I want this resolved now, Col. Myers. Do you understand?" "Yes, Sir. It will be done ASAP", stated Myers.

Col. Myers had dispatched Grimm to Columbia to deal with a situation that was quickly becoming unstable. While relative to any mission, Col. Myers also understood that a full-blown war could escalate any moment if the operation went south. The last thing he needed was to deal with a conflict in Central America. This was the type of mission that Grimm was made for. Sending just the right message producing fear and destroying the will of the opponent to strike back. While Col. Myers was sure Grimm would successfully complete the mission, he still harbored some doubt. Grimm had been off since the Trinity mission. Grimm took it hard that he was not allowed to finish her off at the hospital, and she was the only target to ever live when the Grimm Reaper was dispatched. Of late, Grimm's assignations had taken on a slightly sadistic approach. The targets were deserving, in Myers' opinion. He didn't pay this hunch much attention, but subconsciously, he had registered the change in Grimm.

Col. Myers truly believed in his mandate. While he understood his organization was not without its flaws, his operations directly affected the lives of American Citizens. He believed in the larger purpose of creating a globally aligned world. Balance was needed in the war-torn world. Sometimes, that meant dealing with the less than upright citizens, the mob, Triad, the smugglers, and drug dealers to accomplish the mission. So dealing with Raúl was just another piece on the board that needed to be manipulated to achieve a higher purpose. If Grimm got a little carried away, then it was an inevitability.

Medellín, Columbia

Grimm sat in his hotel waiting for the green light on his mission. He had been waiting for a mission just like this. Ever since that bitch Trinity had been allowed to live, he had not been the same, which bothered him. Trinity had become an obsession, an itch that couldn't be scratched. The Melina hit was just what the doctor ordered. She was easy to spot when he arrived in the county. It is evident that she didn't come from money. Everything about her was about excess and extremes. Everything she did screamed; I need attention from the shopping excursions to the red BMW 735 she drove.

Raúl's wife Melina was a striking beauty. Just under 5'8", weighing about 130lbs. She was a picture of what a typical American would call an exotic beauty, with long wavy raven-colored hair to curves that would make any woman jealous. Grimm guessed that she was about 28 years old, but the most striking feature about Melina was her eyes. Melina had green eyes, which was a rare trait in this part of the world. After spotting his target, Grimm had immediately determined this would be his opportunity to work out his Trinity frustrations on her. Up until now, all his targets had been men. While he had taken sadistic pleasure in torturing a few of them to work out these frustrations, they were men. They just didn't provide the mental release he needed. Everything was okay now because he now had Melina. He would systematically dismantle her carefully crafted façade until there was nothing left but her naked soul. After she realized her life was a lie, he would then fulfill the parameters of his mission… Send Melina's head back to Raúl in a box.

Grimm had slept well that night like he did before every mission. Around 2200 hrs, he received the confirmation codes for the task. His last thoughts before he drifted off were of Trinity's head exploding when his 50 caliber round penetrated and exited from her skull. Grimm had been up before dawn as usual and drove to his surveillance point. Grimm smiled at the thought of personal protection. Raúl always had at least 2 black SUVs protecting Melina, point, and rear security. Each vehicle had at least 4 guards, all armed with H&K assault

rifles. All cars were armor protected to include Melina's BMW.
Taking Melina out when she was driving would be difficult.
After weeks of surveillance, Grimm had decided to initiate
Melina's kidnapping during her morning jog. There were only 2
members of her security detail that could actually keep up with
her running. The 2 SUVs were strategically positioned in the
middle of the route and at the turnaround point to accommodate
this. The 2 members who ran with her employed a point and rear
security posture, staying about 100 meters ahead and to the
rear.

Grimm calculated that the most optimal point of assault would
be after the halfway point. The hilly topography provided the
ideal ambush point.

Grimm nicked-named the point man "Piggy" because of his
larger-than-life nose, shaped like a pig's snout. He named the
rear guard "Scarface" due to the nasty scar that ran down his
left cheekbone.

Piggy had just come over the crest of the target hill. Grimm
waited approximately 10 seconds to ensure that Piggy couldn't be
seen falling as he fired his Glock 34 with Suppressor, which
penetrated Piggy right between the eyes. As planned, when
Melina crested the hill, she would think Piggy had fallen and
rush to his aid. That sprint would buy Grimm the extra 8
seconds he would need to incapacitate Melina before Scarface

74

arrived. As Melina stopped short of Piggy's body, that was when she noticed something was wrong. There was blood pooling around Piggy's head. Before she could scream, Grimm stepped out from behind the tree, slightly to her left. As she turned around to scream, she saw Grimm's fist come around to strike her in the midsection driving all the air from her lungs in one loud whoosh. Melina couldn't even breathe. Forgot about screaming. She doubled over, her body curling into the fetal position as she fell. Grimm never let her hit the ground. He swept her body up with his left arm and held her upright as his right hand placed a cloth around her mouth, crushing the small glass ampoule within it in a single motion. Within 5 seconds, Melina was fully incapacitated, giving Grimm just 3 seconds to pull his Glock from his waistband, assume a kneeling position, and fire. Taking Scarface out just as he had done Piggy exactly 15 seconds earlier. With both bodyguards down, Grimm quickly lifted Melina on his shoulder and ran back to his beat-up Land Rover, a vehicle of choice for the locals. Based on his calculations, he had approximately 30 minutes to escape the AO (area of operation) before the other guards found the bodies and started a full search. Grimm moved the bodies to the shrubs, which would buy him another 15 minutes or so.

Zombie Room - Bookes Ave, Gaithersburg, Maryland

While Kenny and Trinity were in the Zombie room, Joshua retreated to his converted small workout room. Joshua had been troubled of late with his conflicting feelings for Trinity. His sleep was disturbed, making him feel was out of balance. So Joshua decided instead of being the 3rd wheel with a room full of techno geniuses, he would take this time to meditate. As of late, Joshua had been out of balance because of the incident with Trinity. In the past, a good meditation session always brought Joshua back into balance, but not this time. As Joshua sat and meditated, he became more and more frustrated. No matter how hard he tried to flush the thoughts of Trinity from his mind, it did help. With every breath, she invaded his calm. He slowed his breathing, tried sinking deeper into the moment. Whenever he got close to moving his chi to the next charkas, "Trinity" invaded his calm yet again.

Joshua had been at this for the past hour to no avail. He was just about to give up when he detected an all too familiar presence entering his room. Joshua could sense Trinity with his eyes closed in a room full of people. Trinity wore no perfume, but she emitted an indescribable scent. To make matters worse, whenever Trinity was around, Joshua vibrated. It was like receiving an energy boost when she was near. There was no way to explain it other than feeling like a mild electric shock was coursing throughout his body. At first, Joshua thought it was only him who felt it, but once he touched Trinity, she nearly fainted, and he had to grab her. During that moment, they became lost in each other's eyes. Both knew without a shadow of a doubt that there was something more going on between them than just student and teacher.

As Trinity took another step through the door, Joshua softly said, "Hello, Trinity." "How did you know it was me?" "Trinity, I feel you all the time. Sometimes, your presence is so overwhelming, I just want to take you in my arms and kiss you until nothing else matters in the world." "To be truthful, I realized of late that I do not come alive until I am near you, but I know I can do nothing about my feelings. It would be inappropriate, and helping you is the most important thing that I can do for you."

Trinity came around and sat in front of Joshua. Joshua had his eyes closed. Trinity could see the moisture threatening to leak from his eyes. Joshua didn't realize that Trinity was also crying with the ache and conflict that she felt at that very moment. Joshua sensed Trinity sitting in front of him. The connection was so strong between them now he thought he was going to lose this mind. Joshua finally spoke very slowly. Trinity had to strain to hear what he said. "Trinity, I don't know if I can keep doing this. I have always been independent, self-sufficient; I have never needed anyone before. The military taught me to be a warrior through and through. I thought that was why all my previous relationships failed because I could not be what they needed me to be. I was wrong. They say there is a soul-mate out there for everyone. I always thought that was bullshit. Some fairytales to sell more movies and books. Once I might have believed that with my childhood love. I knew I loved her from the moment I first laid eyes on her. So from Kindergarten to the 12th grade, I fought to finally win her over. When I finally won her over, it was everything I hoped for, but it didn't last long." Trinity asked, "What happened?" "That's for another day, Trinity. Ever since I have struggled with relationships. There was always something missing. I would blame them for the breakup, but I have come to realize the problem was me over the years. I was looking for them to make me happy, which was impossible. Trinity, I am now a happy person. I thought I knew what I wanted in life. Even with you, I have been brutally honest with you to help you. I never set out to fall in love with you. Through the process of helping you, I saw you. The real you unfiltered. I have never seen or thought it was possible to truly see someone other than fighting with my fellow comrades in war. I fell in love with who you were long before I fell in love with your outer beauty. It's hard to look at you now because I feel like I have betrayed your trust."

By now, the tears were freely flowing down Joshua's cheeks. He did nothing to check them. "Trinity, I'm in love with you. I don't know what to do, but I promised you I would train you. I am a man of my word. I just need to ask you for one favor." By now, Joshua's head was down, and tears dropped to his lap as he asked, "Trinity, will you please kiss me just one time so I know what it feels like from a woman who means everything to me? Afterward, I will never say another word and just focus on getting you trained. I would do anything for you, Trinity, but I need this one thing, so I know my feelings are not a lie."

Trinity was in tears also. Inside, she was so relieved that Joshua felt this way. He was so professional that Trinity couldn't read his true feelings sometimes. Only during times of intense training did she sense that he cared more for her than he showed. Trinity gently took Joshua's face in her hands and raised his face. "Look at me, Joshua." Joshua opened his eyes and saw that Trinity's tears were a match for his. Trinity leaned forward and kissed Joshua. The kiss was unlike anything that Joshua had ever felt. While he has imagined kissing Trinity, the actual act of kissing Trinity was surreal. Her lips were soft and supple. They molded perfectly around Joshua's bottom lip as he kissed her upper lip. What started off as a gentle kiss of tenderness mingled with uncertainty quickly turned into one of passion and longing. Longing for the unknown. In Trinity, Joshua had found his equal in everything: intelligence, the ability to train hard with a no-quit attitude, and integrity. Now it seemed like they shared the same intensity in passion.

Joshua untangled himself from Trinity and just gazed into her eyes. "I'm sorry, Trinity. I don't know what came over me. I was not expecting this. I was out of place. I promise that will never happen again." Trinity smiled at Joshua. At the horror that was so clearly revealed on his face. "Joshua, please shut up before you say something stupid. Do you really believe I would have kissed you if I didn't want to?" "No." "Do you think I didn't feel what you just felt?" "No." "Then stop fighting what we have been feeling for each other, but afraid to do something about it. You taught me how to live again, Joshua. Something that I thought I would never be able to do after I lost Robbie. Please don't take that away from me by being stupid." At that moment, Kenny walked in and froze. "Hey guys, when are we going to get something to eat. I'm starving?" Once again, the techno genius strikes again with his inability to have any ability to read the room. Joshua just shook his head then he and Trinity both burst out laughing at Kenny and at the fact that something marvelous had just happened. "What?" said

Kenny. "Nothing Kenny, let's go get something to eat." With that, all three left Joshua's house and headed to get something to eat. The difference this time, both Trinity and Joshua wore a much-deserved smile.

Undisclosed Safe House - Medellín, Columbia

Grimm stared at Melina's eyes staring back at him, challenging and defiant, as she slowly came awake. Melina calmly said, "I've been raped before asshole, there is nothing else that you can do to me that hasn't been done before." Grimm just shook his head and smiled, "O ye of little imagination. The fun is just beginning." With that, Grimm took out his Vindicator knife that he had grown fond of and began creating his masterpiece. Grimm thought back to when Melina was alive. She lived three days, which had impressed Grimm. Grimm had stripped Melina naked and tied her up with her hands hoisted above her head. She had two choices based on the slack Grimm had put in the ropes. Stand on her tiptoes or dislocate her shoulders. While Melina was beautiful, temptations of the flesh had long lost any interest to Grimm. Even if he wanted to rape Melina, which was no longer possible because of the torture he had endured at the hands of the Taliban. It had taken Delta 3 weeks to find him through his subcutaneous locator because he was held deep in the Tora Bora caves of

Afghanistan. It was not until the Taliban was moving MSgt. Daniels that a patrol intercepted the locator while on a separate mission to contact an informant, who knew the location of Daniels. After Delta had eliminated the Taliban squad, Daniels was medevacked and examined at the base hospital. It was then discovered what was done to Daniels. While Daniels' penis could still be used for relieving himself, that was all it would ever be used for again. The Major on staff had insisted that they send Daniels back state-side to undergo plastic surgery, but Daniels refused. His teammates, while they disagreed, completely understood Daniels wanting to go back out there and make them pay. It was their ever-presence, not leaving Daniels side, that finally convinced the Major to change his opinion. The loaded M4's didn't hurt either. After Daniels' recovery and his first mission back, Master Sergeant Nathan Daniels became known as Grimm from that point on. Wherever he went, it was like the Grimm Reaper had entered the room.

Grimm had cut a small flap of skin loose on Melina's breast then clipped a small ½ lb. weight to the torn skin. While this hurt, Melina quickly learned that giving up and just hanging by the ropes caused the tear to increase at a much more rapid pace, and the level of pain was unbelievable. If that was not enough, Grimm had placed these weights all over her body. Melina screamed until her vocal cords ripped. Melina was beyond pain. Her body had thankfully shut down at some point during the torture, or at least that is what Melina had hoped happened. It was not until Grimm came back into the room the next day with a blow torch that Melina realized just how wrong she was.

For every scream from Melina, Grimm felt a little better. This was what was in store for that bitch Trinity. *She would pay.* Grimm silently sent a mental message to Trinity as the light of life was finally extinguished from Melina, *Your time is coming, Trinity. Not today or tomorrow, but I promise you, the Grimm Reaper is coming for you.*

By the time Grimm put his Vindicator away, he had experienced what could only be called a mental orgasm. It is the same feeling he experienced on his first mission after he recovered in Afghanistan. As Grimm was sealing the Tegrant Shipper with dry ice, he smiled at the thought of Raul's reaction when he opened the box and saw Melina's head with eyes staring back at him. Grimm added a little surprise, Melina's cut-off breasts showing the strips of torn-off skin to ensure that Raul truly got the message.

Joshua didn't mention anything of the previous day's conversation when she arrived. Instead, he launched immediately into training. Trinity was sweating profusely. Joshua had intensified her training. Just when things were getting comfortable, he would introduce a new aspect of training. In addition to Tai Chi, Joshua had now incorporated calisthenics into their workout. Partner assisted exercises, he called it, isometrics or dynamic tension. Joshua didn't believe in lifting weights. He said lifting weights was an unsustainable form of exercise.

Trinity was feeling a close bond with Joshua. They were working closely over the past 7 months. It wasn't sexual, but there was no mistaking their strong connection. The closeness they shared doing isometrics was some type of energy connection. He seemed to always wear shorts regardless of the temperature outside. One day Trinity asked Joshua why he seemed oblivious to the weather. Joshua responded, "It's what I'm trying to teach you, Trinity. The ability to manipulate your energy and the energy of the environment around you. We each have, for lack of a better word, an aura or energy field. Chinese medicine teaches us that in a healthy person, this energy moves freely throughout our bodies. When we are stressed, this causes blockages in that energy flow; hence, why people feel better after a massage. The knots or stress are temporarily removed, and the energy starts flowing again. However, this is not sustainable because we haven't addressed the underlining reason for the knots forming to begin with. Tai Chi is the perfect blend of martial arts, self-defense, and moving without stress. The following concepts, once mastered, make Tai Chi the grand ultimate. The first step is learning how to recognize when our bodies are experiencing stress. The second step is to take action to manage the stress. In the beginning, Tai Chi is very frustrating because our goal is to reteach the body how to move without stress. Like a child moves without limits, without a care in the world. Most Westernized Tai Chi programs only focus on learning a form, typically Yang Style 24 step. They never go into mastering movements, the breath, and learning about energy.

Once you start to learn to master movement, then you know to maintain your health by cleansing your body of impurities through breathing and the circulation of energy. More importantly, you learn to eliminate stress in your life. Studies have shown that 75% of all medical-related problems can be traced back to stress. I tell my students all the time, the body has everything within itself to heal itself. Case and point, there have been people diagnosed with terminal cancer and told they have 6 months to live. Seeking different solutions, those folks turned to Tai Chi and QiGong to help rebalance their energy. Their bodies cured the illness that they created in the first place.

The ultimate state of Tai Chi mastery is the ability to defend yourself with Tai Chi. Tai Chi is probably the least understood martial arts for that very reason. People only think of it as something that old people and women do in the park. I was one of those people when I first started. Tai Chi is considered the Grand Ultimate or Supreme Fist. When you learn to move without stress and engage your energy when fighting with Tai Chi, you will be amazed at how effective Tai Chi is as a form of self-defense.

We will focus a lot internally during this journey that you are on with me because that is where the problem lies inside our own heads. A key fundamental part of what I am teaching you is to stop blaming others for your problems and look in the mirror."

"At some point during our training, you will notice that during the basic of movements, you will immediately start sweating. This is the first indicator that you are learning to breathe correctly and generate more energy internally. You are also learning to enhance your energy by absorbing energy from the environment. I know this might sound crazy, but that is how I can walk outside in the dead of winter with shorts and a light jacket." Trinity responded, "No, it isn't difficult to believe. There are moments when I train with you that it actually seems like you are glowing or when I feel the energy radiating off you. Sometimes when we touch, I feel jolts of electricity that make me jump."

Joshua stared at Trinity a few minutes then said, "Interesting. I would not have expected you to notice those types of things for at least another 6 to 12 months." "Enough training for the day. I just wasted 30 minutes talking your head off about what most people will call nonsense," smiled Joshua.

"Let's pick up where we left off yesterday. I don't know if you have an answer yet, but I want to talk to you again and emphasize just how dangerous of a situation you find yourself in right now."

"Joshua, please don't treat me like an unworldly person. For Christ's sake, I work in a division of the government that doesn't exist. While I might not have gone to war like you, I have seen my share of reports of actions conducted by people like you because of our intelligence to various agencies. And at times, our own shadow paramilitary force might have conducted."

"Joshua, I might be delusional about the chances of success, but I want to make them pay for the death of my Robbie. He didn't deserve this. It was me. My choices in life that lead to his death, and if I die trying to fix this wrongdoing, then I can't think of a higher purpose in my life.""

"Trinity, are you sure? Because once you start down this journey, there is no turning back. Once these guys know you are coming after them, they will come after you in full force. There will be no half measures this time. They will outright send in an assignation team."

"Yes, Joshua. I understand what I am saying. I want to make them pay and will do whatever it takes to prepare for this journey."

"Ok, Trinity. For now, don't talk with anyone. Just go about your everyday life as if nothing is going on. Be normal. It is the absence of your routines that will make you stand out. Give me a few days, then you and I will need to have a serious talk about what your next steps are. We will have to intensify your training. You just can't be good. You need to be great. I'm going to take you through 4 phases of training.

- Phase 1: I need to teach you not to be afraid. When you can attack me, and I honestly have to start taking your attacks seriously.
- Phase 2: I will teach you how to strike the body with devastating results. Your strikes have to have intent, purpose.
- Phase 3: I will teach you to defeat someone like me. We will focus on being where I least expect you. Trying to stop someone like me is unrealistic if you take me on head-to-head. I am just too strong but learning to not be there when I strike you is. Once

you have mastered the ability to move then, we will be ready for the last phase.
· Phase 4: Full-out sparring. Operational security, personal security, and electronic security have to take on a whole new meaning. Beyond what you do at ORD."
"We have a lot to do, Trinity. How long it takes to master the skills you require is up to you. Understanding the concepts I am teaching might come in a moment, but preparing for that moment, unlearning a lifetime of bad habits might take years."

Trinity left Joshua in conflict. She had spent all night committing to herself that she would not rest until Robbie's killers paid for what they had done. Tonight, Joshua tells her that it might take years before she will be ready, if at all. She wasn't some inexperienced want-to-be. While she didn't have operational experience, she did very well in the selection process to be a field operative for ORD. Trinity thought, *Maybe I should just proceed on my own and use the resources at my disposal to make them pay.* These were the thoughts that played over and over again in her mind. As Trinity was downing her second shot of vodka that she realized it had been almost 6 months since her last drink. The fact that she had been sleeping and she was in shock at the realization that she had been at relative peace. Trinity knew this was due to Joshua with a shadow of a doubt. As much as she wanted to

go it alone to get it over with, she knew she would wait.
In that moment of understanding, she remembered something
that Joshua had told her earlier on.

"Trinity, I don't know what happened to you to cause you
so much pain, but I do know this. I have been allowed to
see a glimpse of your future. You are fast approaching a
choice, a nexus where you will have to make a decision. If
you take one path, I see destruction and the possibility of
a quick death. If you take the other path, there is a
chance. While slim, there is a chance of success. I know
this sounds cryptic and even crazy, but I was compelled to
say this. I know this doesn't mean anything to you right
now but remember these words carefully because they will
make sense when the time is right."

Sure enough, Trinity sat back as she sat the glass of
vodka down and said, "Well, I'll be damn. He was right.
That son of a bitch was right. How did he know?" Well, if
Trinity had any doubts before now, they were gone. She
would follow Joshua.

As Joshua described it, the art of movement was no
longer an active thought on Trinity's part. After two
years of training with Joshua, Trinity no longer thought of

what she did with Joshua as Kung Fu training. "The human mind is incredibly complex Trinity. The average human has over 60 thoughts per minute. Through training and meditation, the goal is to bring those thoughts down to 6 per minute. Have you ever heard of people that saw their whole life flash in front of them at the time of death? Others have said time seemed to slow down, and they could recount every vivid deal of the incident?" "Yes," responded Trinity. "That is the mind putting all its energy into helping the body survive. Unfortunately, most people only achieve this level of advanced thought patterns when their life is at stake. Martial Artist and World Class Athletes have achieved this same level of focus through intense training. Hollywood gives us clues all the time. Think about the movie The Matrix when Neo was fighting Mr. Smith at the end. At one point, they appeared to be going in slow motion, then they were shown fighting at an incredible speed. Sifu Peng taught me that no matter how fast the opponent comes at you, if you can focus the power of your mind, then their movements will slow down. It will look like you are moving at incredible speeds to someone watching, but to you, they will be moving in slow motion. That is the art that I am trying to teach you, Trinity."

"When we teach our students forms, regardless of the
style of martial arts, the goal is to teach movement.
That's why a Master will say there is only "movement" when
you reach a certain level. The style of martial arts
allows the teacher to retrain the body to move naturally.
There are no higher levels of martial arts, only movement.
When you remove the stress from the body, it will move
naturally and respond accordingly to any threat. The only
wrong movement is to not move at all."

Joshua threw a vicious hook with his right arm. Instead
of connecting, Trinity had ducked under the blow and
stepped to her left to deliver a palm strike to Joshua's
right side rib cage. Joshua instinctively stepped back and
flowed with the blow as the impact connected, absorbing
then redirecting the energy. As Joshua continued to step
back and to the left, he delivered a back fist aimed at
Trinity's temple. Trinity's arm came up to block the blow
with her forearm. At the point of impact, Trinity relaxed
her arm the way Joshua had taught her, be steel wrapped in
cotton. This will allow you to deliver internal energy to
the point of impact while preventing you from getting
injured. At the same time, Trinity was delivering a
Phoenix-Eye strike with her left hand to Joshua's nerve
cluster right at the base of his neck.

Joshua immediately ducked and received a glancing blow to his skull vs. a paralyzing blow to the base of his neck. Taking advantage of his position, Joshua hooked his right arm underneath Trinity's armpit. As he continued to circle Trinity, he brought his left arm around Trinity's neck to cut off her Carotid artery with this bicep and forearm. As Joshua's arm was closing in around Trinity's neck, she raised her left arm to prevent Joshua's move. At the same time, Trinity drew her left foot back to slam into Joshua's shin. Sensing the intent of the blow, Joshua had no choice but to disengage. As Joshua backed away, Trinity quickly twisted to her right, delivering an elbow strike. Joshua used his left hand to block the elbow strike while delivering a ridge hand strike to Trinity's throat. She promptly avoided by spinning to the left.

This battle repeatedly continued with strike counter strike. Knee strike to thigh, block with a palm strike to the top of the knee. Elbow strike countered with an elbow strike. Straight punch block then turned into a pull-down; going with the pull-down motion, Trinity spun then delivered a back-fist to Joshua's head. Joshua instinctively ducks to spin into the direction of the blow while at the same time releasing his hold on Trinity so he could get behind Trinity off her line of attack. At that point, Trinity spun, so they were facing each other. Joshua then delivered a toe kick to Trinity's shin. Trinity countered by moving her left leg slightly to the side, thereby only receiving a glancing blow.

Trinity then brought her left knee up, trying to strike Joshua's groan, which was promptly blocked with a palm strike. Without knowing it, their mock battle had attracted an audience outside the studio. Trinity and Joshua no longer thought about what they were doing. Their battle had turned into pure movement, a dance of sorts. Trinity was amazed at how she moved. It was as if she had practiced these moves a thousand times before. Had known every strike Joshua was going to make before he threw it. It was, as Joshua said, at some point when the mind was no longer occupied with the useless bullshit. You reduced your thoughts to that elusive 6 thoughts a minute. Your brain would then unconsciously access the universal knowledge source. In that place, all things were possible. Whether it was to solve a question that plagued you, it was there to take the initiated mind. The audience stared in amazement at how fast the two combatants were moving. Some of the strikes were so fast they couldn't be detected by the audience.

Finally, Joshua stepped away and held his hands up to signal an end to the sparring session. Then he hugged Trinity and said, "Congratulations, we have finished your training. It's time to take this operation to the field." Outside, both Trinity and Joshua turned to see the audience applauding their performance. With a wave of his hand, Joshua acknowledged the crowd then led Trinity to his office.

Muhammad Rashad and his team were preparing to deploy to the US through the drug pipeline via Raúl's cartel. While the greeting was less than ideal upon arrived in Columbia, Raúl's men made every effort to accommodate his team's wishes and provide them with the required resources. When Muhammad was first contacted in Iraq, he thought this opportunity was too good to be true. 2 years ago, Muhammad had lost his family, a wife and 3 kids, to a drone attack. Muhammad just stared at the TV with tears of anguish and hate while the Americans claimed to have killed a high profile, Al-Qaida target. Such western lies, Muhammad thought. At first, Muhammad tried to go through governmental channels to expose the lies. For his troubles, Muhammad received $50,000 for each of his family members that died with the condition that he stop pursuing his media campaign against America. Both Iraqi and American governments representatives came to his house and expressed their deepest sympathies for his loss. They explained how going after Al-Qaida was necessary to secure the future of Iraq. A fund was explicitly created to help families rebuild after being caught up in the crossfire.

Muhammad remembered that conversation as a Chinese national approached him with a plan to strike back at the country that destroyed his life. A plan that would finally take the fight to the soil of America so they would feel the horrors of war up close and personal. Instead of watching it on CNN or reading about it on page 16 of the NY Times. Wu outlined how his government was unhappy with the US having so much influence in the Middle East. Using this influence to keep China from ever challenging the US' status as the supreme Superpower in the world. Muhammad thought Wu was honest because he clearly stated this war is about oil and who controls it. His country only wants a fair playing field. Wu noted that he had gathered 30 individuals who had experienced the same pain as Muhammad. They selected Muhammad to lead this group because he had been the most vocal and had prior military training.

The plan was to take these 30 men and women to China and train them to launch a war of terror on the homeland of America. Unlike other attacks designed to immediately insight terror and kill people in a localized area, the plan was to attack American's infrastructure, which was virtually unguarded. This way, Muhammad and his team could attack multiple locations before America's law enforcement agencies could mount a defense. Wu was clear that this was a suicide mission because they would be caught at some point, most likely after the 4th or 5th attack. After the 4th attack, his teams would be given a high-value target to incite the most psychological damage and end their mission with a suicide bomb.

Muhammad and his team had been training for the past 8 months. Now, they were in Columbia preparing for the mission to begin. His team had been trained in chemical, biological, and explosive ordnance warfare. They also received weapons, martial arts, and language training. His entire team could now have conversations in English to ensure that they blended in. His team was broken down into 6 five-person units spread throughout the county to ensure maximum confusion and chaos. Targets included everything from water treatment facilities to power grids. They were also to target oil refineries. The final mission targeted everything from schools (especially elementary schools) to critical bridges and tunnels and heavily attended venues like sports arenas.

Col. Myers had just received notification from his contact that Muhammad and his team had successfully penetrated the US border. Col. Myers was standing in front of the bank of monitors briefing the committee. The greyed-out face of North America spoke quietly but firmly. "Col. Winters, this operation cannot fail. The successful execution of this mission is critical to the continued funding of the US military and to keep key elements of extremists from gaining control of the Middle East oil reserves. We abhor the killing of innocent lives, but this is necessary. The current US administration is on the verge of making peace with a faction in the Islamic, Al-Jahar, that is secretly undermining all the work previously gained over the past 10 years. That cannot be allowed to happen. Once in power, we have discovered plans that they will basically hold the world's oil hostage. One of their major objectives is to take back Israel from the Jews. That is their overall objective besides making billions from the oil-dependent countries. Unlike the 1st Gulf War, we have uncovered they are prepared to detonate nuclear bombs to ensure that no one comes to retake the country once secured. It's still unclear, but somehow, they have discovered that we are looking for a specific artifact. We are still trying to find that leak, but that is immaterial at this point. Col. Myers, for now, our desire to find this artifact is not your concern. Just know that if it falls into the wrong hands, the world will be forever changed. It was buried long ago for a reason, but now it is time for it to rise, and we need to be in control of it. The mission of Muhammad is crucial. They must make sure American stops being complacent in their relative isolation. No one cares anymore about the 3,000 lives lost during the 9-11 attack. We must wake the sleeping giant. This is one of the reasons you were selected, Col. You understand the need to allow the military to complete its mission without interference from politicians. We have to enrage people of American so much that they will allow the military to destroy the Al-Jahar faction entirely."

"Col. Myers?", this time it was the figure from Germany that spoke. "How is the cyber preparation going for this operation?" "Ma'am, Billy's team is almost ready to release the virus. This virus is designed to attack the two main mobile operating environments: OS and Android. Since most companies allow employees access to company email via these devices, we will exploit that weakness. Most organizations still utilize Microsoft Exchange to run their mail servers. Once released, a security flaw gets exploited. While not dangerous, this virus will create an electronic trail that will lead back to Al-Jahra and ISIS. The NSA will quickly identify the virus and believe that it was designed to create confusion so it could erase crucial data of the terrorist operation in the US. While in fact, the NSA will discover that an error in the code, unfortunately, allows some of the computer tables from being completely rewritten. Thus pointing the NSA to a joint Al-Jahra and ISIS operation. So once the operation begins, Billy will release the virus. If it all goes according to plan, from start to finish, we estimate that the complete operation will take about 6 weeks."

The Germany committee member continued to speak, "Col. Myers, what do you estimate the causalities to be in the US?" "Direct action causalities are estimated around 20,000 killed immediately from either explosions or biological agents. Probably another 10,000 due to secondary exposure to biological agents and another 2,000 due to panic."

Germany slowly shook her head, then said, "It's sad to destroy so many lives, but, unfortunately, it is necessary. Al Jahra and ISIS must be destroyed before they find the Ark of the Covenant first. And if the Ark wasn't enough, their plan to destroy 1/3 of the world's oil supply will cripple the world's economy. That can't be allowed to happen."

Col Myers turned and asked 1LT Brennen to give him a status report of Grimm setting up the dead drops for the insertion team as the monitors went dead. The teams were instructed to hold up for approximately 1 month before the commencement of operations. To blend into the community and get folks used to them and not suspect them. They were all given $100,000 in cash to pay for expenses. Each team was set up in a safe house. So far, 2 teams had made it to their designated safe house. The target

cities were Houston, TX; Las Vegas, NV; San Diego, CA; Chicago,

IL; Richmond, VA; Philadelphia, PA. The cities were selected

based on a mix of population, diversity, income per capita, and

psychological impact. So far, the teams had arrived in Houston

and Las Vegas. After reviewing the team status, Col Myers told

1LT Brennen to make sure he was advised of the teams' progress

when 4 of the 6 teams were in place. All contact with the teams

were to be contacted through dead drops for the remainder of the

operation. No direct contact was authorized to ensure

operational knowledge was compartmentalized if one of the teams

was captured. Muhammad didn't even know the designated target

cities other than his own team in Philadelphia. Raúl provided

each team leader with a sealed envelope with instructions that

it wasn't supposed to be opened until they arrived in the US.

Col. Myers was pleased. So far, the operation had gone off

without a hitch. While personally, Col. Myers was not happy

about the potential loss of American lives. He had seen the

effects of war firsthand and how horrible it could be. While

the US Military and contractors had suffered over 7,100 American

Casualties in Iraq and Afghanistan war and over 51,826 wounded

soldiers, the loss of civilian lives was staggering. There are

over 1,455,590 civilian deaths from violence in Iraq, as

reported by "justforeignpolicy.org." Afghanistan civilian

deaths are estimated between 18,000 and 20,000. While direct deaths caused by US soldiers account for a fraction of that number, their lives still weighed heavily on his conscience. Eliminating elements like Al Jahra and ISIS was paramount in his mind. If those factions continued to go unchecked, the death tolls would continue to rise. This was always a soldier's dilemma, knowing that the use of overwhelming and uncompromising force violent execution, while unpopular, would ultimately lead to fewer deaths in the long run. Just like it had been revealed that the 9-11 attacks were allowed to happen, so would these attacks, initiated and executed by a shadow organization.

Kenny ran his version of the facial recognition program nonstop since they had first uncovered Daniels' identity. The goal was to try and establish a pattern or some degree of predictableness so Joshua and Trinity could formulate a plan. However, things were not going as planned. Daniels never stayed in any one location too long. He had an affinity for avoiding his face appearing on camera. While his tattoo made things somewhat more identifiable, it still was a shot in the dark, especially if Daniels was wearing long sleeves. Kenny was not your average techno-geek. Kenny modified his program to find a cross-match between the facial recognition program and cell phone signals.

Kenny was going to keep searching for Daniels' cell phone through pinging and triangulation. Based on the location of each time the software identified Daniels, he would use his GPS program to determine the cell phone towers in the area. Hacking into their log files was child's play.

The more matches Kenny got, the easier it would be to narrow down Daniels' whereabouts. Denver was the first location he found Daniels. There were over 300,000 unique SIM signatures. The next match was in Dallas, which Kenny uncovered three weeks ago. There were over 500,000 unique SIM signatures at that location, but here is where the beauty and simplicity of the process were. By running a simple comparison of SIM's at both locations, Kenny narrowed the matches to five SIMs. Now Kenny needed just one more place to get a lock on Daniels' cell phone. Based on these five unique SIMs, Kenny modified his search parameters to track their signature and focus on the CCT output efficiency. While Kenny still had the original search parameter running just in case he was wrong about the cell phone triangulation. Kenny felt confident he would have a match in the next day or so. The odds were 300,000 to 1 that five matches would turn up in two cities over 789 miles away from each other. The odds that there would be multiple matches in a third location were 3.5 million to 1. Kenny smiled, knowing the numbers were on his side. Kenny couldn't wait to share the latest update with Trinity and Joshua.

The following day Kenny briefed Trinity and Joshua on his findings. They now had Daniels' cell phone and were tracking his movements. With Trinity's analyst background, she was curious about Daniels movement. She asked Kenny to backtrack Daniels' activities over the past six months. Trinity ran a similar search as part of her job at ORD. A couple of high-profile killings were seemingly connected to Daniels. Still, the events of the past few months were what alarmed Trinity. Trinity had noticed a developing trend. The one that caught her attention was the high-profile assignation of a drug cartel lord's wife, Melina. The classified report that Trinity reviewed had revealed the nature of death. The shocking details of this torture kept Trinity from eating the rest of the day. The fact that Daniels could be traced to a known drug lord and to multiple trips aboard signified a potential problem.

That night Trinity and Joshua met for their regular training session to continue to hone her skills. Joshua landed a punch. While pulled, it still stunned Trinity and landed her on her back. "What's wrong, Trinity? When fighting, the enemy doesn't care that you are sick, injured, blinded by the blood pouring into your eyes. He wants one thing and one thing only…. your death. If it's easy, great. If he has to work for it, the more gratifying. You can never take a break. You must always be alert, ready to strike at a moment's notice because you might not have a second chance. Anyway, that's enough for today." Joshua reached out a hand to help Trinity up. "Now you going to tell me what's bothering you?"

Trinity let Joshua in on the information she just received about Daniels' sadistic nature. While Trinity had been preparing for this ultimate battle, realizing who she would be up against had her thinking about whether she would even survive. The thought of her enemy torturing her for his own pleasure weighed heavy on her mind.

Trinity was tough mentally and physically. She has been through a lot with the death of her son. At one point, to the brink of the abyss, she wanted to take her life but still held on without understanding why. During Special Forces training, this was referred to as survival instincts. "Perhaps the most obvious case is the fight-or-flight response," the SF instructor was saying. "When you are faced with danger or stress, a biological trigger helps us decide whether to stay and fight or get the heck out of there - flight. Adrenaline is released into the bloodstream, our heart rate increases, blood is pumped more quickly into our muscles and limbs. Our awareness, sight, and impulses all intensify and quicken. Early man faced many dangers, and the fight-or-flight response evolved to help them evade or battle those dangers to survive. Today, it's what allows an ordinary Joe to rush into an ambush to pull a comrade out of the line of fire or a mother to lift a car off her children -- a phenomenon known as hysterical strength. Those who listen to their bodies will survive.

Those who don't will come home in a body bag." Trinity displayed the same characteristics as his Special Forces comrades. He was proud of what Trinity had accomplished so far. She had fought back from the brink and endured the endless training sessions to hone her body to become a weapon to fight for her beliefs.

"So, where do I begin?" Trinity said. "I started looking into the data that Kenny was processing. It's amazing how easy it is to connect intelligence when you can start connecting seemingly unrelated data now that Kenny has given me the Rosetta Stone. When I started running Daniels' SIM locations to significant events, I realized something is going on that is much bigger than my personal vendetta against Daniels." Joshua interrupted, "Wait a second, Trinity. I thought there were four possible SIMs that Kenny still needed to eliminate to find Daniels." Trinity replied, "That's not a problem, Joshua. Based on the five possible SIMs, it is no problem to run a global search against those SIMs. Really, Joshua, we are, after all, the Operational Division of Homeland Security. We have access to the computers at NSA. I will put in a request; the queries that those guys can run are amazing. The specification on their system is highly classified. When our division was formed, we felt it was more efficient to use other agency resources with expertise instead of reinventing the wheel. Case and point, currently, as of 2013, the fastest computer documented in the world is a supercomputer called Tianhe-1A. Those supercomputers consume large amounts of electrical power, almost all of which is converted into heat which requires cooling. The Tianhe-1A, which is in China, by the way, consumes 4.04 Megawatts of electricity. The cost to power and cool the system can be substantial, e.g., 4MW at $0.10/kWh is $400 an hour or about $3.5 million per year. The computer power of the Tianhe - is 223 petaflop/s. For us layman, there is an estimated 300 billion stars in our galaxy. Tianhe-2 can run 100,000 times as many calculations per second as there are stars in the sky. NSA's supercomputer is much faster. NSA probably has 50% of the smartest mathematicians and computer geeks in the world working for them. So why waste our time trying to best what is already the best? We didn't. That is why we have a mandate to force inter-agency cooperation." Joshua had to admit, he was impressed with Trinity's knowledge.

"It appears that Daniels' movement can be traced to multiple high-profile killings throughout the globe. A few questions immediately come to mind. What are the motives behind these killings? Who is pulling Daniels' strings? Someone like him doesn't go rogue. He is following orders versus acting out of a random want to kill. What really raised the red flag was his recent involvement with a drug lord out of Columbia by the name of Raúl. Raúl must have really pissed someone off because his wife was tortured and sent back to him in pieces. The flesh was peeled off her in strips. Her head and breast were mailed back to Raúl in a box. Someone wanted to send a strong message to Raúl to get back in line. When I dug some more, I realized that Raúl was expanding operations into Europe instead of North America. Someone with a lot of clout made sure that one of the most powerful drug lords in South American did what they were told. Based on some working assumptions, whoever it is could have easily taken Raúl out. Still, they didn't because they need him and don't have time to put a new leader in place or deal with an all-out cartel war, so they did the next best thing. They sent a message he wouldn't forget. Finally, I made the connection between thirty Iraqi foreign nationals flying into Columbia very close to the same time that Raúl was sent this message. There is something bigger going on."

"I believe that Daniels' was responsible for her death. She was tortured in the most gruesome way. He made her suffer beyond imagining. Based on a report we picked up from the DEA, it appears she was tortured for three days. From what we discovered about Daniels and his time in captivity, it's evident that he has a deep psychological need to exact vengeance out on women. When I read the DEA report, I will tell you, Joshua, I was taken back and slightly concerned about going after Daniels. Can you imagine the depths of his psychosis? In all honesty, he has me a little afraid." With that last statement, Trinity's eyes started to water.

Joshua spoke at last, "Trinity, there is no simple answer for you. From the very beginning, I have cautioned you on fulfilling this need/desire to exact vengeance. Trust me, when you kill someone, it does something to you. It takes away from your soul. I have seen people like Daniels in combat. They snap and turn into guiltless, mindless killing machines. We are taught our entire life not to kill. Every religion teaches us it's wrong it is to kill. But the military tells you it's okay to kill for your country. Inside of you, you understand that it is wrong, and you have to find a way to co-exist with these competing sets of values. Some people cry. Some become withdrawn as they try to figure it out. Some immerse themselves into books, games, drinking, or even religion as a means of coping. Those are the ones that will eventually figure out how to deal with it. Maybe not well, but they will figure it out. It is the ones that start keeping count. Putting notches on their belts. We call it keeping score. Those are the ones who have the potential to turn into the Daniels of the world. I am not saying that torture didn't give him the right to be bitter and seek revenge. Still, the enemies were always just over the next mountain ridge in this never-ending war of terror. Something snapped in Daniels just like in all others like him. In reality, they probably should not have allowed him back into the war zone after he was liberated by his fellow Delta Force comrades."

"Trinity, I have been teaching you in the hopes that you might find a different way. I have killed my share of enemies for the United States of America. Most of them were just fathers pulled away from their homes to fight because someone threatens to kill their family if they didn't fight. When you search their bodies and see family pictures, you realize they are not much different from you. To be truthful, only a handful of truly evil people needed to be killed, in my view. Unfortunately, the military teaches you that you may go through some "innocents" to get to them. There comes the point that you ask yourself, what am I fighting for? Trinity, if not for my Sifu, I could have easily turned out like Daniels, but I found a different path. One that allows me to understand that sometimes, there is no easy answer. Sometimes people die for the greater good, or in some cases, it is just them or you. It is my hope that by training you, you will find that place of balance and peace. One day, if you ever come across Daniels that you kill him, not because of what he did to Robbie and you, but because he is a blight that needs to be removed from the face of this planet."

Trinity continued her analysis of the Daniels/Cartel connection and how this tied into the Iraqi Foreign

Nationals in Columbia. According to the DEA data, Raúl had one of the most prevalent pipelines of drugs and people into the United States. It was speculated that Raúl controlled or highly influenced at least three prominent Mexican Drug Lords. In Columbia, Raúl had grown into the largest trafficker of drugs, sex trade of underage minors (both girls and boys), and smuggling Hispanics into the United States. Raúl blackmailed the families of these illegal immigrants into paying 10% of what was sent back to them. If they refused, he threatened to turn them over to ICE, where they would be deported at best. Worst, they would be incarcerated. Two things about Raúl that concerned Trinity:

One: With Raúl's reach, who is powerful enough to cower Raúl by torturing and killing his wife and more importantly, why would someone want to?

Two: With Raúl having the most extensive pipeline into the U.S., what was the connection with the Iraqi nationals?

Between her training at ORD and the lessons learned from 9-11, she was a firm believer in the philosophy "there are no such things as a coincident." With the appearance of Daniels in Columbia around Melina's death, coinciding with Raúl's expansion into Europe, there was something significant in the works.

Who does Daniels work for? As much as she wanted to say what happened to her and Robbie wasn't connected, she couldn't. Avenging Robbie's murder was her single driving purpose once she came out of her Depression. It's what drove her, shaped her world. Now Joshua's words came back to her. "Learn from my lessons. I'm teaching you in the hopes that you won't repeat my mistakes. Dealing with Daniels is much bigger than Robbie's death. Daniels is just part of the blithe that needs to be removed from the face of this planet. If the cause is just that will sustain you when money paid to a mercenary will not be enough to make them fight against impossible odds."

Without a doubt, Trinity knew something big was about to happen again on United States soil. Something either on par with 9-11 or more significant. The next question: What is the target, and when will they strike? It was evident that she couldn't trust her own agency. While she felt that Joshua and Kenny were excellent resources, would it be enough? Even with Joshua's network of ex-military special operators, would it be enough to stop what will happen, especially if the government was involved? Even with World War II and Pearl Harbor's attack, many historians still can't understand how the attack was ever allowed to happen. With the intelligence available on the Japanese fleet at the time, it was inconceivable that Japan could have launched such a decisive surprise attack. It was almost as if the entire government and military forgot how to communicate. A calamity of errors lead to the single largest loss of life in one day in the history of the military. Trinity's master's degree was in Geopolitical

Studies from Boston University. Her thesis was titled

"Understanding the Hidden Origins of War Beyond the

Commonly Postulated Theories." Her focus was primarily

around the influence of corporations on government

decisions to make war or not, the power behind the

perceived power. Beyond the geopolitical ramifications of

winning a war, who benefits the most economically from war?

Before the United States entered World War II, it was still

recovering from the Great Depression. Nothing the

government did was enough. Americans were barely getting

by. With our entry into World War II, the entire nation's

industrial engine was primarily focused on manufacturing

equipment for the war effort. This indeed was America's

Industrial Revolution. Trinity's paper went on to describe

the Keynesian economic model. Keynes argued that the

solution to the Great Depression was to stimulate the

economy through some combination of two approaches: a

reduction in interest rates and government investment in

infrastructure projects. By reducing the interest rate at

which the central bank lends money to commercial banks, the

government signals to commercial banks that they should do

the same for their customers. Investment by the government

in infrastructure injects income into the economy by

creating business opportunities, employment, and demand and

reversing the imbalance mentioned above. During his

presidency, Roosevelt adopted some aspects of Keynesian

economics, especially after 1937, when, in the depths of

the Depression, the United States suffered from recession yet again following fiscal contraction. But to many, the true success of Keynesian policy was seen at the onset of World War II, which provided a kick to the world economy, removed uncertainty, and forced the rebuilding of destroyed capital.

Coming out of World War II, the U.S. was a Superpower, not just because of military might but because of their economic power. The corporations that were built during World War II became worldwide leaders of industry for decades to come. So, it was speculated by some theorists that the attack on Pearl Harbor was "allowed" to happen; to wake the sleeping giant. Who had the authority behind the politicians? Who benefited from the 291,557 American soldiers that died fighting for this country?

It was theorized that the same type of mistakes that led to Pearl Harbor was present again during the 9-11 events. The intelligence was there, but critical information wasn't passed on to the right people because of inter-agency bureaucracy. Her paper explored all aspects of the hidden reasons behind war, and to ignore the conspiracy theorist would be a big mistake. Both Pearl Harbor and 9-11, both according to theorists, should have never happened. That is unless someone in the government wanted it to happen. The forensic evidence of the data revealed that the breakdown in critical information being shared was the link that allowed these atrocities to happened. Either to a

114

violation of protocol or a superior holding onto data.
Whether it was for personal gain or the fear of being under
the microscope for reporting wrong information. Based on
the thesis, the war on Terrorism came on the heels of a
major U.S. recession. When you apply the Keynesian model
to 9-11, you will find that the United States didn't have
the economic lift as it did during World War II. The
United States remained in a recession. The United States
war industry had become so specialized that only a handful
of companies benefited from the war; however, look at the
changes that came about post 9-11: The Patriot Act, the
FBI's Carnivore Monitoring Program, the TSA, the global use
of the Millimeter Wave Scanner Technology, are just a few
of the significant policy changes that have affected our
way of life.

Trinity thought, *So, why go back to Iraq?* All the
evidence used to justify going back to Iraq, the 2nd time
was briefed by Secretary of State, General (Retired) Colin
Powell. Once the war was started, teams of investigators
searched without success to find the evidence presented by
Colin Powell. At the end of his first term, Colin Powell
resigned. He felt used. He had gained the hearts and
confidence of the American people during and after the 1st
Gulf War. Now that was used against him to start an
"Unjust War."

*And now, here we go again, about to allow another
terrorist attack to happen on American soil. For what?*

Trinity thought, *What can I do to stop it this time? I'm sure if I asked the analyst of Pearl Harbor and 9-11 the same question, their response would be much different this time.* Something kept nagging at the edge of Trinity's subconscious. She knew she was missing something. Not seeing the complete picture. Joshua even said something about a mission in Iraq and letting another warlord live for some geopolitical reason. The attempt on her life for stumbling across some damaging information against the Vice President, which she still hasn't figured out yet. They were all connected. She just couldn't put it together. She needed to meet with Joshua and Kenney to see if they could figure out what was happening collectively.

Col. Myers could no longer ignore the intelligence being generated around a breach of operational security. Someone was piecing together "Operation Scimitar," and all signs pointed to Trinity. He thought for sure she could no longer be a viable threat with the death of her son. She was suicidal based on the last psych report he had reviewed. She was clinically depressed and was a borderline drunk. Then she did something totally unexpected, she started training with a Kung Fu teacher named Joshua. He was teaching her Tai Chi, and his business was legit. However, his concern began to shape when Trinity started improving and when her boss sent in

his sitreps. Col. Myers was keyed into the fact that
Trinity was remembering and trying to affect an outcome
beyond finding out who her killer was. Steps needed to be
taken to keep Trinity at bay. Col. Myers felt Joshua might
deserve another more thorough review because Trinity had
improved so much. On closer inspection of Joshua's
background, it was uncovered that Joshua was ex-Delta
Force, Special Forces A-Team Captain, and a Ranger Platoon
Leader. He had served in some tough spots, fighting in the
war on terrorism. A few missions came back classified,
eyes only, and redacted. This fact didn't concern him
because those missions in Iraq coincided with the
activities of the Directorate. From Joshua's team's
perspective, these missions were a cluster fuck that nearly
got his men killed; the Directorate has scored these
missions as complete successes. These missions happened to
be part of the opening moves for a larger mission that now
included Operation Scimitar, which was finally playing out
the final act. The Warlord that was Joshua's target was
critical to the Directorate's plans for the artifact's
recovery. If anyone other than Iraqi nationals were caught
looting Iraq's national treasures, looking for the Ark, it
would have created world-wide condemnation. This kind of
attention could set them back for many years.

What was unexpected was the fact that one of the Iraqi
Factions within the Shia Arabs would discover what the
Directorate was searching for. Not only had they figured

out that a mysterious outside benefactor was using a rival to search for the Ark of the Covenant, but they might have figured out what the Ark did. Intelligence suggested that they had hatched a plan that would allow them to take on Israel, head-to-head, and eventually retake their land. The Directorate absolutely did not need the Middle East up in flames with an all-out war with Israel; hence, the current plan to have the U.S. military back in Iraq and eventually a permanent presence occupying the entire country. It was done with the MFO (Multi-Force and Observers) Mission in Egypt, which established a permanent presence between Egypt and Israel after the Egypt Israel Syria War in 1973.

If nothing else, Col. Myers believed in following protocol. The fact that Trinity and Joshua were training together, no big deal. The fact that both had connections to past and present operations, again, no big deal. What, however, was a big deal was that Trinity's behavior had changed since meeting Joshua. She was now asking more questions and piecing together parts of Operation Scimitar. Degrees of separation weren't enough anymore. Protocol dictated to eliminate all threats, and now Trinity had become a threat: She was asking questions about Raúl and Melina with the DEA; The communication that was intercepted by Trinity to the Vice President of the United States; The request for more information on Grimm. It was time to eliminate a potentially growing threat. However, contrary to what was said to Grimm, Col. Myers had no intention of using him to eliminate Trinity.

Col. Myers turned and called out to Jennifer. "Yes, Sir," Jennifer replied. "Get the leader of the Night Stalkers on the line. I believe his name is Thornton. Jennifer, when you get him on the line, please forward to my office." Without waiting for Jennifer to answer the order, Col. Myers turned and headed toward his office. As Col. Myers was sitting down, the intercom buzzed. "Thornton is on line 1, Sir." "Thanks, Jennifer. Put him through." After the call was transferred, Myers waited until the secure LED turned green, indicating that he was now on a wholly scrambled and shielded line and could communicate freely. Once secured, all recordings were halted for the duration of the call. The only checks and balances were a log file that he was required to maintain as per protocol. This log file was sent to Central Security Audit. It was matched against other logs to ensure a double-blind check occurred. The log file was finally compared against the gaps in the security recordings. There were no chances taken to ensure there were no leaks or spies among the ranks.

"Thornton here. How many I help you?" "I have a job for your Night Stalkers." The Stalkers were the equivalent of the U.S. Military's Delta Force. Under his command, Myers had spies, assassins, paramilitary, night stalkers, and mercenaries at his disposal. His forces were designed to fight, sustain, and win in any theater in the world if the scope of the operation was limited in size and duration. He loved using the Night Stalkers because they were recruited from the ranks of the military's elite, Delta, Seals, Special Forces, Rangers, PJs, & Force Recon. They followed orders without question.

"Thornton, I'm sending you over a file on a female named Trinity Winters. She is an analyst with ORD. I need you to eliminate her. Make it look like a mugging gone badly." "No problem, Sir. Any specific timetable?" Myers paused for a few seconds wishing he didn't have to take these actions but finally responded. "As soon as possible, Myers Out."

Trinity, Joshua, and Kenny sat around the central command and control planning table in the Zombie Room. They were in the process of brainstorming, trying to collate all the different data points to see if they could piece together what the overall objective was. Nothing was off the table. The command console had a 50-inch LED screen embedded into the table. Kenny had reprogrammed the Microsoft Kinect to allow individuals to interact with the touch screen. This enhancement allowed Kenny to create a virtual whiteboard just by waving his hands through the air. The added benefit, he could quickly re-arrange data to portray a different line of thought. "A few things are clear," Trinity stated. "It is obvious someone wants the United States back in Iraq. The question is, why go back to Iraq for the 3rd time? The 1st Gulf War made sense. The 2nd war not so much. Now a 3rd war? By engineering another mass terrorist attack on United States soil by Iraqi Nationals, it would almost certainly ensure a long-term U.S. presence in Iraq." Trinity continued, "It's almost as if someone is looking for something and wants to use the U.S. Military as a cover while they search."

"Kenny, can you run a search on anything significant that stands out in the 2nd war besides the obvious?" asked Trinity. Joshua then chimed in, "Trinity, why only search the 2nd war and not the 1st Gulf War?" "That's easy, Joshua. Besides Special Ops, there was no real military presence in Iraq during the 1st war; therefore, I believe whatever these guys were searching for did not become relevant until the 2nd war." "Good point," Joshua said in agreement. Trinity continued, "Look for the fringe Kenny. If you can find something, it might be the key to unlocking this mystery."

"Now the other question, who is behind all of this? Who is this shadow organization? So far, we know that the Vice President is involved along with Daniels and two corporations, the Axion Corporation Int'l, and Prometheus Unrestricted. How widespread does this reach within our government? Who can we rely on for help when we need it? I'm afraid to engage my boss based on how he has been acting. The fact that every time I bring something to my boss, the investigations have been shut down or stonewalled. So, as far as ORD is concerned, I'm afraid they might be compromised as well. Thinking back to my thesis from college, I briefed you both on earlier. I believe this group has been manipulating American foreign policy going back at least to World War II. Sorry that I didn't start my research earlier, but I never thought I would be here at this point in my life either." Trinity smiled sadly.

Joshua took the floor, sensing that Trinity was about to have a moment thinking about how all these events converged, taking Robbie's life. "Based on what we uncovered about my previous failed mission in Iraq with Axion, it stands to reason that there is a thread that connects all of these events. Obviously, uranium was not what they were searching for, and whatever it was, they definitely didn't find it. Kenny, why don't you include Abu Hafez Al-Sheik in your search or the area his faction controlled? Maybe look at old legends, fables."

"Putting my Spec Ops hat back on, the question foremost in my mind is what to do about the potential terrorist that are about to enter this country and what are they planning? I need to start working on gathering my old teammates and resources. It's going to take some time, and we need to prepare. Those 30 Iraqi Nationals could split into multiple teams, causing all kinds of havoc across the U.S.

We have to prepare for everything from conventional attacks to biological to chemical. I hate to say this, but maybe even nuclear. We just don't know what they are planning and what the timetable is. Kenny, the quicker you are with your research, the better chance we have of stopping this. Based on the way events are moving, we need to know what we are up against in the next 48 hours. I'm sorry that so much is on your shoulders, Kenny, but we have no other choice."

"No problem guys, I will do my best." Kenny turned to his computer and started typing, his shoulder slightly slumped with the weight of responsibility.

Kenny knew the key to success was to do something the government had never been successful doing. To be truthful, the government had turned the lack of inter-agency cooperation and bureaucratic red tape into an art form. Kenny often wondered how such incompetence could be the norm with so many PhDs working for the government. The government had the most extensive collection of the smartest dumb people he had ever met. Kenny smiled at that analogy. It's amazing the government could function at all. *Oh well, time to get to work*, Kenny thought.

Kenny started working his magic on three different computer systems. Each one was useful to separately hack into the NSA, CIA, and DEA's server farms. The CIA and DEA's servers were relatively easy to hack into. The NSA

123

was a different story altogether. The NSA had a totally
separate server system dedicated to performing security
sweeps on every server every hour. The most time he had
ever been able to hack into NSA was 10 minutes without the
security server detecting his intrusion and shutting off
the source of the breach. This time Kenny was going to try
something different: create an intelligent trojan horse
virus that would invade every server at once. The goal of
the virus was to infect the RAM on every server. It will
reside on the firmware versus on the operating system.
While not foolproof, firmware viruses made it easier to
evade detection. The secret was to make the initial attack
obvious. Let the virus protection server think that it had
detected a threat. The genius of the NSA's security system
called SIRVS (Security, Intelligence, Reactive, and Virus
System), or pronounced "Sirus," was in how it operated.
Its job was to first identify any threats. If a threat was
identified, it would immediately take that server offline
to isolate and minimize any danger of the virus spreading.
Once the server was separated from the network, SIRVS would
then isolate the virus on the infected server.

The NSA's servers communicated via a totally separate
internet protocol. Designed to make it almost impossible
for a hacker to break into their network. The government
financed an initiative called Next Generation Internet
(NGI) program, which met all its goals except for its
pursuit of a Terabit per second networking in FY2002. This

initiative was intended to drastically increase the speed of the Internet, exclusively used by the U.S. Government. While the NGI Program is completed, Federal agencies are still coordinating advanced networking research programs under the Large Scale Networking (LSN) Coordinating Group. The NSA operated on two different networks, the shared government network under the LSN project and Advance Next Generation Network (ANGN), the backplane for its servers. So, the LSN protocols were taken offline when a server was infected, and SIRVS continued to communicate via the ANGN.

Kenny's trojan horse virus was to create both a transient and resident virus. Being transient would allow the virus to attach itself to the anti-virus program when it is executed. Being resident would enable the virus to locate itself in the memory. It can remain active or be activated as a stand-alone program, even after its attached program ends. Kenny started the process of modifying some old Malware he previously used to hack into several systems. He embedded code that would act as a logic bomb when SIRVS attacked it. He created a tag that would attach itself to the SIRVS software and slightly modify its base functionality. Kenny's virus would gain control of SIRVS, causing it to spread to each system by following its programming logic to immediately scan each system for the same type of anomaly and eradicate it.

Kenny also knew that this type of attack would at most have a life span of about four hours because every three to

four hours, SIRVS did a firmware scan for resident viruses.
So, while an NSA-wide infection was complicated, it was
easy enough for Kenny. The key of Kenny's plan was to
create an automatic shut down for his virus. Every two
hours, it would shut down and stop transmitting. This way,
it would go undetected by SIRVS's firmware scan. The
variable that Kenny could not plan for was the change in
SIRVS's scanning intervals. This was the wild card. SIRVS
changed the frequency and interval of its scans, so this
virus might go undetected for 2 hours or 2 days. Still,
eventually, it would be detected and eradicated. He also
knew that any type of virus had a lifespan of only one use
on the NSA servers because of SIRVS's adaptive nature.

36 hours later, Kenny had completed the virus and was
ready to brief Joshua and Trinity. Joshua could hear the
excitement in Kenny's voice when he called him. He knew
his residential nerd had done it. When Trinity and Joshua
joined Kenny at the command console in the Zombie room,
Joshua couldn't help but feel sorry for Kenny. He had red-
rimmed eyes with bags visibly below them. Joshua's empathy
was a momentary thing because of the excitement clearly
displayed in Kenny's smile.

"So, what have you got for us?" Trinity asked.
"Actually, not as much as I would like," responded Kenny.
"Why did you call this meeting then" Trinity chastised. "I
had to take a day off work, and I can't afford that.
Especially with the scrutiny, I am under. Sam is a hair's

breadth from firing me." Joshua just smiled and laid a hand on Trinity's arm, imploring her to be calm down. "Trinity, give Kenny a second. I've known him a long time, and he wouldn't call us in here unless he had something important to tell us." Kenny took the next 30 minutes to explain how his virus worked. "Now, the true genius lies in how we will collect the information from all three agencies." Joshua just shook his head. Kenny was lost in his own brilliance, and rightfully so. Anyone with an I.Q. of 185 could afford to live in their own world. If employed correctly, they could even be a productive member of society.

"I'm sure you both are aware of how Visual Cryptography works. It is a special encryption technique to hide information in images. It can be decrypted by human vision if the correct key image is used. This type of encryption was proposed by Naor and Shamir in 1994. Visual Cryptography uses two transparent images. One image contains random pixels, and the other image contains secret information. It is impossible to retrieve the secret information from only one of the images. Either transparent images or layers are required to reveal the information. When the random image contains truly random pixels, it can be seen as a one-time pad system and offer unbreakable encryption. This method of encryption has become the norm for most operatives in the world. Mainly because of its security, ease of use, and low cost to operate. As you are aware, my computer system stores information from every website in the world through its special web crawlers that I designed. My virus is designed to send out bits of information to websites throughout the world. Using Visual Cryptography as an example, think about the world wide web as a picture. Truthfully, an image broken down is simply a series of ones and zeros (ex. 100011001). I will call them bytes to make it easier for our discussion. My image is just larger, and utilizing my algorithm of the data stored on our system, I will decrypt this information. Then, Trinity and I can analyze it on our workstations. My virus will only transmit the information that we discussed for our search criteria. These bytes are disguised as part of the internet traffic as individuals search the web as part of their jobs. The goal is to keep the byte transmissions evenly dispersed throughout each agency. It must be low enough that the upload size of the bytes doesn't trigger a response from SIRVS and not create a violation of Internet use protocol."

"When you give me the "G.O.," I will initiate the trojan horse attack. It should take about one hour for SIRVS to recognize that a server has been infected, then another four hours for the virus to replicate. After which, the virus should start transmitting data and continue transmitting data for up to two days on the optimistic side or four hours on the pessimistic side. Conservatively, we should get about a day's worth of data before SIRVS changes its frequency of scanning intervals and detects my virus. Suppose the shutdown function works correctly and they don't change the scanning intervals. In that case, we should be able to get everything that we need from each agency. I am already putting together the SQL queries necessary to quickly get us the answers we seek. All I need is the final go-ahead from you both. Once initiated, there is no going back, and getting information in this manner will no longer be possible."

Joshua spoke first, "Well, Trinity, I say we go for it. I don't see any other option. While understanding the "Why?" is important, I am more concerned about stopping American soil's imminent attack. As we used to say in Spec Ops, "Cause and Effect. While we might never understand the cause of something, we definitely were responsible for the effect." Trinity simply nodded her head, deep in thought. As much as she wanted to utilize the comprehensive resources of her agency and the U.S. Government, she didn't have a choice any longer. Time had simply run out, and Trinity didn't know who to trust. As she turned away, feeling like the weight of the world was on her shoulders, she couldn't help but wonder, was she making a mistake?

"Also," Kenny chimed in, "I was able to put a working theory together as to why they want the U.S. Military back in Iraq for the 3rd time. In 2003, there was widespread looting of Iraq's National Museums. As the full extent of the looting in Baghdad emerged, it became clear that there was nothing accidental about it. Instead, it was the result of a well-planned scheme to plunder the artistic and historical treasures held in the museums of Iraq. Once the museum staff could communicate with the outside world, however, it became apparent that the looting was not random. It was the work of people who knew what they were looking for and came equipped explicitly for the job.

In an interview with Ann Talbot, Dr. Dony George, head of the Baghdad Museum, said, "I believe they were people who knew what they wanted. They had passed by the gypsum copy of the Black Obelisk. This means that they must have been specialists. They did not touch those copies."

The U.S. reluctance to act cannot be explained by any lack of warning. Professional archaeologists and art historians had told the Pentagon of the danger of looting beforehand. Dr. Irving Finkel of the British Museum told sources that the looting was "entirely predictable and could easily have been stopped." "Now that we know about the conspiracy ongoing in our government, I can't help but to believe that the military was ordered to focus their efforts elsewhere.", stated Kenny.

"I believe that this mysterious organization found something that has led them to something significant in their ultimate agenda. They have been steadily pursuing this agenda since 2003 and are willing to start another war to achieve their objective. Whatever it is, they want to use the U.S. Military to provide cover for their operation. Among the artifacts that have been stolen were the sacred vase of Warka, a 5,000-year-old golden vessel found at Ur, an Akkadian statue base, and an Assyrian statue. None of the other artifacts identified as stolen had any significant value beyond their monetary worth. After several more hours of research, I was able to eliminate the sacred vase of Warka. On the other hand, the Assyrian statue was believed to hold clues to the whereabouts of the Ark of the Covenant. This information came from an obscure article written in the Biblical Archaeology Review. Last year, CNN reported that Ethiopia was the resting place of the Ark. I, however, believe that the CNN report is wrong. Considering the current events leading us to Iraq."

"Any clue as to what the Ark does?" asked Trinity. "Good question Trinity. I haven't been able to determine, with any reliable accuracy, what it does.", said Kenny. "There are several theories, but one common thread that runs true is that it contains ultimate knowledge. The theories range anywhere from biblical to alien conspiracies. Considering my belief about the bible and how it was written by individuals who confused technology as miracles or mystic events. I believe all these references are linked but biased by man's own selfish beliefs and fears. What if the Ark was, in fact, a source of knowledge but some kind of alien-based computer technology?"

Trinity and Joshua just stared at Kenny for a moment taking it all in. "Since this is only my theory based on all the articles I have read so far, I wouldn't make any operational plans based on it. However, I will continue to do research.", said Kenny. "Regardless of what we believe, this organization wants something badly in Iraq and will do anything to get it. The only clues we have steer us to the Ark of the Covenant." "I'll continue my research and start working on uploading the virus."

With their approval, Kenny took his seat at his workstation to prepare his virus for launch. Trinity and Joshua both left with a lot to do and a lot on their minds.

It had been 30 days since Joshua and Trinity had given Kenny the go-ahead to hack into the government's database. The virus had worked perfectly. Kenny's virus had successfully infected the servers. It had transmitted data for 3 days on the NSA's servers, 5 days on the CIA's servers, and 6 days for DEA's. The visual cryptography program collected over 300 GBs of data associated with Trinity and Joshua's search parameters from the last transmission. While initially disjointed, Kenny and Trinity were able to piece enough information together to help Joshua formulate a plan of attack. It was discovered China's Ministry of State Security (MSS) had dispatched one of its best operatives Wu Liang to Iraq. He had been

operating there for six months when thirty Iraqi Nationals
had received visas to travel to China. Not in numbers to
attract attention, but all thirty Iraqi Nationals in
Columbia had never returned to Iraq over six months. The
CIA database had been collecting data about the MSS
training camp for the past 5 years. It was believed that
members of the Taliban had first learned how to create
improvised explosive devices or (IED) from training camps
deep in China sponsored by the MSS. An IED is a bomb
constructed and deployed in ways other than in conventional
military action. It may be built of conventional military
explosives, such as an artillery round, attached to a
detonating mechanism. Roadside bombs are commonly used.
IEDs are generally seen in heavy terrorist actions or in
unconventional warfare by guerrillas or commando forces in
a theater of operations. In the second Iraq War, IEDs were
used extensively against US-led invasion forces. By the end
of 2007, they had become responsible for approximately 63%
of coalition deaths in Iraq.

The MSS was first suspected of being involved in the
training of the Taliban when a Delta Forces team had killed
a known MSS operative Ng Yu Wei in 2009. It was a typical
night op designed to take out the leaders of the Taliban.
During the operation, the Delta unit encountered extreme
resistance. 2 members of the Delta team were killed, and
several received minor injuries. The team leader had to
call in air support from Apache helicopters to avert an

all-out mission disaster. During the after-action assessment, it was then that the Delta team discovered Wei and several members of the Snow Leopard Commando Unit were among the Taliban dead. The CIA pieced together critical information that had eluded them on how the Taliban had become so adept at unconventional warfare.

The CIA had lost track of the thirty Iraqi Nationals. Still, the DEA had reacquired them in Columbia two months ago. While the DEA didn't know who they had acquired, Trinity and Kenny quickly identified these Iraqis. Based on the photos from the Chinese visas and the fake passports of the Iraqis as they entered Columbia, the thirty were an identical match.

The NSA had been tracking MSS activities *as it relates to activities* beyond teaching terrorists how to make IEDs. The US Government was confident that the US Military could now competently deal with IEDs thanks to the efforts of the US Explosive Ordnance Disposal (EDO) Military units. The EDO had been the point of the Pentagon's Joint IED Defeat Organization (JIEDDO). JIEDDO used its experience in Iraq. Its members spent their time analyzing roadside bomb attacks over the last decade. Leading efforts to build technology to find and defuse these explosive devices to create effective counter-IED technology and techniques. Everything from Handheld Detectors to Vehicle Mounted Sensors to Drones and Robots to Video Game-Like Trainers.

While the JIEDDO was constantly having to evolve its counter technology efforts to match the terrorists developing IED devices, it was a battle that was finally under control. The NSA was worried about the rumors that the MSS was now training terrorist groups to use Biological and Chemical warfare. China had known for decades that its military was no match for the US Military in a head-to-head conflict, even with its billion-man army. With the projection of power that the US Naval Carrier Fleet afforded the US, China was effectively confined to the Asian-Pacific region of the world. China wanted a way to deal with the US. Politburo had listened to MSS's recommendation and approved their strategic approach to dealing with the US. The MSS wished to emulate the cold war tact between the US and the USSR, where the intelligent agencies were on the frontline of the battlefield. The NSA was worried about China's ambitions of expansion into Japan, Taiwan, and Siberia. Japan and Taiwan for the territorial buffers and their global technological, industrial might. For Siberia, China wanted the oil-rich regions to supply energy for its growing infrastructural needs. The ever-increasing global markets of China had everyone worried, especially the NSA. The NSA had been tracking down leads that the MSS was experimenting with Anthrax.

Kenny's briefing went on to explain to Joshua that most people do not understand Anthrax. While the news media glamourized it as this white powder in envelopes just to get ratings. Anthrax is still relatively unknown to the public. Anthracis, commonly known as Anthrax, is a member of the genus Bacillus family and forms dormant endospores or spores for short. They can survive in harsh conditions for decades or even centuries. These spores can be found on all continents. When inhaled, ingested, or come into contact with a skin lesion on a host, they may become reactivated and multiply rapidly. With a sly smile, Kenny also admitted that some of his information was taken shamelessly from Wikipedia.

Anthrax commonly infects herbivorous or plant-eating animals that ingest or inhale the spores while grazing. Ingestion is believed to be the most common route by which animals contract Anthrax. Carnivores living in the same environment may become infected by consuming infected animals. Anthrax does not spread directly from one infected animal or person to another; it is spread by spores. These spores can be transported by clothing or shoes. The body of an animal that had active Anthrax at the time of death can also be a source of anthrax spores. Due to anthrax spores' hardiness and their ease of production in vitro, they are extraordinarily well suited to use (in powdered and aerosol form) as biological weapons. Such weaponization has been accomplished in the past by at least five state bioweapons programs — those of the United Kingdom, Japan, the United States, Russia, and Iraq — and has been attempted by several others. It's believed China is on this list with a first full-scale attack planned for execution on US soil.

The NSA report theorized that China's intended delivery vehicle for their weaponized Anthrax would be an air dispersant via a low-yield bomb designed for maximum dispersal. Similar to the way a dust initiator bomb works. This way, the spores are inhaled versus being digested. Inhalation anthrax infection starts primarily in the chest's lymph nodes before spreading throughout the rest of the body, ultimately causing severe breathing problems and shock. Inhalation anthrax is the deadliest form of Anthrax. Infection usually develops within a week after exposure, but it can take up to 2 months. Without treatment, only about 10 - 15% of patients with inhalation anthrax survive. However, with aggressive treatment, about 55% of patients survive. With widespread infection, aggressive treatment will be next to impossible.

To get the maximum exposure possible, detonation would need to occur in a venue that would attract many people. An enclosed sports venue would have the most impact. This would allow the spores to be contained in the structure and nothing to escape outside into the atmosphere. So now, Joshua's team had a list of wide-ranging attack vectors to plan for. Anything from infrastructure attacks to limited terrorist attacks on small groups of people to chemical or biological attacks. Now the question was how to track

these groups. Lucky for us, Kenny already had a plan.
Some assumptions needed to be made, but Kenny was sure that
the same methodology used to track Daniels' movement could
track these terrorists. This would be a two-fold brute
force attack analysis. Since we have pictures of all the
Iraqis, utilizing all the CCTV and security cameras would
be straightforward using facial recognition.   While this
would take up ample data storage and CPU processing power,
both were relatively cheap and easy to add to Kenny's
customized system.   The other key component was to track
their cell phones, which would be more difficult but not
impossible. The working assumptions are the

1. Cells will have disposable cell phones.

2. They would have been activated about the same time.

3. There would not be a lot of communication once the
    operation started.

4. Each cell will be operating independently and operating
    off a predetermined set of targets.

Kenny would first try and determine if 30 cell phones
were activated within a brief period within the vicinity of
one cell phone tower around the time the Iraqis arrived in
the country. Even if that number was larger than thirty,
it would still be manageable. Once these cell phone
numbers were identified, Kenny would run a cross-reference
query against those numbers on every tower in the US the
same way he did Daniels.

Joshua stood over Trinity as she laid in the prone position with an assault rifle firmly against her right shoulder. "Slow your breathing. Fire after you have exhaled your breath and are at the resting position. Slowly squeeze the trigger; when it fires, it should come as a surprise." Trinity had Joshua in her head coaching her. She had been at the range for over 2 weeks now with Joshua's team of ex-special ops buddies. They were in Texas at Peter Cullum's ranch in Waco, Texas. This would be their base of operations to try to stop the terrorist attacks from happening. There were 20 guys on the range, either zeroing weapons or just re-familiarizing themselves with various weapons. Another 20 were rehearsing squad-level battle drills. Since coming to the ranch, Trinity had been trained on every weapon imaginable: Glock, Smith and Wesson, Beretta, Browning, Bushmaster, Colt, Heckler Koch, and Ruger. Firing various handguns, assault rifles, machine guns, and sniper weapons. Joshua made sure she was familiar with the various hand grenades from smoke, frags, WP, and flashbangs. Explosive familiarity was also part of her training. Every day was something different, a new weapon system, a new simulated target, another mission. Still, one thing was constant over the past two weeks: physical conditioning. Every morning at 0430 hours, the day would start with warm-ups following by a 5-mile run. The pace was always brisk. As everyone was getting back in shape, several team members threw up the first few days, but Trinity was impressed. No one ever quit. These guys were hardened by years of fighting in some of the worst terrains in the world. They were conditioned by fighting an enemy that wouldn't quit.

Based on Joshua's estimates, they still had about two more weeks of intensive training before Joshua felt comfortable engaging the enemy. Left on the training agenda: MOUNT operations; SERE (Survival, Evasion, Resistance, & Escape); NBC (Nuclear, Biological, & Chemical); Guerilla Warfare; and Martial Arts Training.

Bravo Team was in overwatch position providing security while Alpha Team was preparing to breach and assault the kill house as part of their MOUNT training. Two - two-man sniper teams were also positioned. Sniper Team 1 was tasked to take out enemy snipers and/or delay reinforcements from engaging. Sniper Team 2 was tasked with taking out the 2 sentries posted on lookouts at opposite ends of the building complex. The teams used the M21 sniper rifle made by Rock Island Arsenal. At half a klick with the 7.62 mm sniper rifle suppressed, Sniper Team 2 would be able to take out both sentries with no issues.

Joshua was with Alpha Team directing the breach and assault. For this last and final MOUNT exercise before the teams deployed, live humans and real munitions. Charlie and

Delta Teams were acting as the combatants with hostages. While dressed as civilians, both Charlie and Delta wore full body armor, including Kevlar helmets, goggles, and face shields. Alpha Team was equipped with their standard armament with the exception, they would be utilizing rubber bullets. It was expected that the assault team would fire two round center of mass followed by one round to the head as rehearsed. The sniper teams used live ammunition while not targeting the sentries; they were supposed to hit the designated targets next to the guards.

Alpha Team split into two fire teams consisting of five men each. Fire Team 1 split and headed to the front door, while Fire Team 2 headed toward the back door. Explosives were set on each entry. One team member from each fire team was set up by the windows preparing to lob Flash Bang grenades as soon as the doors were breached. Their job was also to remain outside to ensure no one escaped the four two-man clearing teams. On Joshua's signal, Sniper Team 2 took out the two sentries while at the same time, both explosives were triggered. The team had learned the hard way in Afghanistan the value of quickly breaching a door. Al-Qaeda started using foot-long bolts that made it near impossible to simply knock down the door with a kick or battering ram. Until the U.S. changed tactics, quite a few high-value targets escaped through bolt holds while their soldiers brought them precious seconds with their lives. With the shock of the explosives followed by the Flash Bang grenades, fewer soldiers were killed or wounded because they now had the element of surprise. The explosives also served a more vital function. It safely triggered any booby traps that might have been set.

With the breach successfully executed, the four two-man clearing teams swept through the house. From Fire Team 1, Joshua and Mac swept left to clear the first room. Sam and Mike went straight down the hallway. From Fire Team 2, Tom and Dan moved straight into the main room, taking out two tangos, trying to recover from the flashbang effects.

James and Paulie moved left to clear the master bedroom. In ten seconds, five tangos were down with three more rooms to clear. Sean and Bennie were crouched low under their respective window, sweeping the area back and forth. They were making sure no one engaged team six while the clearing operation was underway. Tom came on the net shouting that one tango had managed to escape and headed toward the back door. James turned just as the tango was emerging. Before the tango could bring his weapon to bear, James fired two rounds center mass followed by a single head shot. In less than thirty seconds, each team member reported "all clear," and the kill house was cleared of all tangos, a total of ten in all.

All teams converged on the kill house to conduct an AAR. Tactics were discussed, and kill shots were evaluated. Each rubber bullet was coated with a fluorescent dye, so it would leave a mark upon impact. One of the clearing team members suffered minor injuries when he was shot upon entry into the bedroom. He killed the tango, but not before he was shot in the thigh. After everyone was satisfied with the AAR and no more lessons were to be learned, teams rotated. By the end of the day, Trinity was exhausted. While her designated position was either sniper spotter or guarding the team's six, she switched as part of the clearing teams. She was amazed at the level of professionalism displayed and the detachment of emotions shown when a team member was provided a critique. When a team member was killed during the assault, the AAR was conducted. That team would immediately conduct the drill again. While there were only two clearing houses, they were built with sliding walls to constantly change the house for a different look and feel.

A few days later, satisfied that the teams were ready, Joshua brought Kenny in to brief the teams on the latest movement activities. Kenny stood in front of the team members and began the brief. "While training has been ongoing, unfortunately, the terrorist strikes have already started. So far, three confirmed attacks have taken place: a sub-power station in Houston, a water pumping station in Las Vegas, and another sub-power station in San Diego. I'm assuming the other teams are still moving to their designated cities. So far, the authorities are assuming these attacks are gang-related violence as part of some initiation. Only local authorities are dealing with it. No other agency has made a connection with the attacks yet."

Kenny continued, "Tracking the other terrorist cells might prove to be difficult right now due to the communication pattern of the cells: one text to signal arrival at the designated city; one text to signal attack initiated; and one text to signal attack successful. This is the pattern I've been able to attribute to the cell phones I am tracking and correlating with the attacks that have successfully been carried out so far."

Joshua stepped up and thanked Kenny, then laid out the attack plan. "Priority one, we have to neutralize the threat with minimum collateral damage. Our goal is to be in and out like a ghost, unseen. Remember that our law enforcement elements are ignorant of the threat. Unless the engaging unit is the FBI's HRT unit, they are most likely incapable of dealing with the threat. If US law enforcement engages, do not engage; escape and evade to designated rally points in your area of operation. We cannot afford to be captured or identified. We are vigilantes as far as the world knows.

Bravo Fire Team 1 will deploy to Houston. Fire Team 2 will deploy to Las Vegas. Team Charley, your entire team, will deploy to San Diego. Team Delta is the designated reserve unit to assist any team in need. Team Alpha will be responsible for figuring out the larger endgame and deploying to Iraq. Trinity, you will be attached to Alpha Team. As crazy as it sounds, these terrorist attacks are a distraction for something else, something more significant. Someone wants the US back in Iraq for a reason, and we need to stop that from happening, but more importantly, figuring out what they are looking for.

Bravo Fire Team 1 had established their base of operations in a vacant office building two blocks down the road from the Athens Hotel Suites on Clay St, Houston, TX. In conjunction with Kenny, Peter, the team leader, selected this location because it was conveniently located near the Toyota Center (home of the Houston Rockets) and the George Brown Convention Center. If all other attempts to stop the terrorist failed, the final attacks would likely occur at one of these venues. While Peter was confident, it would never come to this. A career in Special Forces taught him to plan for the worst-case scenario. Expect nothing and be prepared for everything.

Peter's Team was in the process of doing a weapons and equipment check. Each team member had disassembled their weapons and performed Preventive Maintenance Checks and Services or PMCS.   Peter was in the process of cleaning his M4 with suppressor. Allen was applying a light coat of machine oil to his M21 sniper rifle. Max was checking the pre-loaded 200-round plastic magazines for his M249 Squad

Automatic Rifle. Manny also carried an M4, and Karl was cleaning his Heckler & Koch HK G36 assault rifle.

The Team was focused. Knowing that they were all that stood in the way of innocent Americans dying for reasons that mattered to only a handful of rich pompous guys that were trying to control the world. *Well, not this time,* Peter thought. *This time his Team will stop the bad guys before any lives are lost.*

Aban and Hakim were in the process of studying the schematics of the wastewater treatment facilities of Houston. Aban was surprised by how much information was readily available on the Internet. Houston's Wastewater Treatment System collects, conveys, and processes wastewater from an estimated 3 million people. The system consists of approximately 6,950 miles of sanitary sewer lines, over 425,000 services connections, over 380 sanitary lift stations, 40 wastewater treatment plants (5 primary and 35 satellite), and three major sludge treatment facilities. Aban and Hakim discussed how feasible it would be to destroy 2 or 3 of the major wastewater treatment plants.

"Hakim, in order of priority, the following plants warrant additional on-site surveillance: Harris County Mud No 119 Water Treatment Plant; HED Environmental Systems; and Gulf Coast Waste Disposal Authority." Aban said,

"Remember, the main goal of the attacks at these facilities is to disable the facility versus creating an obvious terrorist attack. The treatment facilities being targeted are still utilizing chlorine gas as the chemical agent for disinfection. The goal is to destroy the chlorine gas containment units. If the chlorine gas is released, it may threaten the facility employees and the public near the affected facilities. This gas can be deadly if inhaled and, at lower doses, can burn the eyes and skin and inflame the lungs. While this outcome is hoped for, these attacks aim to degrade the infrastructure that creates the illusion of American supremacy. Hakim, take away America's infrastructure and their convenient way of life, and America will become just another third world country."

The sun was just setting as Aban and Leyla conducted surveillance of the Harris County Mud No 119 Water Treatment Plant. Meanwhile, Hakim and Jamail investigated the HED Environmental Systems.

As Aban was studying the facility, he noticed significant upgrades to the facility's perimeter security. Far more than they were briefed when they were training in China. Their online research of the Bioterrorism Act of 2002 required drinking water utilities serving more than 3,300 people to conduct vulnerability assessments and develop emergency response plans.

After two days of surveillance, Aban and Leyla discovered the following: The installation of a 12-foot fence with three rows of barbwire running along the top of the fence angled outward. There were parameter security cameras in place now. While there were no guards in place, there was a central access point with a guard shack. So far, it appeared that the guard shack was staffed from 5am to 6pm. The guard locked the sliding gate fence and secured it with a Neulock-Bolt when leaving for the day. Aban also ran an electronic sweep of the water purification plant. There was one WEP secured network that corresponded to the Harris County Mud No 119 Water Treatment Plant. It was called HarrisSecureNetwork. Aban thought; pretty *original… not*. It appeared that they were using a Cisco SR 500 Series Secure Router. While good, it was easy to hack, especially with the back-door passwords provided by his Chinese handler. Aban smiled; everything *was made in China*.

Consequently, the Chinese Government had access to just about everything manufactured in China for other countries. By hacking into the network, Leyla could disable the security cameras and the automatic alarms that were built into the systems. Links that notified plant supervisors if systems were compromised and link to the local fire and police responders. To cover her footprint, Leyla went into the routing tables to delete any presence of her guest login. She then added a false trail that would point to the site manager as the individual that had disabled the system during a routine maintenance check and failed to reactivate it.

Based on the Intel gathering so far, defeating the security systems and gaining access to the facility would not be a problem. Aban wanted to make sure that his team hit every facility at the same time. Although this was a direct violation of his orders from China, he didn't care.

He wanted the Americans to suffer the way his family suffered. While life under Saddam Hussein was hard, it still was a way of life. At first, when the Americans came in to liberate the Iraqi people, they were cheered, only in the beginning. After defeating the Iraqi Army, the Americans pulled back and allowed the lawless gangs and religious fanatics to govern. That is when life became impossible. Daughters and mothers were raped. Sons and fathers were executed. Life was one terror after another. When the Americans finally moved back to restore order, it was too late. Their heavy-handed approach had resulted in the death of his family when a bomb from a drone strike took out his house instead of the Al-Qaeda facility next door. As reparation for his losses, he received $2,500 for each family member killed, totaling $10,000 for his wife, daughter, and two sons. *America would pay. It was time to bring the war to their shores and incite terror and sleepless nights for the infidels.* Aban didn't want a quiet build-up. He wanted to make a statement. He was prepared to die, so in his mind, it didn't matter. Little did Aban know that his thirst for revenge would have the opposite effect with Peter's team stalking him.

Two days after the surveillance mission, Aban's team was ready to proceed with the first set of attacks. Everything was in place for a simultaneous attack. While a violation of their orders, Aban's team was of one mind. America would pay, and the impact needed to be significant. Both teams had secured access to their respective facilities. Aban's team had just finished adjusting the chlorine's main feed-line regulator valve. The team had increased the feed pumps by 200% of the recommended flow capacity. It reduced the flow regulator to a quarter of the ability. Based on Leyla's calculations, it would take approximately 30 minutes for the feed valve to fail. Once failed, Chlorine gas would be released into the atmosphere. Based on the pump operating at 200% of flow capacity, the 10,000-gallon Chlorine tank would be empty within two hours.

Just perfect, Aban thought. *While not as devastating as I would like, it will still create a major inconvenience for Houston*. Leyla sat and listened to Aban more out of shared pain than any real sense of loyalty. Leyla believed in following a man's orders, as was the Muslim way, but she thought Aban was reckless. Leyla knew from the start this was a suicide mission. Still, she wanted every opportunity to make the Americans pay for the tragedies inflicted on the Iraqi people. Leyla thought back to the conversation last night, where she had finally convinced Aban and Hakim of the beauty and simplicity of her modified plan. It wasn't that she was more competent, but Leyla truly understood the cold-blooded nature of revenge. Now was not the time to rouse suspicion with the authorities. A full alert would make it impossible for their final sacrifice. By rigging the system to fail via a computer malfunction served three purposes:

1. It would increase downtime while the engineers tried to figure out where the software glitch originated.

2. By not making the attack obvious, it allowed the team to continue to operate with relative ease.

3. Finally, engineering a slow leak creates an opportunity for more collateral damage. Emergency responders will not be aware of the problem until it's too late, mainly because all security alarms will be disabled. The team finally agreed this approach would have the most desired outcome.

Leyla smiled to herself and thought. *At least these idiots will not ruin my chance of revenge.* Leyla knew while these men all suffered under the hands of Al-Qaeda, her suffering was the worst. She would not only exhibit the physical scars but the mental shame of what they did to her. Before they executed her husband and son, they raped her repeatedly to make her family an example for the community if they didn't side with Al-Qaeda. Laying there

151

helpless was nothing compared to the fact that they were going to let her live. At least her husband and son would die quickly. Al-Qaeda truly understands terror. Her whole family was dragged out in the street naked. Before they were killed. The brutes first cut off their genitals, then they were beheaded for the community to watch. Then they doused her entire body with gasoline and set her afire. They made sure they put out the fire before she died to ensure that the shame and lesson would continue for a long time to come. Now Leyla wrapped entirely from head to foot to hide her shame vs. being a traditional Muslim woman. Hassan and Rashad would be avenged if it was the last thing she did, and Aban's stupidity wouldn't stop her.

Peter and his team were watching the news and staying clear of the quarantine area. Kenny had called an hour earlier with a possible hit on the terrorist cell phone. There was nothing to do other than wait and prep their gear.

So far, over fifteen thousand residents had been treated and released for respiratory irritation due to the chlorine gas; and 300 residents were in critical condition in the ICU. Another twenty thousand residents were displaced, waiting for the all-clear to go back to their homes.

Peter just shook his head at the senselessness of it all. He vowed to himself that this would be the last time these terrorists struck in this city and got away with it. Just as Peter turned back to the news, his cell phone beeped, alerting him to a new message. Peter hated not being back in Delta with his Hi-Tech toys and superior communications gear. He hated having to use disposable phones, but they didn't really choose the matter. Having to fly below the government's radar screen left them with little choice.

Peter opened the message from Kenny. He had pinpointed the terrorist's location to two different hotels: Rodeway Inn Houston and Athens Hotel Suites. "Okay, team, we have two targets. Let's prep the surveillance gear for a recon mission. We also need to be prepared to execute and take the targets out, so bring your full assault gear. We might not get more than one opportunity to get these assholes." Karl chimed in. "So Boss, we have two target locations and only one fire team. Are we going to divide and conquer or take out one objective at a time?" "The later Karl. I don't want to risk not having enough resources to accomplish the mission. We are going to take out the Rodeway Inn Houston first. I only hope they are isolated cells and can't warn their other terrorist buddies."

"And worst-case scenario, Boss," asked Karl.

"Either the terrorist will go to the ground or continue executing against their planned targets. I,

153

however, believe they have a contingency plan. Once compromised, the terrorist will execute against a suicide plan and take out as many targets/civilians as possible."

Manny, the team's commo expert, spoke up. "Boss, I want to get Kenny in on our recon mission. If there is increased communication between the cells, having Kenny monitoring cell phone traffic might make it easier to find the other cell if they bolt." Peter replied, "Make it so, Manny. We leave in the next hour."

Manny and Allen were in overwatch on top of the Fort Bend Music Center next to the Rodeway Inn. Allen handled the M21 sniper rifle, with Manny acting as the spotter with his M151 Spotting Scope. While the distance to the Inn was less than 100 feet, Manny's job was to check reinforcements and give the team enough advance warning when the police were dispatched. From their vantage point, they had a clear view of Southwest Freeway, US-59, and Westpark Drive. Plenty of time to ensure that the assault team could exfiltrate with no chance encounters with authorities. Harming innocent law enforcement officers was senseless as well as a violation of the rules of engagement.

Peter, Karl, and Max were parked in the Rodeway Inn parking lot. Peter was thankful that Joshua chose to go with the more modern 2016 Ford Transit Connect Van XL Wagon versus an older model. Being in an urban environment, Peter felt the trade-off of speed and power far outweighed the anonymity of an older vehicle. Kenny had provided instructions to Manny on how to disable the GPS system that comes standard in today's vehicles. Peter laughed when he thought back to Kenny's briefing on how Big Brother is always watching. "And the funny thing is," Kenny stated, "we enable Big Brother to always track and monitor our activities. Everything from smartphones to satellite radio. On a vehicle, the following system needs to be disabled: OnStar, Sirius, and those vehicles equipped with cell phone technology for in-vehicle WIFI." Kenny continued to describe the teams' precautions, especially with all the surveillance measures being employed at the city and state levels. "The federal government does not have a need to have a nationwide network of surveillance systems. Homeland Security, NSA, FBI, and CIA all had the capabilities to tap into the local surveillance networks. Never use EZ-Pass toll systems. Try and stay on local roads as much as possible. When driving, always wear a baseball cap and sunglasses. Modern-day facial recognition software has issues when you introduce caps and shades into the mix. Try and always drive with the windows up to ensure that cameras can't get a clear picture of the inside cab."

Peter's team had taken all these precautions when the team had moved into position. They infiltrated around 0300 hours to ensure Manny and Allen could get set up with a minimum chance of being spotted.

Manny and Allen were also utilizing the latest sniper ghillie suit specially designed by Kenny. All the sniper teams had been outfitted with these specially designed suits. Kenny's suits accomplished two goals: making the wearer virtually invisible and masking the wearer's heat signature. Kenny employed hundreds of tiny cameras that continuously took pictures of the surrounding area and fed the images into the suit's microprocessor, sending the thousands of images to LED screens. So, in essence, the sniper became invisible. The only drawback to the suit occurred if the sniper had to make rapid movements from one position to the next. Considering the hallmark of a sniper was the ability to move very slowly into their position, quick movements weren't an issue unless the sniper had to E&E (escape and evade) in a hurry. The system was designed to automatically go into E&E Mode base on GPS positioning. If the system detected rapid changes in position, the computer would immediately go into E&E Mode. This instructed the cameras to go into video mode. The result would be a continuous stream of images to the LED screens. Both modes made the sniper team invisible.

Peter was impressed with the new technology that his sniper team was utilizing. Even though his assault team was only 200 feet away from the Fort Bend Music Center, Peter couldn't discern their location. It was now 0800 hours, and so far, no one fitting a middle eastern description had exited the hotel. The team packed MRE's for two days, and Peter made it clear nothing was left behind. One of the unpleasant sides of operational security was to pack out all waste to include human waste. *Shit in a bag… Oh, the joys of special forces. The things we learn to endure to defend this great country*, Peter thought.

Around 1300 hours, Manny reported that they had spotted two males that appeared to be of middle eastern descent. His team had accounted for the staff and hotel guest vehicles based on their recon except for 3 cars. Peter concluded that those two had to be the terrorist they were after. Max was the only one on the team not in tactical gear if an up-close recon was required. Peter dispatched Max to go into the lobby and see if he could get close enough to clone one of the terrorist phones. Max was selected because of all his team members. He was the most nondescript. Max would never be considered a special forces operator at 5'7", sandy blond hair, pale complexion, sporting a three-day-old shadow, medium build, bordering on the skinny side. Little would anyone know that Max was a Yondan (4th Degree Blackbelt in Aikido), put simply, a bad-ass when it mattered.

Max entered the lobby and immediately spotted the two targets. They were in the process of getting coffee, so cloning the phone shouldn't be a big deal. Max took his cell phone out and initiated the clone sequence. He walked over to the coffee station and started making a cup of coffee with sugar and cream to ensure the phone had time to complete the cloning process. Max was within three feet of the targets. Close enough for each phone's Bluetooth to communicate and pair. Max used his Bluetooth Plantronics Voyager Edge SE headset, pretending to have a conversation with his girlfriend. So far, the targets had not noticed him. Unfortunately, he couldn't make out their conversation, which was okay if he cloned the phones. Max received a beep in his headset, indicating the phone had successfully cloned with the target. At that point, Max turned and walked to the restroom to relieve himself. Shitting in a plastic bag with team members hovering around was not his idea of fun, especially since he had left the team over 5 years ago. As Max walked into the restroom, he smiled, knowing he wouldn't have to hold his shit any longer.

Manny was listening in on the target's conversation via the cloned cell phone. It was evident that the terrorists planned another attack. This one was designed to provide significant interruption to the power grid. They planned to attack two power substations simultaneously. Because one group's phone was cloned, Manny was able to look at the phone log to get the other member's phone numbers. This information was then provided to Kenny. Peter's team now had real-time tracking of all 4 terrorists in Houston. Kenny used state-of-the-art continuous pinging technology, which he hacked from the NSA computer server. Kenny could now give Peter's team the terrorist location within 50 feet. Based on this information, it was apparent that the terrorist cell was split into two groups.

The first power substation was identified as Zenith substation northwest of Houston. Karl and Allen had already been dispatched to recon and develop a plan of attack. The second target was the Gibbons Creek substation. Peter and Max were currently conducting a recon of that location.

While not optimal, Peter had decided on a simultaneous assault plan. It was Peter's hope that they would neutralize one set of terrorists and try and capture one or more members from the other group. Peter would lead the assault team on Gibbons Creek power station with Karl and Max. At the same time, Manny and Allen would take out the other terrorist from a sniper position.

Peter's team had reassembled back at the hotel after their respective recons. Peter laid out the plan of attack. Based on the volume of calls from each cell phone, Peter had identified each terrorist as Tango 1, 2, 3, & 4. Tango 1 was considered the leader; Tango 2 was assumed to be second in command. Peter's team was tasked with the capture of Tango 1 and Tango 3/4. Allen was charged with eliminating Tango 2 and Tango 3/4.

Peter continued, "The terrorists were coordinating their attack for Wednesday, August 4, 2016, at 0300 hours. We have two days to prepare for our assault team. Under no circumstances can we let these terrorists succeed. Hundreds may die without power. In most years, Houston averages a daily maximum temperature for August between 92- and 97-degrees Fahrenheit; however, Houston was amid a heatwave with temperatures exceeding 98 degrees on 5 separate days in July. August is Houston's hottest month overall. Gentlemen, without these two power substations being operational, residents in Leon, Madison, and Grimes counties will suffer numerous blackouts. Without air conditioning, hundreds if not thousands could die or be hospitalized from dehydration, heat exhaustion, and heat strokes."

"Allen, Manny. Take them out. Simple as that. Exfiltrate after you complete the mission. Leave no trace of your presence. Let the authorities find their bodies and evidence."

"Karl and Max, we have the hard job. If we can capture Tango 1, we might assist our second Fire Team, plus Teams Charlie and Delta. We can give our brethren any leg up, you better believe, we damn well will give it to them. The cost of failure is just too great. Karl, you will go in with me to secure Tango 1. I will carry non-lethal munitions to disable Tango 1. Karl, if things start going south, take them out."

"Remember, team, we are a ghost in and out without a footprint. You have 24 hours to rest and prep your equipment. I want us in place and waiting at least 4 hours before the terrorist cell attacks the substations."

"Any questions?" After a moment of silence, Peter stated, "You know the drill. Let's get some guys and save lives!!!! Dismissed."

With that, the team members went about the task of final equipment check and mental preparation.

Zenith substation was located south of House Hahl Road, between Katy Hockley Cut Off-Road and the Grand Parkway. Karl and Allen discovered in their recon that there was nothing near the substation. They would set up in a field directly east of the substation. The plan was to park approximately 2 klicks east off Sharp Rd then hike to their designated sniper position. Manny parked the SUV, having moved the vehicle about 1/2 klick north of Sharp Rd. Manny and Allen got out of the Jeep and covered it in camouflage netting. After shouldering their rucksacks and weapons, they proceeded west approximately 1.5 clicks to their sniper position. While not necessary because of the darkness of night, they both activated their ghillie suit's active camouflage technology. Manny marveled at the technology and shook his head in amazement as Allen disappeared directly in front of him. The night vision goggles did little in assisting Manny in spotting his partner. Manny could only track Allen through the IFF (Identification Friend or Foe) beacon.

After 30 minutes, Manny and Allen settled into their sniper positions with clear visibility of the substation. It was now 0100 hours. There was nothing to do but wait, an activity that any sniper team, while used to, still created an opportunity for doubt to creep into their psyche. Doubt about their chosen profession, about the people they were tasked to kill, and doubt about their souls after this life has ended. Only through years of mental discipline did an operator learn to quiet the voices and doubt. Learn to calm the ghosts of all the dead they had sent to their makers. Both Manny and Allen settled into their mental routine without speaking. There was no need. The mission and the belief that what they were doing was right were the only things that mattered. That's how operators survived. Anything less than total commitment to the mission meant death.

Peter and his team had a more difficult task. The Gibbons Creek substation is in Grimes County, approximately two miles north of State Highway 30 and County Road 244. The substation was located about 100 meters east of the Gibbons Creek Coal Plant. The only cover was a group of trees to the northeast of the substation. The chatter from

Tango 1 made it clear that the only way to successfully take out the substation was to kill the security guards at the coal plant. The coal plant had two guards operating out of the guard shack. Every hour, one of the guards would do a perimeter sweep in a golf cart. Team 1 would eliminate the roving guard and dress in his uniform to get close to the stationary guard based on what Manny could pick up. Once stopped, destroying the substation would be simple.

Peter's recon of the Gibbons Creek substation revealed just how difficult capturing the Tangos would be. The guards at the substation made the task even more difficult. Based on the tactics of the guards, Peter could tell they had some military training, probably regular Army. Because the coal plant was so remote, the ex-soldiers were sloppy and, over the years, had been lulled into a false sense of security. The guards were armed with a sidearm; it appeared to be a Glock 17. The guard making the rounds kept an M4 carbine assault rifle in the passenger seat of the golf cart. The guards made it impossible for Peter to use his non-lethal 12-gauge shotgun because of the noise involved. Therefore, Peter opted to use the DELTA Light Ball instead. While the additional stunning/distraction from a concussive bang grenade is absent, the DELTA Light Ball emits a high-energy 400-lumen strobe effect for three flashes. Peter counted on the DELTA to confuse the Tangos long enough for his team to use Tasers to disable them.

Karl would still carry his traditional combat load in case Murphy decided to raise his ugly head. Murphy's Law dictates that what can go wrong will go wrong. Hence why Karl is armed and their counter to Murphy. Years of black ops missions in Iraq and Afghanistan had taught Peter the hard way to always be prepared for the unexpected. Max would carry identical gear as Peter to maximize the opportunity to capture the Tangos.

Peter had determined that the Tangos' most probable axis of attack would be to move along Route 244 until the cover of the woods masked their approach to the coal plant. Peter's team would ambush the Tangos after they exited their vehicle and started approaching the coal plant to eliminate any chance of collateral damage.

It was 0130 hours, and Peter's team was strategically set up to view any traffic coming down Route 244. Peter knew he was taking a chance, one by having all his resources deployed to Route 244, but this was the best possible course of action given his options. Also, with having to split his team, he really didn't have another choice. Peter started to second guess his decision to capture Tango 1. Maybe he was putting his team at risk. Simply eliminating the Tangos would significantly reduce any chance of casualties, but the potential intelligence gained outweighed that risk.

The team was also prepared to execute against Plan B if the Tangos managed to take a different route to the substation. The destruction of the substation would be the signal to implement Plan B: mount vehicles and immediately deploy to the substation with the intent to engage and destroy the enemy by all means necessary.

This plan would result in the loss of 2 security guards and a substation. While not optimal, at least the Tangos would be eliminated, and their activities contained. If all went well, the ongoing terrorist threat to Houston in a few hours would be eliminated.

At 0200 hours, Max spotted a vehicle approaching with only the parking lights visible. Max remembered his training when driving at night with just night-time running lights. It was a test of courage. With modern GPS and off-the-shelf NVGs, driving at night was almost a cakewalk, even without lights. Max squawked his radio twice to indicate a vehicle was approaching from the north. If one squawk was heard, it would have suggested a car coming from Karl's position to the south. A few minutes later, Max squawked three more times, indicating a positive identification of their target. As planned, all members of Peter's team started to converge on his location. The goal was to shadow the Tangos until they parked the vehicle and were about 100 meters into the woods. Then at that point, they would proceed to incapacitate the Tangos.

Peter saw Karl and Max both approaching his location. They had already acquired the targets. They were just parking their SUV about 20 meters into the wood on the West side of Route 244. Peter was relieved that they had guessed right about the route the targets would take. Once all members had made it to the rally point, Peter signaled for team 2 to activate their camouflage uniforms. Each team member virtually disappears before Peter's eyes. The team started moving off in a direction that would take them on an intercept path to initiate their ambush.

Peter and Karl were set up waiting for their targets. It was agreed that Peter would take out the lead Tango and Karl would take out the rear Tango. Max was positioned in an over-watch position with his silenced HK G36 assault rifle, ready to take out either Tango should the need arrive. He switched out his M249 SAW with Karl's weapon because the M249 was a squad automatic weapon and couldn't be silenced. Max needed to place one shot and take down a Tango without potentially injuring his teammates. The Tangos were about 5 meters from the kill zone. Peter and Karl prepped their DELTA Light Ball and started their silent 30-second countdown before throwing the DELTA Light Balls. At 5 seconds, Peter squawked twice. All team members closed their eyes. Both Peter and Karl hit the activate bottom and threw their DELTA Light Balls at the targets. This was the first time that Peter had ever utilized these in a combat situation. The results were beyond expectation. The first strobe of 400 lumen DELTA Light Balls had the effect of overloading the NVGs. Most NVGs were equipped with a high-intensity light monitor that senses when the ambient light exceeds a predefined intensity and immediately shuts down the device. When the Tangos removed their NVGs to see, the second strobe activated. The strobe would not paralyze people. It caused disorientation and other psychophysical effects. And just in case the targets hadn't opened their eyes yet, a third strobe activated.

After the third strobe, a bell chimed to indicated to the team that it was safe to open their eyes. After the chime went off, both Peter and Karl closed in on the targets. While it looked like both were incapacitated enough to bind them, Peter and Karl both fired their M26C Taser at the max distance of 15 feet. Tasers utilize Electro-Muscular Disruption (EMD) technology. Tasers deliver a powerful 50,000-volt electrical signal to completely override the central nervous system, resulting in muscle spasms until the target is in the fetal position on the ground. Peter smiled… their plan worked, and both targets were lying on the ground. As agreed, Peter and Karl would wait until Max arrived to bind the marks if another charge was necessary. After Max tied both Tangos wrists behind their backs with flexicuffs and gagged them, Max commented to the team that one of the targets was a female. They were all surprised to discover, while it didn't matter, it came as a surprise that a Muslim female was involved.

15 minutes later, both targets were secure and in the back seat of the 2016 Ford Transit Connect Van XL Wagon en route to the team's rally point. Karl was on prisoner watch while Peter drove, and Max was trailing in the target's SUV. On the way back to the vacant office building 2 blocks down the road from the Athens Hotel Suites, Peter received a text from Manny. The text was simple, "MC" for mission complete. Manny and Allen's mission had gone according to plan. The authorities would soon discover the other two terrorists. While it would be hard to identify the terrorist because of the result of the 7.62×51mm NATO cartridge entering and exiting the terrorist head from Allen's M21 sniper rifle. The message would be unmistakable. Two individuals were dead, carrying enough explosives to destroy the power substation. While these individuals and who killed them would be a mystery, the fact that a significant event was averted wouldn't be missed. It was now 0630 hours, and the team was now traveling on US 77 North headed back to Peter's ranch in Waco, Texas, for interrogation. The team visibly relaxed after they had linked up Manny and Allen and headed back to their secure base of operations. Peter was satisfied as he drove the 4.5 hours back to his ranch that his team had met all mission requirements and left Houston without leaving any footprints of their presence.

Baghdad, Iraq

Trinity was looking out the window of the Al Rasheed Hotel Baghdad, located off Yafa Street. Looking at the Unknown Soldier Monument, Trinity thought about all that transpired to bring her here. She was happy that she would finally get a chance to fulfill her dreams to defend her nation. Trinity also understood none of this would have happened without the death of her son Robbie. His death brought her the resolve and perseverance to fight when all that she believed in was an illusion. Knowing that ORD was a pawn of a shadow government pulling the strings that would draw the US into another protracted conflict with Iraq set Trinity's blood on fire. She knew that the conspiracy reached the Vice President of the United States, but that was just the tip of the iceberg. Someone wanted the US back in Iraq and was willing to kill countless American soldiers and Iraqi citizens to accomplish their goal. Trinity hoped that the state-side operations were going well. She knew that Joshua was getting an update from Kenny via a specially designed encryption program installed on his laptop.

Joshua had called the team together in the waiting room of the adjourning suite to go over the sitrep he deciphered from Kenny. "Guys, I'm not going to sugarcoat it. The news is not good. While our teams were successful in stopping the terrorist, we suffered significant causalities. Bravo Fire Team 1, under Peter, was able to capture the terrorist cell leader in Houston. While not helpful, he gave us enough answers for Kenny to analyze how to optimize our Delta Team and locate the cells in Chicago and Richmond. Both teams were successful in neutralizing their targets based on this intel. There were no causalities with either Fire Team, but there were minor civilian causalities. The news out of Chicago is not good. So far, overall, 87 civilians were killed, and over 200 were hospitalized with various injuries. The cell in Chicago, realizing that it was about to be captured, took off on a high-speed chase through downtown Chicago. Mick, the Delta Team Leader, called off pursuit when the Chicago Police took up the chase. They followed at a discrete distance until activities terminated in Millennium Park. This must have been one of their planned targets because it wasn't by chance, they rigged their SUV to explode. Unfortunately, Millennium Park was having an event with well over 1,000 people in attendance. The police determined a few high-profile targets that needed to be defended and sent squad cars to form roadblocks. Fortunately, there was a roadblock in place at Millennium Park. The police were able to engage the vehicle and partially disable it. The SUV still hit the barricade with significant force to break through. The SUV rolled to a stop a few hundred meters past the barricade before a combination of police fire and damage to the vehicle halted it. A few seconds later, the car exploded. I guess the terrorist realized this was as

close as they could get and detonated their explosives.
The explosion killed 87 people, and another 200 were
hospitalized. Luckily the police were able to engage the
vehicle early. If not, the causality total would have been
much higher. Our worst fears were confirmed, however. Our
teams recovered Anthrax from each of the terrorists they
eliminated before the authorities found it in all
locations.

Altogether, our teams successfully engaged and
eliminated the threats in Houston, Las Vegas, and Richmond.
You already know about Chicago. The Bravo team was
redeployed to Philadelphia based on updated intel from
Kenny. For the most part, their mission was successful.
Andrew and Billy suffered from gunshot wounds but will make
a full recovery. Philadelphia, however, suffered severe
infrastructure damage from waste treatment facilities to
power substations. The terrorists took out the substation
powering 30th Street Station before Peter's team could
eliminate the threat. The resulting loss of power stranded
commuters from Washington, DC to Boston, MA. Amtrak got
enough diesel engines into service to start offering
commuters 75% of its typical service routes after 3 days.
Unfortunately, SEPTA and NJ Transit have continued to
suffer due to the loss of the substation. Both no longer
have diesel engines in their inventory beyond maintenance
and repair service engines. SEPTA operated with increased
bus services, taking passengers along the 30th Street

station route and commuters to other train stations. SEPTA is currently working at a 60% service level efficiency. NJ Transit is utilizing bus services to transport passengers back and forth to 30th Street Station. ETA before operating at standard efficiencies is another 3 to 4 weeks.

The awful news comes out of San Diego. John's Charlie Team suffered 100% casualties, and the terrorists were, for the most part, successful in their mission goals. It appears that the terrorist had help from a well-equipped and experienced military unit. They were well trained based on the reports that Kyle transmitted to John before the entire Charlie Fire Team 2 was taken out. Kyle's Fire Team was ambushed as they were moving into place to take out the terror cell. Like in Houston, the cell split to maximize the potential damage. Initially, the news reported the slayings as ex-Military, killed in a drug-related deal gone bad. It wasn't until the actions of John's team that the authorities declared the activities of both teams as connected and called them a vigilante group of ex-military personnel. While their actions saved tens of thousands of lives, this kind of para-military action was unacceptable. They should have involved the proper authorities as soon as they became aware of the plot. The news media, on the other hand, was hailing Charlie Team as heroes of the highest caliber. The ambush of Kyle's Fire Team allowed the terrorist to destroy a kindergarten school via a suicide car bomb that killed 135 children and 20 teachers, with another 200 students and teachers injured.

John's Fire Team 1 followed their targets to Petco Park, the home of San Diego Padres. John's team was prepared to take out the cell at their base of operations. Still, it was interrupted by the same para-military unit. The brief gun battle allowed the terrorist to escape. As John's team retreated to their vehicle to follow the terrorists, Sal was wounded but still able to continue. As John chased the terrorists, he knew he had no choice but to violate mission parameters. After the ambush of Kyle's team and the subsequent school bombing, he didn't want to take a chance and allow his target to explode their Anthrax at the baseball game. The last report from John was that Sal was lying down suppressing fire to let the rest of the team pursue the terrorists into the stadium. Eyewitness accounts reported there was a running gun battle in the stadium with what look liked military personnel chasing two men of Middle Eastern descent. Two police officers willingly admitted they were confused by the actions of the ex-military men. By all accounts, the ex-military men had them dead to rights.

Still, instead, the two assailants lowered their weapons. They ran after the other two assailants who were pursuing the two Middle Easterners. At that point, the officers fired several rounds, striking Len and Mikie, who later died on the way to the hospital. John and Danny's heroic efforts clued the authorities in on what was actually happening. Witnesses stated two Middle Easterners ran down the stairs of K entrance. At that point, two military-type individuals fired and hit both men. While down, one of the men clearly wasn't dead and pressed something in his hand. Seeing this, both military guys ran and threw their bodies over the man. At that point, a lot of white powder was thrown into the air.

It took almost a week for the authorities to make sense of what happened. Final reports say if John and Danny had not thrown their bodies over the bomber the collateral damage would have been much more significant. The fact that John and Danny were wearing body armor helped to contain the explosion. As it stands, there were still over 1,000 fans exposed to Anthrax, currently being treated at the local hospitals. There were also 40 people killed between the explosion and stray bullets from the ensuing gun battle outside the stadium. Based on the equipment of both groups, it was concluded that the ex-military personnel was part of the same team. The authorities were still trying to figure out who killed the team of heroes. The authorities were actively searching for the other assailants that escaped the stadium police."

Now that John's team was identified, the news outlets were sharing their military history and hailing them as heroes. Their efforts prevented the worst terrorist attack in the history of the United States.

At this point, all 30 terrorists were accounted for, but they still managed to do considerable damage. The loss of the Charlie Team was unexpected and tells us, whoever is moving the chess pieces behind the scenes has unlimited resources and political connections. That's the only way the other team could have disappeared so completely. The US Government is contemplating what the next steps are. Still, it looks like they are leaning toward an air campaign and special operations on the ground in Iraq. That's good news for us because it will allow us to move more freely.

"Team, we have got to figure out what is going on. We have to find this ancient artifact, or you can bet, whoever is pulling strings will continue until the US has a large contingency of troops on the ground."

Trinity sat back in shock. It was hard to believe that so many individuals had already lost their lives. She was devastated to hear about Charlie Team. While she didn't know these men closely, she had trained with them for months and knew they had families that depended on them. Now those wives and children will never see them again because of her. While logically she knew this was flawed thinking, emotionally, she knew these men would have been ignorant of the threat altogether if not for her. Joshua noticed Trinity sitting by herself, crying as she stared out the window. Joshua knew precisely what she was thinking. Anyone who has led troops in combat and lost soldiers carried that same look. The unmistakable look of guilt and shame.

Joshua approached Trinity and put his arm around her shoulder as he sat next to her. At first, Trinity tried to pull away but realized Joshua wasn't going to let her. She finally turned to Joshua with tears in her eyes and said, "Oh Joshua, what have I done? All those good men, and now they are dead. How am I going to live with myself?" With that, Trinity buried her head into Joshua's shoulders. The Alpha Team cleared out of the adjourning suite to give them space. Every one of them understood. Joshua silently looked at each team member and thanked them with a nod. Knowing what was coming didn't make it any easier, but Joshua proceeded anyway.

"Trinity, you can't take on the burden of what happened to Charlie Team. They did their job. The only comfort that I can give you is the fact that those men died for what they believed, and I can guarantee you… If Charlie Team had known they were going to die, they still would have chosen to fight to the end, knowing that their actions saved innocent lives. Anyone in this room would do the same. We understand what's at stake and willingly accept the ultimate price to stop threats to our country. Trinity, I'm not going to lie to you. This is going to be tough. Consider this though, how many innocent Americans would have died if you chose not to pursue this? I know this doesn't make it easier, but knowing it does help to cope." Trinity just nodded. Not trusting herself to speak right now.

They held each other for what seemed like 20 minutes before Joshua suggested they go outside and do some Tai Chi. "Learn to be in the moment, Trinity. It's one of the few lessons that will help you cope and survive in our line of work. Let's go."

Hill Flats - Washington, DC

Senator Kelsey Ryles sat down heavily in his mid-18th century Italian Armchair. Senator Ryles had been a Senator for Oregon for the past 10 years. Unlike many Congressmen and Senators, who lived in their offices because they couldn't afford to maintain two separate residences, Kelsey lived in a Hill Flats luxury 1880 brownstone. The first residential block across the street from the Library of Congress and Folgers Shakespeare Theater. These brownstones had been renovated, which was perfect for Kelsey because he could disguise his custom additions and mask the waste output with the other general contractors. While he sat, he poured himself a shot of his prized Macallan 25-Year-Old Fine Oak Highland Single Malt Scotch Whiskey. At fifteen thousand a bottle, Kelsey savored the exquisite flavor explosion of fruit, vanilla, and wood smoke. As he sipped his Scotch, he thought about how close he had come to losing a crucial vote that would have sent the US Military back to Iraq. Being the Chairman of the subcommittee that funded all black operations, he had a great deal of political power on Capitol Hill. Fortunately, this was an election year, and no politician in their right mind wanted to risk their chance of being re-elected.

Kelsey had asked the President to call a meeting with the Chief of Staff, Chairman, and Vice-Chairman of the Armed Forces Committee. He also requested that the Chairman of the Joint Chiefs of Staff be in attendance. Kelsey had laid out a logical argument about the pitfalls of sending troops back to Iraq. The NSA presented a rational debate about the terrorist's connections with ISIS and Al-Qaeda. Still, Kelsey knew they were too convenient a target. He had utilized his position to initiate a deeper probe. Kelsey realized a long time ago that the NSA relied too much on electronic intelligence (ELINT). The CIA relied too much on Human intelligence (HUMINT). Kelsey learned that a balanced approach always worked best. Kelsey utilized his contacts at the Defense Intelligence Agency (DIA) to uncover a Chinese connection. He convinced the meeting participants that a more focused response was the only viable option until they could use the CIA to probe the Chinese link in more detail. Coupled with the polls that showed the US population had no appetite for another protracted war in Iraq, everyone agreed despite the death toll. Besides, at any given time, the US could always send troops back to Iraq. The Joint Chiefs of Staff Chairman then took over the meeting and laid out a predesignated plan that called for the combined use of special ops, the Air Force, and the CIA drone force. This strategy would send the right message to the terrorist and subdue those in the US population and politicians demanding action. After the meeting, President Mitchell had confided in Kelsey that he was relieved with this approach. The last war had cost Mitchell, his son, and this country thousands of dead soldiers. If history was any indication, another 10 years of fighting was a price just too high in a region that will continue to be unstable for centuries afterward.

After Kelsey had finished his Scotch, he got up from his chair and moved over to his bookshelf. Kelsey adjusted his favorite books in sequential order. First, "The Stars in Their Courses" was moved out at a 30° angle. Next, Kelsey readjusted "Theatrum Orbis Terrarum" to a 10° turn, followed by "Voyage de la corvette l'Astrolabe" to a 90° position. The following 3 books were removed then inserted in rapid succession: "Codex Seraphinianus"; "Le Caucase pittoresque"; and finally, "Mr. Barnes of New York." With the last book sliding back in place, there was an audible click followed by the left side of the bookshelf sliding backward then to the left into a hidden recess. Kelsey then stepped down two flights of stairs, where he passed through multiple layers of enhanced security.

The first was a retina scan followed by a complete handprint analysis. While each of Kelsey's fingers was being scanned and verified, a tiny needle extracted a DNA sample of Kelsey's index finger for analysis. As usual, all security checks were passed with no issues. A keypad appeared from behind a sliding panel. Kelsey entered his 25-digit alphanumeric code. At that point, a green light illuminated the entranceway, opening the 8-inch-thick titanium door. The final check after entering the correct code was an IR scan measuring for thermal signatures. If more than one signature had been detected, the entranceway would have been illumed in red light. The red light was accompanied by a microscopic mist that would react to anyone not vaccinated with the counter toxin, producing instant paralysis. Over the years, Kelsey and his associates had learned the hard way how easy it was to be captured, tortured, and drugged until they gave up entrance codes. Just having a member's body was enough to defeat the first three layers of security. As a failsafe, protocol dictated that only one associate enters the Sanctuary at a time for this reason. If the associate was unconscious or dead and didn't enter the abort code within 90 seconds, the hallway and Sanctuary would detonate, eliminating all traces of the Sanctuary.

Kelsey stood still as he entered the room and greeted the Artificial Intelligence Life Interface (AILI). "Good afternoon, AILI." ""Good afternoon, Kelsey. Please enter so that I may secure the Sanctuary." Even unknown to Kelsey, the last check was a voice and stress analysis. A self-destruct sequence would initiate if the system didn't recognize the voice pattern or sensed the associate was in distress or compromised.

As Kelsey sat in his chair in front of the command console, AILI closed the Sanctuary's titanium doors and the bookcase upstairs. "AILI, connect me to Lucas Jacquot in Belgium." "Right away, Kelsey."

AILI initiated the protocol necessary to create a secure link to Lucas. Unless Lucas was already in the Sanctuary, it could take a while before a safe connection was established. Communications with his comrades could be conducted via Sanctuary to Sanctuary or face to face. Even in emergencies, an associate would receive a non-secure communication stating there was a message awaiting review. Kelsey sat and drifted back to how they had reached this point. Being a clone was something that Kelsey never got used to. His body had changed over the centuries based on the evolution of man, but his base consciousness was always Sanarian. All these centuries, and Kelsey still longed to be back in his original host body. Kelsey needed to speak with Lucas to discuss the final preparations. He was convinced the Illuminati or the Committee, as they have been known for the past two centuries, were finally ready to openly attack the Guardians, Kelsey's associates. The two groups directly resulted from a mutiny on his ship that crashed on Earth over 350,000 years ago. This war between the two groups had been going on for so long. Kelsey was tired and wanted it to end, but for the sake of humankind, he knew he and his team had to keep fighting.

The crew of their star cruiser, called "Alpheratz," meaning bright star, were from the alien race known as the Sanarians. The Sanarians were from the Sombrero Galaxy, approximately twenty-nine billion light-years or nine million parsecs from Earth. The Sanarians were in an intergalactic war spanning thousands of galaxies with another species called the Xanduran. Their ship had been on a recon mission when it was hit by a particle beam from a Xanduran scout ship. The crew of the Alpheratz managed to destroy their ship, but not before suffering severe damage to the ship's hull, life support systems, long-range sensors, and worse of all, the ship's matter|anti-matter Stardrive. Scanning their database of habitable planets, Be'lima (now Kelsey), the ship's Captain, decided to head toward the third planet from the star in the Min'ta system. The inhabitants of Earth now call it the Solar System located in the Milky Way Galaxy. Without the Stardrive, it would be impossible to make it back to the Sanarians nearest outpost for repair. The First Officer, Xan'lima, argued they were better off putting the crew in their hibernation chambers, activating the emergency beacon, and setting a course for the outpost in the Andromeda Galaxy. Which were approximately two-and-a-half million light-years from the Min'ta system or seven hundred and seventy-eight thousand parsecs.

Be'lima listened to Xan'lima before issuing final
commands to the ship's navigator to set a course for the
Min'ta system. Xan'lima tried to protest again, but the
intensity in Be'lima's stare silenced him immediately.
Be'lima knew now was not the time to take chances. Their
mission had been a success. With the information stored in
their ship's AI, they had the key to defeat the Xandurans
in battle. Their mission had been to capture and secure an
enemy vessel. Access to their databanks indicated another
race of aliens named Ja'narans had been successful in
fighting the Xandurans. The information stated the
Ja'narans were in the Min'ta system on the fifth planet.
The Min'ta system had been marked as off-limits in the
Xanduran computer system. The planet they inhabited was a
gas giant with a gravitational force equivalent to
23.6N/kg. Soa'limae, the ship's scientific officer, was
excited when she learned of the other alien species and
their location. Their technology would allow them to
function for only 3 to 5 hours on the planet's surface due
to the extreme gravitational forces. If the aliens could
live on this planet, then they had to have highly advanced
technology. Technology that would be capable of helping
them defeat the Xanduran Empire. Kelsey kind of smiled
inwardly when he remembered saying, "The enemy of my enemy
is my friend." That quote had been used so many times in
Earth's history with little understanding of where it
originated.

So, in Be'lima's head, it was an easy decision, continue with the mission. Land on the third planet, which was compatible with their physiology, repair their Starship, then proceed to the fifth planet and make contact with the Ja'narans. Xan'lima's plan was too risky. With the damage sustained to the ship, the crew would be practically defenseless while hibernating. Not to mention, they would have to initiate their emergency beacon if they had any hopes of being rescued. While the Xandurans didn't control this galaxy sector, they did have scout ships out in force, as evident by the one that damaged their ship. Somehow the captured enemy crew must have successfully gotten off a distress call before our jammers could block all communications. Even so, Ped'lima, the ship's security officer, was reasonably sure that there were no additional ships in the sector based on previous Sanarians ships passing through. The damage to their ship proved just how wrong that assumption was. It was just too many unknowns to risk the trip to the outpost.

Kelsey absently rubbed his right arm even though this body was a clone and didn't experience the trauma Be'lima's body suffered in their crash landing on Earth. The ship's doctor had no choice but to amputate Be'lima's right arm, which was pinned inside of the twisted wreckage of one of the interiors retaining walls. While his cybernetic replacement arm was better than his original arm, Be'lima still missed it and occasionally felt the pain of losing it. If only that was the least of what troubled Be'lima, now Kelsey. Kelsey could no longer remember all the lives Be'lima's clones had lived. But the most painful memory was the betrayal of his First Officer and best friend, Xan'lima. The mutiny had caused so much turmoil and death for both his crew and the inhabitants of this world. Worst yet, the death toll would only increase unless his team figured out how to stop the Committee.

Recounting the crash, Kelsey remembered, without their sensors, the Alpheratz flew directly into the path of the asteroid belt in the Min'ta system. Roughly between the orbits of the planets now called Mars and Jupiter. The Alpheratz suffered yet more damage to the hull and ship's deflector shields. During the entry into Earth's atmosphere, the ship's deflector shields failed utterly when the Alpheratz entered the upper extremities of the atmosphere. The frictional interaction with the air molecules decelerated their ship, and the lost momentum was converted into heat. Temperatures reached over 5,000 degrees Fahrenheit because the re-entry corridor angle was too steep. Without the deflector shields, the Alpheratz spun out of control. It crashed into the Sahara Desert in a place now known as Giza. The crash's impact killed 10 of his crew members, with another 15 suffering various injuries, including himself. 3 more crew members died later due to their injuries, leaving a total of 35 left alive.

The debate began almost immediately over what to do. Xan'lima and Soa'limae believed they should use all means necessary to conclude the ship's repairs and set course for the outpost. Soa'limae had deduced that they could genetically evolve the hominins species based on the current evolution of the local population. To repair their ship, they needed a workforce capable of extracting the necessary minerals and manufacturing capabilities to repair their ship. The most challenging task would be the computer technology, which was crystal-based, to improve their ship's AI (artificial intelligence). With the ship's systems damage, crucial advanced technology necessary to mine and refine the raw materials for repairs was offline. It would take millions of workers to mine the diamonds to create the crystal-based circuits for the ship. For each circuit that needed to be repaired or built, the workers would have to collect over one million metric tons. It's the crystallized form of carbon created from extreme pressure and heat that leads to the creation of diamonds. Diamonds are incredibly hard because they have crystallized in a particular atomic shape that resulted from heat and pressure on Earth at a depth of 140 to 150 kilometers. Soa'limae continued to discuss how they could use these Diamonds to replace the manufactured Nelatimium initially used in the circuits. The Diamonds would have to undergo a compression process that would fuse the carbon in the Diamond molecules beyond what nature intended. The molecular structure of a Diamond has a tetrahedral unit composed of five carbon atoms, with one carbon atom sharing electrons with the other four. The enhancement manufacturing process would create a unit with cells comprising up to several thousand carbon atoms sharing electrons with the others. This new structure would allow for almost zero loss of electrical conductivity and an absolute necessity for the AI and onboard computer functions to operate and execute nearly one hundred trillion calculations per second. While good in its current form, a diamond has limited thermal conductivity and can only remove 12% of the thermal energy generated. At these computing speeds, the circuit board material must have near-perfect electrical conductivity to eliminate all resistance, creating thermal energy.

Kelsey couldn't help but marvel at how the Committee manipulated humans into believing diamonds were valuable as rare jewelry. When diamonds are cut for the 5C's, they are not actually cut, they are ground down, and only dust is left. The extraction of diamonds during mining operations will produce tons of waste rocks. Within the waste, rocks are hundreds of worthless diamonds. Through this process, the Committee has been making the required diamonds necessary to create new circuit boards and CPUs. The Axion Corporation was contracted to sift through this waste material, remove and return any viable diamonds then grind the unusable portions to dust. This dust was then put into a furnace for final processing; however, the dust was shipped to a holding facility located in a remote region of South Africa.

In addition, the workers would mine and refine the ore necessary to produce the titanium needed to repair the hull. While the planet didn't have the raw materials required to produce Salitanium, Titanium would make the Alpheratz space worthy with the addition of the repaired deflector shields.

Soa'limae theorized, with the augmented workforce doing most of the manual labor, they would finalize the ship-wide repairs with a smaller number of enhanced hominins. They could have the ship repaired in approximately seventy-three solar cycles around the Min'ta star based on his estimates. The biggest obstacle to the plan would be the genetic enhancements to the hominins. That was the unknown. Soa'limae estimated if they ran into any problems, the delay could potentially add ten to fifty cycles to the plan, one hundred more cycles at the outset.

Once repairs were completed, the only way to escape the gravitational pull of this planet would be to initiate the matter/anti-matter Stardrive. The magnetic pulse drive did not generate enough thrust to achieve escape velocity. By activating the Stardrive, the Xandurans would trace the source point and send a scout ship out to investigate. That's why their protocol mandated that any expedition had to be 100 light-years away before initiating the Stardrive.

This exponentially increased the number of locations the Xandurans would have to investigate. They didn't have the resources to do that, but their task was much more manageable if the source point was close to an inhabited planet.

Be'lima listened to the plan and turned it down without a second thought. Not only would the Xandurans destroy this planet by harvesting its resources, but they would also discover the aliens on the fifth planet. As they passed the planet, the short-range sensors could pick up numerous electronic and biological readings. The Xanduran database stated the last engagement with the Ja'narans had ended with the Ja'narans' ship crashing on the fifth planet. It had taken three Xanduran battle cruisers and five scout ships to destroy one Ja'naran ship. Before being overwhelmed, the Ja'naran ship had destroyed all five scout ships and one of the battlecruisers. If the Xandurans discovered the ship wasn't completely destroyed, then all hopes would be lost. Be'lima couldn't afford for that to happen. The Ja'narans were their only hope. While the two aliens were technologically matched, the Xandurans employed hybrid drones to do their fighting. They increased their fighting force exponentially with every world they conquered by turning the population into drone soldiers. The numbers game was just not on their side, and they were losing the overall war. Their commanders were performing brilliantly and winning battles. Still, with every Sanarian ship loss, the tide of the war increasingly turned in the Xanduran's favor.

While Xan'lima and Soa'limae agreed openly with Be'lima, they secretly started to plot against their commander. Be'lima's plan would condemn the crew to live out their lives and die here on this un-evolved planet. Based on protocol, Be'lima stated the High Military Command would dispatch another recon mission to accomplish the same thing. They would most likely be able to achieve the same results as his crew and fulfill the mission. Be'lima knew he had no choice but to condemn his team to die without ever having a chance to see their home world again.

Six months into making basic repairs on the Alpheratz, Be'lima uncovered a plot by Xan'lima and Soa'limae to control the ship. Be'lima was disheartened to discover that only 10 of the 35 crew members were loyal to him and the mission. Everyone else wanted to go back home and felt the risk of discovery by the enemy worth it, and as far as this planet was concerned… there was no intelligent life here, so what did matter if the enemy harvested it. Be'lima had seen countless worlds develop in his lifetime. Noticed how the spark of life could blossom into something extraordinary and how quickly it could be destroyed. Having been a party to the destruction of numerous worlds, Be'lima just couldn't be responsible for destroying another world due to his actions.

Alpheratz - Sahara Desert - 350,000 BC

Be'lima knew what was coming. While he didn't know how long he had before Xan'lima made his move, his death was inevitable if he didn't make a counter move soon. So far, he had been able to identify nine other crew members who would continue to follow his orders. Be'lima felt fortunate because he had the mission-critical positions in his crew on his side. He had Ped'lima, the Weapons Officer; Sa'limae, the Medical Officer; and one of Medical Technicians, Kec'lima. The ship's Computer Technician and System Administrator for the AI, Mec'lima, and Ja'limae. Two of the ship's engineers, Na'limae and Xi'lima. Final two members from the Security Team: Ca'lima and Va'limae.

The plan was simple, remove critical ship systems from the Alpheratz to make it impossible for Xan'lima to execute against his plan. The team plotted to remove the computer core for their AI. While this would severely hinder Xan'lima's team from performing complex analysis, it would by no means eliminate their access to the ship's database of knowledge. The ship was equipped with backup computer systems. The rest of the plan included removing the access key to the ship's navigational system, the decipher key for the communication's array (the matter/anti-matter energy source that powers the Stardrive). Finally, they would remove the DNA Matrix Sequencer that enabled the crew members to clone themselves in an emergency when their host body was dying. Previous explorers learned the hard way the dangers inherent to deep space missions that encompassed years. While the hibernation chambers allowed the crew to survive prolonged periods when traveling between galaxies, its functions could not repair severe damage to the host body. The deep sleep slowed all bodily functions allowing the body to quickly heal itself when minor injuries had occurred.

Xan'lima was furious to learn that Be'lima and nine other crew members had escaped. They had successfully crippled crucial ship functions that ensured the failure of Soa'limae's plan. The loss of the DNA Matrix Sequencer taken by Be'lima would make a viable workforce a blunt force trial and error versus a precision operation. Dr. Soa'limae had presented an updated report that outlined how his plan could succeed. Still, it would require a timetable encompassing tens of thousands of solar cycles instead of one hundred cycles initially estimated. It would require the capture and experimentation of the local chimpanzee population using Sanarian DNA to artificially impregnate the female chimpanzee. This would be a complex process and would require the diverse DNA of the many breeds of chimpanzees. The modern-day scientist called this geological period the Miocene. The fossils uncovered show a clear lineage divergent from that of chimpanzees. The fossils also show an ancestry full of side branches and evolutionary dead ends. Little did modern scientists know, these evolutionary leaps were the direct result of Dr. Soa'limae's experiments. Those dead ends turned out to be the incompatibility of Sanarian DNA and chimpanzee DNA.

In early experiments, Dr. Soa'limae used the chimpanzee as surrogates to incubate Sanarian offspring the same way he did with the Sanarian females. The eight female Sanarian's that remained with Xan'lima willingly volunteered to be surrogates for Dr. Soa'limae's experiments. They would be the host for the first wave of Earth-born Sanarians. With the hibernation chambers, they could, in theory, have up to 3 infants in one solar cycle. Unfortunately, Dr. Soa'limae could not get the females to bring the infants to term. The fetus' kept aborting before it reached its third stage of development. After two females had died in the process of Soa'limae trying to extend the pregnancy to term, the experiments were terminated. It was determined that something in Earth's environment made childbirth incompatible with female Sanarian physiology. Three solar cycles had been lost before these experiments were concluded.

The chimpanzees fared no better than the Sanarian females. Dr. Soa'limae concluded he would have to create a hybrid Sanarian using chimpanzee DNA. Trying to find the right DNA combination was going to be a time-consuming process. Not only is figuring out the correct genes to turn on but having the patience to let the stable hybrid-Sanarians develop before the next round of experimentation began. In their quest to map the human genome, modern scientists were still losing to understand the human DNA. The human genome contains around 20,000 genes, that is, the stretches of DNA that encode proteins. But these genes account for only about 1.2 percent of the total genome. The other 98.8 percent is known as non-coding DNA. Most scientists agree that while some non-coding DNA is essential, it most probably does nothing for us at all. The explanation is simple, Dr. Soa'limae turned off those genes.

Dr. Soa'limae and his two assistant scientists woke up every ten thousand years to check on the development of the hybrids. If the combinations developed sufficiently during those periods, then the next round of generic manipulations would begin. Archaeologists have been successful at tracking Soa'limae's work. The distinct phases of the hybrid's evolution are now known as Ardipithecus, Australopithecus, Homo Erectus, and Humans. Once the hybrids evolved to the stage of Homo Sapiens, Dr. Soa'limae woke the critical members of the crew so they could start making preparation to repair the ship. Soa'limae told Xan'lima it would take a few thousand years before the technology was in place to achieve the repairs necessary for their ship to be flight worthy. The human brains were now sufficiently developed. The crew could use telepathy to manipulate human development while hibernating. Dr. Soa'limae did warn Xan'lima that the human race was still

194

very fragile. The process that created the hybrid-Sanarians produced an alarming number of deaths during childbirth. It was only in modern history when doctors started tracking infant mortality rates. Bearing a child is still one of the most dangerous things a woman can do. It's the sixth most common cause of death among women ages 20 to 34 in the United States. About 15 per 100,000 pregnancies result in maternal death. While Dr. Soa'limae had no way of tracking the mortality rates before the 1600s because humans were not keeping records, the numbers were even more dismal.

Dr. Soa'limae explained Sanarians were on average seven-and-a-half feet tall, weighing approximately 280lbs. A Sanarian infant, on average, is 2 feet tall, weighing 50lbs. Even splicing the genes to create hybrids still couldn't reduce the risk altogether. The hybrid wombs just couldn't handle such a large delivery. Many offspring and mothers died during childbirth. Soa'limae went on to explain, as technology improves, so shall the successful delivery of infants increase. "To counter the obstacle of surviving the birthing process, Xan'lima, you have to implant biological instincts to procreate," said Soa'limae. "This is a simple numbers game. Until technology improves, we have to have warm bodies to help us accomplish our goals."

Xan'lima and others used telepathy to communicate with humans to guide the course of their development. Unfortunately, this process was not an exact science because this equipment was designed to allow Sanarians to communicate with their homeworld over vast distances. While communication was now possible, the hybrid brain was not developed enough to accurately understand their commands. The humans called these interrupted attempts of communication prophecies and wrote them down. In the beginning, most prophets went crazy because the nature of using telepathy simply overwhelmed their minds. These early prophets could no longer distinguish between reality and their visions. They had to be, literally, chained like a beast, and a scribe would always be present to record their words no matter how wild and outlandish they were.

As humans continued to evolve, Dr. Soa'limae started waking more frequently to conduct more targeted experiments. Some were successful, some were not. Each cycle, Soa'limae would continue to activate dormant genes to develop hybrids closer to the Sanarian-base DNA. These cycles brought about extraordinary humans that Xan'lima implanted imperatives that forever changed the course of humanity. Some of the greatest rulers and spiritual leaders were the result of advanced gene manipulations by Soa'limae. Buddha, Jesus, and Muhammad, to name a few spiritual leaders. Exceptional military leaders included Alexander the Great, Genghis Khan, Attila the Hun, Sun Tzu, Napoleon Bonaparte, and Hannibal. Samson and Goliath were examples of physical enhancements genes initiated to bring humans closer to the Sanarian stature. King Solomon was the wisest man who ever lived. Unfortunately, he couldn't handle the visions given to him. The genes gave him unsurpassed wisdom, which Solomon squandered because he could not control his lust. An unfortunate side effect of activating this specific gene sequence. A mistake that Soa'limae did make again. Solomon had 700 wives and 300 concubines. When Solomon was not overtaken by lust, he did many great things over his 40-year reign. Solomon built the first temple on Mount Moriah in Jerusalem, a seven-year task that became one of the wonders of the ancient world. He also built a majestic palace, gardens, roads, government buildings and accumulated thousands of horses and chariots. After securing peace with his neighbors, he built up trade and became the wealthiest king of his time. His example set the stage for modern commerce, the cornerstone for gathering the materials necessary to repair the spaceship. At one point, Soa'limae even activated the immortality gene. The results were staggering. Methuselah lived to be 969 years. LP Suwang was rumored to be between 200 and 500 years old. Chen Jun lived to be 444 years. Devraha Baba lived for over 750 years.

Kelsey remembered when Ane'lima, the Navigational Officer, set up a secure commlink with Be'lima. Ane'lima briefed Be'lima on all that had happened and the ultimate plans that were being set into motion. It was probably 4 solar cycles into the mutiny when Ane'lima could no longer stomach the unconscionable experiments Dr. Soa'limae conducted. Losing his wife in the first cycle, trying to conceive, was bad enough. Watching the horrible mutations as the hybrids were born was too much to tolerate. Yet Dr. Soa'limae continued her experiments as she tried to find the correct DNA sequence to create a Sanarian-hybrid.

In most cases, even when the hybrids were brought to term, the surrogates died because the host womb was incompatible with the size of the hybrid. Ane'lima recounted the screams of the poor animals and how something had to be done to stop Soa'limae. At one point, Be'lima told Ane'lima there was nothing that could be done. If he genuinely wanted to help, he would have to continue as if nothing had changed. Helping them from the inside was the only way to stop Xan'lima and Soa'limae's plans. While not happy, Ane'lima understood and agreed to do as Be'lima wished. Anything to stop the insanity.

Kelsey thought back to the horrible things he and his team had authorized on behalf of saving humanity. They called themselves the Praservare or their modern-day name, The Guardians. While there was nothing the Guardians could do to stop the forced evolution of humans, they could slow it down. And slow it down, they did. Throughout the history of humankind, The Guardians have been doing their best to slow down the technological advances of mankind. Be'lima and his team accomplished this by introducing some of the worst plagues in the history of humanity. Smallpox killed more than 300 million people worldwide in the 20th century. The Spanish Flu took 50 to 100 million lives in less than 2 years. The Black Death slew 75 - 200 million people from 1340 - 1771. Malaria is still killing approximately 2 million people per year. Finally, AIDS, which has taken 25 million lives from 1981 through today.

While tragic, Be'lima knew the human population would recover, but each death still disgraced his karma. The end justifies the means had long since lost any relevance to what Be'lima and The Guardians would do in the name of saving humanity. The enemy would destroy this world, harvest its planet's resources then use all the animal and human populations for food. There was no winning once the enemy became aware of a newly inhabited world. The Sanarians had tried before to stop the Xandurans from harvesting a planet. Still, the Xandurans swarmed planets with hundreds of ships, making it impossible to stop them. The Sanarians have tried several times to mass enough ships to stop the swarm. Still, they have never been successful, and their loss was just too high to continue trying. So, Be'lima ordered Ce'limae to create bio-engineered plagues to wipe out segments of Earth's populations with a heavy heart. These plagues were introduced when mankind was on the verge of taking an evolutionary leap in technology and science.

Hill Flats - Washington, DC

"Kelsey, I have Lucas available on secure communications," said Aili. "Patch us through, please, Aili."

"Lucas (Ped'lima), this is Kelsey. Thank you for responding so quickly to my requested communications."

"It wasn't a problem at all, Kelsey. What's so urgent?"

"Lucas, I believe the ancient war with our brethren is finally coming to an end. The Committee is getting closer than ever."

"It's been a long time since I've heard my native name. For you to use it now is significant, Be'lima".

"It is, Lucas. I believe the Committee has finally figured out how to track the ship's components. It was only a matter of time before technology evolved enough to track them down." "We need allies in this final battle. Soldiers to engage the Committee. Now that this world has reached globalization and instant communications, the Committee is moving events faster than ever. It's a matter of a few years to get the ship operational to get the components and gain access to the ship. If that happens, I might have to activate our fail-safe protocol. Unfortunately, the fail-safe protocol will, in all likelihood, wipe out up to 70% of the world's population. Ce'limae has been working on a new strain of flu. She has been working indirectly with the CDC, WHO, and certain pharmaceutical companies to secretly create the deadliest flu strain. Based on the results of the Spanish flu, which killed approximately 100 million people, it was decided to continue down this path.

Ce'limae, now Dr. Brenda Calms, worked as an epidemiologist for a small pharmaceutical consulting firmed called, PatientZero, Inc. They had become the number one called firmed whenever an outbreak occurred. Dr. Calms was the CEO with 5 doctors, 3 research scientists, and 8 lab technicians. They were initially privately funded by the Guardians, but now the company is very profitable. They had 3 to 5 doctors deployed across the globe at any given time responding to their request for assistance in dealing with some type of outbreak.

Ce'limae engineered a new strain of flu called the Avian Flu or Bird Flu. H5N1, as named by the CDC, is a highly pathogenic avian (bird) flu virus that has caused severe outbreaks in domestic poultry in parts of Asia and the Middle East. When Ce'limae released the strain in the early 1900s. It wasn't until 1961 that the H5N1 strain was first isolated in birds in South Africa. There are many different strains of avian Flu: 16 H subtypes and 9 N subtypes. Only those labeled H5, H7, and H10 have caused deaths in humans. While Ce'limae couldn't stop the direct crossover of the avian flu from bird to humans, she was conscientious about keeping the avian flu from being spread via human-to-human transmission. December 1983 marks the first time scientists decided the best way to stop the spread of the avian flu among birds was to euthanize more than five million birds. Since then, tens of millions of birds have either died or have been euthanized to limit the spread of H5N1.

Ce'limae genetically engineered the Flu viruses so they will continue to change and mutate. These changes can happen slowly over time or suddenly. These mutations are called Antigenic drift and Antigenic shifts.

Antigenic drift is when these changes happen slowly over time. These changes occur often enough that the human immune system can't recognize the flu virus from year to year. Therefore, everyone is encouraged to get a new flu shot vaccination each year. The flu vaccine protects individuals against that season's three or four most common flu virus strains.

Antigenic shift is when changes happen suddenly. This occurs when two different flu strains infect the same cell and combine. A shift may create a new flu subtype because people have little or no immunity to the new subtype, potentially causing a very severe flu epidemic or pandemic.

"Lucas, the avian flu has the potential to make the Spanish flu look like a common cold. Ce'lima is prepared to create an antigenic shift. I do not want this to happen. The World Health Organization has identified H7N9 as a perilous virus for humans. Of all the mutations, that has the highest likelihood to produce the greatest result.

That is the strain she is prepared to mutate, creating a variant that can be spread through human-to-human contact."

"Kelsey, I've known about these plans since Ce'lima first designed the avian flu. Why the call? What's changed?"

"To be truthful, Lucas, I am tired of killing millions of humans for the sake of saving the human species. I no longer believe the end justifies the means. I believe humans have finally reached a stage where they might be capable of helping us defeat the Xandurans. Besides, at this point, they have evolved to be our children and possibly more. The hybrids that Xan'lima created are now more Sanarian than the native creatures we first encountered. And even if we do launch this new strain of flu, the Committee is now too well protected. Their organization will survive by retreating into their bunkers until the crisis has passed. In the end, I truly believe the Committee will be stronger and able to operate with impunity if we create a power vacuum within the nation-states."

"Recently, I have come across a group of individuals that are successfully challenging the Committee without directly understanding who they are fighting. I propose that we aid them in their quest and eventually bring them into the fold. As you are aware, there have been numerous terrorist attacks in the US in recent weeks." After acknowledgment from Lucas, Kelsey continued. "It was the work of these individuals that stopped the terrorist from accomplishing most of their goals. The Committee wants the US military back in Iraq. Because of this group, I was successful in limiting our engagement to surgical operations with Special Forces, airstrikes, and using the CIA's drone force."

"Lucas, I believe we have to change our strategy if we want a chance to win. Thousands of years and advances in technology have finally leveled the playing field. All these centuries, we have merely been delaying our brethren, and now a delaying strategy is no longer a viable option. Maybe we should consider changing our definition of what winning means. While I am not proposing this right now, I have been reconsidering our ancient war with our brethren. Our priority should still be to stop the Committee from finding the ship's components so that Xan'lima can't repair the ship. Still, humans have evolved and truly might be capable of helping us in our fight. We have seen examples of what human societies are capable of when they evolve beyond their pettiness. Our DNA combined with the chimpanzees and how Dr. Soa'limae unlocked the hybrid's genome has created a super-race capable of becoming so much more than we are. You were there, Lucas, when the Mayans simply disappeared from the face of this planet. I read the report. The energy they generated when their linked minds joined for a common purpose of evolving was nothing we had ever seen before. While this event hasn't been duplicated since the potential is there within humans."

"We probably need to call a meeting of our team in the next few months to discuss future strategies. But for now, Lucas, we have to extend our help to this covert team trying to stop the Committee. That's where you come in. We have tracked their movements to Iraq. The leaders of that team are Joshua Palmer and Trinity Winters. I am sending over the information we have collected on them via AILI. They will be reaching out for resources through their contacts, but it will be limited at best. The state of affairs in Iraq has deteriorated since the US Military pulled out. Joshua's group is made up of ex-military Special Ops types. Still, there is only so much they can accomplish without adequate resources. We need to assist them through our back-door channels because a team is hunting them from the Committee. They are called the Night Stalkers. They are deadly and efficient and have unlimited resources backing them. They were responsible for taking out one of Joshua's teams in the states. Now the Committee has dispatched them to Iraq. If Joshua's Team was just searching for the artifact, we wouldn't need to assist them. They are more than capable of handling anything that could come up in Iraq, from random secular violence to roaming bands of thieves, but the Night Stalkers… Joshua's team will not stand a chance. The Night Stalkers are the best with equipment the Committee has armed them with.

They come from the same stock as Joshua's team, but the tactical gear will make the difference in any engagement. The Committee is close to finding the Ark of the Covenant. We must stop that from happening, and our best bet is to support Joshua and Trinity's Team. Until we meet to discuss a potential change in strategy, we have to stay the course."

"No worries, Joshua. Give me a few days, and I will get everything in place to support them."

Thawra District - Sadr City, Iraq

Joshua and Sam O'Donnell were meeting with their contact, Omran al-Zahawi. Joshua and Sam had served together in Iraq during the 2007 Surge, called Operation Imposing Law. It was a bad time to be an American soldier serving in Iraq. Relationships between the Iraqis and Americans took a wrong turn in 2003 and had only gotten worse. During a security screening, the Chairman of the District Council got into a confrontation with elements of the 2nd Armored Cavalry Regiment and a team from the 490th Civil Affairs Battalion. The conflict led to a shoving match that resulted in the Chairman being shot by an American soldier. The death of the Chairman caused a serious setback in relationships. It led to increased violence, from which the district never recovered. Joshua and Sam were part of Delta Force B Squadron working with the Central Intelligence Agency's elite Special Operations Group (SOG). This joint task force's mandate was to cripple the opposition's leadership structure, making it impossible to organize adequate resistance against Operation Imposing Law.

During their time in the Thawra District, Joshua and Sam's team made numerous contacts. Some would lay down their lives with the team, like Omran al-Zahawi, and others would lead them into an ambush without hesitation. Working in Sadr City was problematic. Sadr City was built in Iraq in 1959 by Prime Minister Abdul Karim Qassim in response to grave housing shortages in Baghdad. Originally, Sadr City was named Revolution City. It provided housing for Baghdad's poor. Omran had grown up on the streets of Sadr City. His parents had been killed during a round of secular violence when Abu Hafez Al-Shei consolidated his power. Religion was a tool of fear.

Abu Hafez was a master at using fear to break the will of the people. Omran had just turned eight when they accused his father and mother of following the path of Christianity. Abu Hafez accused them of having a Christian bible. He held the bible up before the gathered crowd as his parents were dragged from their house. Hafez preached for one hour about the virtues of the Muslim faith and the wrath that Muhammad promised to all infidels. With that, Abu Hafez ordered his parents to be doused with gasoline, then he personally tossed a torch on their bodies. Omran still had nightmares about that day, remembering their screams that lasted what seemed like an eternity. Abu Hafez turned to the boy being held by his men and said, "Remember this day, boy and learn to follow the ways of Muhammad. Allah is great. Don't forget this lesson. I am gracious, allowing you to live and make reparations for the sins of your parents." With that, Abu Hafez turned and walked away as if he had no concerns in the world. Omran couldn't be heard pleading through his tears, whimpering his family was true believers. "We're true believers," Omran repeatedly said as he kneeled, staring at the charred remains of his parents. Omran wasn't aware that Abu Hafez had heard his words, but it didn't matter. He needed to make an example out of a family to ensure he instilled fear and broke the will of any resistance.

Omran was homeless, living on the streets as a beggar and thief to survive. He vowed, every day of his existence, that he would kill Abu Hafez.

In April 2003, the US Army 2nd Squadron, 2nd Armored Cavalry Regiment established their headquarters at the abandoned Sumer cigarette factory on the east side of Sadr City. Like in every war, a lot of US equipment went unaccounted for. Whether due to ambitious Supply Officers are known as S4s selling the equipment illegally or due to thefts, the 2nd Iraqi War was no different. Between 2003 and 2008, the roadside bomb attacks created chaos within the US military structure. The blue-on-blue killings just added to the mix. The Mahdi Army spearheaded the first

major armed confrontation against the U.S.-led forces in

Iraq from the Shia community. The group was initially armed

with various Soviet-made light weapons, including

improvised explosive devices (IEDs). However, that quickly

changed with the collapse of the many US-trained Iraqi

Divisions. There were many examples of soldiers and police

officers shedding their uniforms and dropping their weapons

on the spot in the face of confrontation. After the US

left Sadr City, the Mahdi Army occupied the Sumer cigarette

factory, which became their Headquarters. Inheriting

equipment, the US Army left behind.

Omran al-Zahawi was a survivor and used his contacts to

create a network where he supplied rival factions with

weapons to medical supplies. Omran disagreed with the

political and religious direction of his country. Every

faction was fucked up in their approach to fixing his war-

torn country. Joshua had a deep respect for Omran. He had

risked his life to save several of Joshua's men when they

were pinned down in an ambush. Omran and Sam had flanked a

machine gun position and taken out 5 Mahdi soldiers, which

allowed Joshua's assault team to break through the ambush

and escape. Omran loved Iraq, and his actions proved he

would die for his country and anyone he thought could help

Iraq. He believed the American soldiers were Iraq's best

chance of living a life of peace and equality for all

Iraqis, including the Iraqi women. Omran was there when

higher-ups ordered Joshua's team to abort the snatch and grab or elimination mission of Abu Hafez Al-Sheik.

After that aborted mission, US Army Special Operations Command (USASOC) ordered the pullout of all Special Operations Forces in Sadr City. Before leaving, Omran vowed to keep fighting and that one day, he would kill Abu Hafez Al-Sheik. Joshua promised to aid him in any way possible. He also informed Omran, this was his last tour, but being Delta meant you never left the brotherhood. The brotherhood took care of each other. No matter where they needed help in the world. "Omran, you are now part of our brotherhood. You have passed the test of being initiated into our ranks by fighting alongside us. We are grateful for your willingness to pay the ultimate sacrifice in defense of our lives. We will never forget you. We will meet again. If not this lifetime, then the next." Joshua then hugged Omran goodbye. During their brief hug, Joshua slipped Omran a note with just a phone number on it. "Use this if you ever need something. Keep it on you in case someone calls," said Joshua. With that, Joshua turned and left, joining his team on the waiting helicopters. It was Joshua's connections that helped Omran establish his first arms connection.

Their developed plan required keeping the rival factions from gaining control until a more acceptable faction stepped forward to help their country. Joshua equated this plan to the cold war and nuclear armament, MAD - mutually assured destruction. If all factions had the same equipment, no one faction could gain the upper hand. It was five years later that Omran had finally got his revenge on Abu Hafez. Abu Hafez and his closest aides moved into another one of the abandoned US Bases. On a cold, moonless night, Omran infiltrated the base that he was intimately familiar with from his days working with Delta. Omran set a bomb on the main gas line leading into the house. When the bomb detonated, Omran watched as all inside of the house burned to death. Abu Hafez's soldiers tried desperately to put out the fire to no avail. So, just like it started, it ended. Omran remembers the quote, "If you live by fire, you will die by fire." He also understood this exact quote now applied to him.

Sam reached out to Omran a few weeks before they left for Iraq. He asked Omran to help him equip a team of eleven soldiers. Sam gave a supply list including assault rifles, heavy machine guns, assault shotguns, 40mm grenade launchers, pistols, sniper rifles, smoke grenades, fragmentation grenades, white phosphorus grenade, CS grenades, flash-bang grenades, claymores, det cord, RDX explosives, gas masks, combat knives, NVGs, communications gear, body armament, helmets, shooting glasses, and MRE's for at least a five-week duration. He also needed transportation; armored vehicles and at least two helicopters with rocket launchers and machine guns. Sam asked for mounted Gatling guns on the helicopters if possible. If not, a mounted 50 caliber machine gun with depleted uranium rounds would work just as well. Sam requested black Humvees with two mounted 50 caliber machine guns, an M60 machine gun, and a mounted MK 19 automatic grenade launcher.

Omran expected this call. One of his suppliers previously told him that a former colleague would be coming back into theater. Whatever equipment they needed would be provided without question. Omran started to protest that the situation in Iraq was difficult right now. Before he could say another word, his arm's supplier told him that this order would be fulfilled by higher-ups. "Just put the request in Omran. They will receive the best available weapons that money can buy. Money will not be an issue. Charge them your normal fees. The balance will be subsidized by a 3rd party. Don't worry, Omran. You will be compensated for this transaction. By the way, this conversation never took place."

Omran happily told Sam that he would provide him with everything he requested on the other end of the line. Before the call from Omran's supplier, he would have equipped Joshua's team with antiquated Soviet weapons. Omran would have been disappointed and brought dishonor to their friendship, knowing that this equipment would barely meet their needs. The situation in Iraq has deteriorated in the last few years. No one seemed to care what happened to the Iraqi people anymore. Supplies had dried up, and money was hard to come by. Omran was excited to have the opportunity to work with Joshua's team again.

Thawra District - Sadr City, Iraq

Sam O'Donnell finally linked up with Omran al-Zahawi at his warehouse in the industrial complex at the southeastern edge of Baghdad. The complex contained many acres of factories and warehouses abandoned during the numerous confrontations between coalition forces and residents in 2003. Most of the warehouses were abandoned, but Omran made one his base of operations.

Seeing each other, Sam and Omran hugged. Once Sam verified that all was secure, he radioed Joshua that all was clear. Upon receiving the call, Joshua's team moved up from their overwatch position and entered the industrial complex heading to Omran's warehouse.

The team exited the vehicles leaving the drivers in place just in case they needed to make a hasty exit. Joshua and Trinity led the rest of the team into the warehouse.

"Omran!!!! You old devil. Damn, it's good to see you again," said Joshua. With that, the two men embraced like long-lost brothers.

"Come, sit down and share some shai with me," said Omran. It's been a long time since Joshua drank Egyptian Tea. "Joshua, Sam gave me a list of equipment that you needed. It appears that you are arming yourselves to go to war. So, what's going on, and how can I help?" The team moved over to the crates as directed by Sam and started unpacking and inspecting the weapons. While this was being done, Joshua and Trinity launched into a descriptive story about their journey to this point. An hour had passed by the time they concluded describing the events that led to this point.

"Omran, we need your help. First, the weapons support you have provided is invaluable. I'm sure you will tell me how you got access to this equipment at some point. Even with my resources, I wouldn't have been able to acquire this state-of-the-art equipment. Let's not even talk about the cost. The money we agreed upon doesn't cover a fraction of the cost of this equipment. So, spill the beans, Omran?"

Omran hesitated. Joshua knew Omran, and his hesitation was a sure sign that he was holding back information. He would rather remain quiet than lie to his brothers in combat. "Omran, I know you don't have access to this type of equipment. To be truthful, I was expecting equipment that we left behind during our occupation. A lot is going on in this world. To be truthful, we believe we only see a part of the overall picture. Someone or some shadow government wants the US military back in Iraq. Let me tell you, Omran, if the military comes back, it will not be like last time. Omran, do you remember Peter from Delta Assault

Team 2?" "Of course, I do, Joshua. I remember his team saved a group of school kids being held hostage by Abu Hafez Al-Shei's men. I thought they were going to die, but his team was amazing. All the kids were freed with no causalities or losses to his team." "Well, Omran, we lost Peter and his entire team. This silent war that we are waging in the shadows has been costly. Already thousands of Americans have been killed. If not for our team, the numbers would have been in the tens of thousands, if not more. We can't trust our own government. It's compromised. We play a dangerous game of trying to stop the terrorist without engaging our own police forces, who are ignorant of what is going on. Our research has led us here. This shadow government wants US troops back in Iraq to provide cover for a group searching for an ancient artifact. We now believe the second gulf war was just a cover for this search. All those museums that were looted. Did you ever wonder why the military did nothing to protect all those ancient museum pieces?" "To be truthful, Joshua, I was just concerned with surviving from day-to-day. Trying to bring some sort of stability back into my country." Joshua nodded his head in understanding. "Well, we believe they found something during the second Gulf War. Something that our analyst believes leads to the Ark of the Covenant." "Are you serious, Joshua? I personally thought that the Ark was nothing more than a myth. Although I have heard rumors that the Islamic State of Iraq and Syria

(ISIS) believes they might be very close to finding it. Whispers are that the Ark has incredible power. With it, they can finally destroy Israel and reoccupy the Promise Land. I think it's just a ruse meant to give false hope to distract the people from the crushing poverty in Iraq right now."

"Omran, we need your help and your resources besides the weapons that you provided. We know that there is a well-trained and equipped team that is hunting our teams. They may be tracking us now. It's a possibility that Iraq will be the focal point of another long protracted, useless war if we don't find the Ark before this shadow organization or ISIS. We are trying to prevent this from happening. We need the truth to understand what we are up against. So Omran, who are you working with? It's imperative that we know we can trust whoever supplied us with this equipment. If you choose not to reveal this information, we will have no choice but to walk away regardless of what we have been through together. The stakes are simply too high."

Omran finally looked Joshua in the eyes and nodded solemnly. "A few weeks before Sam reached out, one of my suppliers out of Germany contacted me. His name is Hans Krause. He has been a reliable supplier to me for the past 3 years." Omran went on to relay the conversation he had with Hans. "As far as I could tell, Hans was just a messenger. Whoever gave this weapon deal the green light was obviously well connected and wanted to make sure you were successful in your mission. They also informed me that there is a team tracking you in Iraq." "Thanks, Omran, for being honest with us. Give me a second." Joshua excused himself, took out his secure phone, and sent an encoded message to Kenny to track down who was working on their behalf to ensure his team's success. While Joshua was happy for the assistance so far, not knowing the motives of his mysterious benefactors was never a wise move when you were working in the shadows. In his many years as a Delta operative, he had seen it happen time and time again. A friend today was a potential target for capture of elimination tomorrow, especially when you were taking orders from the CIA.

"Omran, we could definitely use your support. While we are confident, we can handle just about any threat, it would be better for operational security. We could use you and a few of your trusted associates to guide us around the city. I would prefer to keep our recon team to just a few operatives along with your associates. We need to keep a low profile unless absolutely necessary. So, for now, the recon team will be Trinity, James, and myself. Hopefully, you will be our primary guide. Do you have any resources that can look into the status of ISIS and their search for the Ark?" Omran thought for a moment, then said, "I have the perfect person. His name is Taha Rassam, an Iraqi professor of Near Eastern Archaeology at the Institute of Prehistory, Adam Mickiewicz University in Poznań, Poland, with field experience from Iraq. Taha is currently in Iraq, working with The National Museum of Baghdad to expand on the theory that Iraq is the Cradle of Civilization. I have been contacted a few times by members of Taha's team to smuggle in certain materials from the US that violate the secular rules of the extreme Shiite party." Trinity chimed in and said, "It's hard to believe that the looting of the museums in Iraq was over less than 48 hours after it began on April 10, 2003."

Omran shook his head. He remembered the sadness vividly he felt as his nation's national treasures were looted. In those 48 hours, over 170,000 museum pieces were stolen. Most were recovered, but Omran despaired because a new generation of Iraqis has grown up without any access to the museums that were once crowded with school children. Omran looked up, "There is a climate of open hostility toward any foreigners, especially American archaeologists. They are now forbidden to excavate in Iraq until a trove of Jewish artifacts is returned by the US government. The State Board of Antiquities is a member of a splinter Shiite party. Taha believes the US Military is just as responsible for the looting of the museums as the thugs that perpetrated the act. Their inaction was viewed as an attempt to diminish the influence of religion and Iraqi pride so democracy could be installed as a means of control. Unfortunately, the American's have some of the best excavating equipment in the world, and Taha needed access to their sophisticated sonar equipment, which we acquired for them."

"I'll reach out to my contact, Raena Alwan, to arrange a meeting with Taha and see how much he knows about ISIS' search for the Ark. If anyone can help us, it will be him. I can almost guarantee ISIS has employed staff from the museum to assist him. Let's meet outside your hotel tomorrow morning at 7am. I should have everything arranged by then." "Sounds good Omran, I can't thank you enough," said Joshua. "And one more thing, Omran, when this is all over and if we survive, I want to track down this mysterious benefactor. I want to understand just who is trying to help us and why?" Omran simply nodded, knowing that look of resolve in Joshua's eyes.

While Joshua, Trinity, and Omran continued to discuss details about the operation, Sam directed the rest of the team to load each vehicle with their weapons in the newly acquired Humvees. The team would be posing as a private security firm to blend in. While their SUVs blended in and provided some armament protection, they were strictly defensive in nature. Having the Humvees gave the team better protection from IEDs and provided superior offensive firepower.

Once the Humvees were loaded, and the team members were outfitted in their personal body armor and armaments, they headed to the safe house that Omran had secured for them. Mike, Sean, and Paulie were tasked with running back to the hotel and retrieving their personal effects. After which, they would rendezvous with the team at their base of operations.

Cafeteria Al Bajaa - Baghdad, Iraq

   Joshua, Trinity, and James sat waiting at the Cafeteria Al Bajaa drinking a glass of iced tea, waiting on the other party to arrive. It had been two days since they had met with Omran at his warehouse. Last night around 1800 hours GMT, Omran reached out and informed him that Taha had agreed to a meeting. Taha wanted to meet at the Cafeteria Al Bajaa because it was the focal point of all things intelligent in Baghdad. Omran, Raena, and Taha strolled into the cafeteria around 1230 hours. Omran spotted the team with a quick wave of Joshua's hand. Joshua, Trinity, and James stood up and extended their hands, greeting and introducing themselves as the three approached.

   Joshua started the conversation, "First, Professor Rassam, I can't thank you enough for agreeing to meet with us on short notice. It is an honor to meet you."

   "Please call me Taha. In some academic circles, titles mean everything, and I use my title as necessary to achieve my goals. Outside those circles, I understand just how little those titles mean to those that do not respect life. Based on what Omran told me so far, I believe you are fighting for life on a grand scale. Therefore, I will consider you a friend of the people of Iraq, which is why I have agreed to meet with you." Just as Taha finished his statement, the waiter walked up to take their order. In Arabic, then in perfect English, the waiter asked what they would like to order.

Taha turned to the table and asked if they didn't mind if he ordered for them. They all nodded their consent. Taha then proceeded to order their meal. After ordering, Taha turned back to the table. "Thank you for allowing me this privilege. Most foreigners who come to Iraq never get a chance to experience the true culture that is Iraq. I have taken the liberty to order a sampling of some of my favorite dishes: Kebabs, grilled meat on a stick; Dolma, stuffed spiced rice wrapped in grape leaves; Biryani, cooked rice with spices and meat/ vegetables and finally Masgoulf, which is seasoned fresh carp skewered and cooked by grilling on an outside grill. While these meals are served at just about every restaurant, I love Cafeteria Al Bajaa because of its location. Located on Mutanabbi Street near the old quarter of Baghdad. It is in the historic center of Baghdad, a street filled with bookstores and outdoor bookstalls. It was named after the 10th-century classical Iraqi poet Al-Mutanabbi. This street is well established for bookselling. It has often been referred to as the heart and soul of the Baghdad literary and intellectual community. This area of Baghdad reminds me of why I am here. My goal in Iraq is to work with the

National Museum of Baghdad to expand on the theory that Iraq is the Cradle of Civilization."

Joshua cut in, "Taha, I wanted to speak with you about your help in finding the Ark of the Covenant."

"Joshua, please. Let's talk business after we eat if you, please. Eating while discussing matters of this importance does not allow one to truly enjoy their meal."

The group continues to have conversations that mainly centered around Taha's work here in Iraq. About fifteen minutes later, the food arrived, and the table began to eat.

The conversation turned back to the Ark after they finished their meal. "Based on what I've heard, it appears that ISIS is getting close to narrowing down the coordinates for the Ark. What I fear the most are the intentions of ISIS after they find it. They are backed by Iran, and they have made it clear they want nothing less than the total destruction of Israel," said Taha.

"And if a war is started with Israel," Joshua said, "then I'm afraid it will be the start of World War III. The moment Israel is threatened, they will use nuclear missiles to strike against any target they deem necessary. The rest of the world knows this, which is why they will quickly come to the defense of Israel. If finding the Ark leads to World War III, then we must find it first."

"While I don't understand what the Ark does, I do know that its discovery will be the catalyst for national pride.

If ISIS finds it, it will be the rally point necessary to win the support of Muslim nations to go to war with Israel," said Taha. "Our nation is already fragile, and I don't think it can survive another all-out war. Secular violence has been a way of life in Iraq for as long as anyone can remember, but an all-out war if we attack Israel will be the death of Iraq. So, I will do whatever I can to assist you and your team, Joshua."

KAP-CARRÉ - Büros nahe Flughafen Tegel - Berlin, Germany
    Colonel Myers was on a video conference with the Research team in Berlin, Germany. The Committee occupied the three floors of the KAP CARRÉ - Offices near Tegel Airport. The office complex was centrally located on the city highway north of Berlin, close to Tegel Airport with a subway station in front of the building. Myers was coordinating with the Research team and the Night Stalkers to find the location of the Ark.

    "Jamie, tell me how the decryption of the codes is going?" said Myers. "As you know, Colonel, Research has been working on decoding these transmissions for almost a century." Before Jamie could continue, Myers interrupted him, "Look, Jamie, I don't need a history lesson. I just want to know how close you are to helping my team locate the Ark?"

The reality was Myers had already been briefed by his
staff. One of the traits that made Colonel Myers
successful in his military career was the fact that he
always thoroughly prepared his soldiers for their missions.
This mission wasn't any different. Colonel Myers
discovered the Committee was operating from a set of
obscure prophecies written by Nostradamus. In 1994, Enza
Massa, an Italian journalist, accidentally found an old
manuscript in Rome's Italian National Library. This ancient
manuscript, dating back to 1629, was titled Nostradamus
Vatinicia Code. It was written by Michele de Nostradame,
generally known as Nostradamus, one of the most famous
prophets that ever existed. The Committee had been
following Nostradamus since he came to their attention in
the year 1517. Like so many others, Nostradamus was
identified earlier and tracked as a potential candidate for
having the intellect necessary to receive communications
from the aliens in hibernating chambers now called the
Illuminati. Nostradamus was so brilliant that at the age of
14, he entered the University of Avignon to study medicine.
He was forced to leave after only one year due to an
outbreak of the bubonic plague. The bubonic plague was a
bacterial infection engineered by the Guardians to slow
down the growth of mankind. In 1538, an offhanded remark
about a religious statue resulted in charges of heresy
against Nostradamus. When ordered to appear before the
Church Inquisition, Nostradamus chose to leave and traveled

through Italy, Greece, and Turkey for several years. There is little known about Nostradamus during his travels. It is believed that Nostradamus experienced a psychic awakening. The reality was that Dr. Soa'limae captured Nostradamus to conduct genetic experiments to awaken dormant genes necessary to enhance his ability to receive telepathic communications from the crew.

In 1547, Dr. Soa'limae released Nostradamus after implanting false memories. Nostradamus returned to France to resume his practice of treating plague victims. After marrying and having six children, Nostradamus moved away from medicine and began studying the occult. It was during this time that he started having visions and prophecies. The writings that Enza Massa discovered in 1994 were only part of his works. The scripts that were recently found were stolen and hidden by none other than the Guardians. While these writings were not as revealing as Nostradamus' original works, their discovery put into context some original passages that made no sense.

The collection of prophecies by the Committee originated in 527AD with the inception of the Saint Catherine's Monastery in the Sinai Peninsula, Egypt. It was there, during meditation, that one of the monks received the first telepathic communications from the Aliens. The other monks wrote down the words to ensure the prophecies were captured when they realized that their brother monk was in some sort of trance. The early attempts at communication by the aliens resulted in the monks and many other prophets' inability to separate visions from reality. They had to be locked away for their own good. It didn't take long for the monks caring for the prophet to realize something extraordinary was happening. St. Antony created a special order to study these prophecies. Over the years, the purpose of the Special Order was lost to all those except the "Order" itself. The Special Order eventually left Saint Catherine's to pursue their original charter as outlined by the prophet monk. *Find the prophecies, secure them, and then follow the instructions without fail.* Those early works of the prophecy contained blueprints for the origin of the Committee. Nostradamus' original works were the most transparent communication from the aliens to date. These documents made it clear what the aliens wanted humans to do. Find critical components to the spaceship to initiate repairs. The humans that assisted in this task would travel the stars with their Gods, their creators. The prophecies were not actually prophecies. They were instructions, an operating manual of sorts. The instructions laid out a path of how to find the components. It would be centuries before the Committee would have the technology to decipher the original prophets' transponder codes, radio waves, and transmissions leading them to the ship's components.

Most everyone knew of Nikola Tesla. What people didn't realize was this research into radio technology was funded by The Committee.

1893 Tesla proposed a system for transmitting intelligence and wireless power using the earth as the medium and gave many lectures on his theory. By early 1895, Tesla was ready to transmit a signal 50 miles to West Point, New York... But in that same year, disaster struck. A building fire consumed Tesla's lab, destroying his work. The Committee believed it was the work of The Guardians that destroyed his lab to prevent the Committee from tracking the ship's components. Finally, by 1900, Nikola Tesla was able to transmit signals from New York City to West Point. Nikola's technology made it possible for the further development of shortwave radio technology versus long-wave radio transmissions. Prior to the 1920s, the shortwave frequencies above 2MHz were considered useless for long-distance communication and were designated for amateur use. The Committee was responsible for passing legislation in each country to ensure no government could figure out those transmitted codes were actually transponder codes for the ships' components. Those transmissions are called Number Stations. The Committee learned a long time ago to hide the truth in plain sight. To create conspiracy theories to ensure the facts remained hidden. No one believed the fringes of society openly for fear of being labeled a flake. So, whereas they might believe, they kept silent and allowed others to fight for the truth. The Committee used this to their advantage.

Research has been refining its methodology of decrypting what short wave radio enthusiasts worldwide call the elusive Numbers Stations. It is a name that refers to several unusual broadcasts that usually start at a particular time, though often from different locations. For the most part, the signals make no sense, and the messages are relatively random. Most think they are spy codes being transmitted by different countries. The messages are so short that there is not enough information in the broadcast to decipher them. The transmissions contain odd elements like music excerpts, a regular attention message, and a string of phonetic letters or numbers. It took Research the better part of 60 years to decrypt the randomness of the transmission to a set of longitude and latitude coordinates. The musical notes translated into a mathematical formula that created the coordinates when the letters translated into one of twenty-six letters of the alphabet. The first sixteen digits represented degrees followed by minutes then seconds going out to two digits. Unfortunately, that left Research to determine the function of the remaining eight digits of the twenty-four-digit transmission code.

Research figured with the Latitude and Longitude coordinates, they would still have enough information to find the components. The rest of the digits were written off as irrelevant. While Research had picked up other transponder transmissions, they felt locating the first component in Iraq offered them the best chance for decrypting the remaining transmissions. The Committee had engineered the First Gulf War as a cover to find the components. Unfortunately, the coordinates led to nothing but an empty spot in the desert. Under the guise of hunting for chemical munitions, the US sent Special Forces teams trying different permutations of the code to find the component. Nothing worked. Finally, The Committee pulled the plug on the mission. The ground offensive of the Gulf War ended two days after it started in 1991.

Research decided to take a different approach. Their hope is that a combination of technology and history would reveal the clues necessary to decipher the last eight remaining digits of the code. So far, the new information gathered by the archaeologist was able to determine that the component was, in fact, the legendary Ark of the Covenant. The second Gulf War was launched as a cover to ransack the Iraqi Museums. Of the items stolen, 4,795 were sealed cylinders containing ancient scrolls. It is in these cylinders that the archaeologists believed they would find the answer. It was thought the thief of these scrolls had to be someone that worked at the museum. It was simply inconceivable that this area had been found and breached by anyone who did not have an intimate insider's knowledge of the museum. The staff was investigated, but many staffers did not return, including Jassim Muhamed, the museum's former head of security. Jassim actually worked for the Committee through several cutouts. Research and archaeologists were finally able to determine how to locate Ark. The last eight digits were codes that corresponded to the phase of the moon. The time of year and alignment of Earth, Mars, and Jupiter were keys to this puzzle. When all elements were in place, it changed the coordinates to the location of the Ark. It was all theory at this point. Still, Research believes they had to go back into Iraq. If Research could verify the concept, they could use this information to find the coordinates for the other components described in the book of prophecies.

Col. Myers knew that the Ark was some sort of computer-based on the book of prophecies. Based on the predictions, it was believed to contain the knowledge of God by the unenlightened, and no human could open the Ark without going blind.

Col. Myers believed Research had finally figured out how to locate the Ark. The Committee had made it clear that they could not accept failure this time. While the terrorist action was successful in terms of causalities and creating fear, it ultimately failed to draw the US back into Iraq. The Committee wanted results and was unwilling to rely on his word that the Night Stalkers would handle the mission. Col. Myers learned early in his career not to question high-ranking officials. He witnessed too many careers ruined because an official's ego got bruised by a subordinate questioning or seeking clarification to their orders. Myers learned to say "Yes Sir" then do whatever was necessary to accomplish the mission and always support his troops. The Committee wanted an insurance policy. To that end, they needed to make a statement so profound that the American people would have no choice but to go back to Iraq in force. The Committee had ordered Myers to assassinate the President of the United States. Then the Committee could guarantee a US presence in Iraq and place a Committee operative, the Vice-President of the United States, to take over the most powerful position of the free world. Based on the book of prophecies, the time to act was now. Events had been unfolding at an alarming rate, foretelling the end of days. While Myers disagreed with the Committee on assassinating the President, he would follow orders. The Committee made him afraid. They were surrounded by an aura of power that made this experience, with high-level political figures, look like child's play.

Col. Myers terminated his connection with Jamie and asked to be contacted when he finished the decryption. Myers authorized Jamie to utilize whatever resources to finish the job in the next 72 hours. Nothing else was more important.

Undisclosed Safe House - BAGHDAD, Iraq

Thornton was sitting in the safe house, briefing his team Night Stalkers. Research had brief Thornton that ISIS (Islamic State of Iraq and Syria) controls the dig site in the wetland in southeast Iraq. Based on the updated decryption algorithm developed with the recovered scrolls, Jamie briefed Thornton that he was 95% confident the ISIS team was digging in the correct location. Col. Myers ordered to sit tight and wait on the ISIS team to find the Ark. It's better to not engage and let ISIS do the work since they were digging in the right area. ISIS had no shortage of forcefully recruited archeologists searching in several Iraqi provinces. ISIS was careful not to capture any American, British, or German archaeological teams in Iraq, not wanting to escalate international military intervention.

"Gentlemen, first and foremost, we need to recover the Ark of the Covenant. This is going to present us with a unique set of challenges. We need to continue to monitor the active dig site controlled by ISIS. We will have both satellite and drone support to alert us when the Ark is found. Wayne, your Fire Team will be tasked with providing human intelligence (HUMINT) on the site. Once found, the goal is to ambush their convoy en route. We absolutely do not want ISIS to move the Ark to a secure location. Wayne, your goal is to shadow the convoy and prepare to execute a pincer ambush. We will deploy two additional Fire Teams to support this operation with an Apache helicopter in support. The other Fire Teams will be deployed via a Black Hawk helicopter, a few kilometers in front of the convoy's route. Once all elements are in place, the Apache helicopter will take out the lead and trailing security vehicles. We can't risk damaging the Ark. Patrick, I want your snipers to disable the other vehicles with single .50 caliber shots. Wayne and Jessie, your Fire Teams will have to clear each vehicle and secure the Ark as quickly as possible. Two Black Hawks will be on station to extract your teams and the Ark on your call." The team leaders all nodded. There was no need for questions; the Night Stalkers were the best and continuously trained various combat drills to include the pincer ambush drill. Instinctively, both Wayne and Jessie checked their MTOE to ensure that CS gas was included as part of their standard equipment. This particular combat drill required a member from each team to fire CS Grenades and Flashbang rounds from their M320 grenade launcher. Disorienting the enemy was the standard operating procedure for the Night Stalkers.

"Our second problem is to find and eliminate Trinity Winters and the team of ex-Special Forces members supporting her. They are also looking for the Ark. We have already tangled with part of this team in San Diego. While we were successful and suffered no causalities, make no mistake, these guys have the same training and chewed the same dirt many of us have. Our superior technology and equipment allowed us to prevail. Yet, these guys still partially succeeded by sacrificing their lives to ensure that the terrorist did not achieve the mass causalities as planned. After losing their comrades, you can bet that Joshua's remaining team members will be even more committed to succeeding. While superior technology is our advantage, don't underestimate what these committed soldiers can accomplish. Just consider the fact that even without our resources, Trinity and Joshua have managed to arrive in Iraq and are searching for the Ark, the same as us. Research is currently monitoring all communications and conducting a satellite facial recognition search for their team members. Based on information gleaned by Research, they have approximately 11 members on their team. It's a given that they will receive support from their previous local Iraqi contacts. It's unknown if that support will include hired guns, so be prepared for everything. Zane, your team has point on Trinity and Joshua. If you cut off the head, the team will dissolve. So, if your snipers have a shot, take it. Engage the entire team but only terminate as a last resort. Don't take any unnecessary chances. Adam, your team will be the designated QRF for this operation. Any questions?" When no one responded, Thornton closed the meeting. "Team Leaders, you know the drill. I want everyone ready to go in one hour. Once prepped, go into a fifty percent team readiness posture. Dismissed."

BAGHDAD, Iraq

Paulie, James, and Bennie were in their hide position currently conducting surveillance on the ISIS archaeological dig site. Thanks to Professor Taha Rassam, the team was able to quickly locate the dig site. With over twenty archaeologists missing from the country, it was not hard to track down where ISIS was holding them at night. From there, determining the dig site location was a matter of surveilling their transportation vehicles. Joshua had only assigned part of the Fire Team Bravo to keep surveillance, hoping that the ISIS contingency found the Ark.

The team had been in place for over a week following standard operating procedures; 1 man down, one on surveillance, and one on security. On day three, Paulie spotted another team doing exactly what they were doing, watching the ISIS archaeological dig site. The other group was good. It was only by chance that Paulie detected the other team. One of their team members had slipped up. Their Operation Security (OPSEC) was based on ISIS security, not spotting them. They never assumed there might be another team out there. Something as simple as one of their guards removing the Velcro cover to check the time while invisible to the ISIS guards gave Paulie and his team the element of surprise. Joshua was motivated by finally catching a break. This other team was probably elements from the team that took out Team Charlie. Joshua cautioned Paulie not to do anything stupid and stay frosty. Time to avenge Team Charlie would come, but only after completing this mission. Joshua learned not to question the universe and to trust that things happened for a reason. They would pay. The negative karma associated with intentional acts of violence would only harm Joshua's team in the long run.

While Paulie's team continued to conduct surveillance, Joshua briefed the rest of the team on the plan. "Team, it's obvious that both teams have reached the same conclusion; let ISIS find the Ark then liberate it from them. Well, here's the change. We will let the other team ambush ISIS, then we will ambush the ambushers. We should assume they will have air support and at least two full Fire Teams with another element in support. We must also assume that they have a command element. So, the other team will have at least twenty combat troops with another five to ten support elements on the ground. We can't match those numbers, but with the element of surprise on our side and support from Omran's men, we might have a chance to not only recover the Ark but take down their team."

"Omran, we need a staging area close enough to the dig site that we can provide both ground and air support within 7 minutes from the time Paulie's team tells us to go."

"Sam, Mike, and Sean, you will be our QRF on-board the Black Hawk. Once the operation begins, you will orbit on station and provide support as required."

"Tom and Dan, you will be on the other bird. Once we confirm the engaged area of operation, the bird will drop you in a strategic sniper position and immediately dust off to provide air support. Your mission is to take out any counter-sniper elements then provide support to our ground elements."

"Mac, Trinity, and I will be the lead assault team with Paulie, James, and Bennie engaging and rolling the enemy's flank."

"Omran, I need you to gather a team of ten men broken into two Fire Teams. I need those teams mobile. So, secure a few more armored vehicles for your team. Your team will need to provide perimeter security and set up blocking positions once the attack commences."

"Let's get prepped. Remember, we have only identified one element so far. Say alert and make sure you are employing counter-surveillance protocols. Make sure you wear hats and sunglasses to block facial recognition software efforts. Remember, our cover puts us in the country for about 6 months, providing contracted security for a powerful Iraqi Minister. If we act the part, we will be invisible."

Paulie and his team continued their surveillance operation. So far as he could tell, their presence had still gone undetected. Now that they knew where to look, James had Bennie spotted three additional men in other surveillance positions. Bringing the total to four men on the opposition's surveillance teams. The dig site located in the wetlands in southeast Iraq was thought to be the biblical Garden of Eden. During Saddam Hussein's rule, the wetland was almost completely drained. The wetlands were fed by the Tigris and Euphrates rivers. The wetlands were the spawning grounds for Gulf fisheries and home to bird species such as the sacred ibis. They also provide a resting spot for thousands of wildfowl migrating between Siberia and Africa.

Saddam Hussein accused the region's inhabitants of treachery during the 1980-1988 war with Iran. He ordered dams to be built and the wetlands drained in the 1990s to flush out rebels hiding in the reeds. While the wetlands were drained, there were several reports of strand incidents occurring in the wetlands. Weird light formations, Iraqi's encountering a strange box and either going crazy or suddenly acquiring the ability to speak an unknown peculiar language. None of these reports could ever be verified because the wetlands were considered a haven for rebels. Therefore, anyone caught in that area was hunted and killed.

After he was overthrown by the US-led invasion in 2003, locals wrecked many dams to let the water rush in, and foreign environmental agencies helped breathe life back into the wetlands. The wetlands once covered 9,000 square kilometers had shrunk to just 760 sq km by 2002 before regaining some 40 percent of the original area by 2005.

Vast, remote, and bordering Iran, the wetlands have been used in recent years for drug and arms smuggling, receiving stolen goods, and keeping hostages for ransom. Saving the wetlands made the process of finding the Ark that much more difficult. The dig team had to construct a barrier around the entire site. After construction was finished, the dig site was pumped to empty the location of water. Pumps could be heard continuously running in the background to keep the area dry.

Paulie and his team had set up operations amid the wetlands. They had commandeered three bellums, long canoe-shaped boats capable of carrying 15 to 25 men. One bellum served as their sleeping and eating quarters. The other was used for their equipment storage. Finally, the last served as their observation platform. The team was outfitted in their specially designed sniper ghillie suits. James had the M21 sniper rifle as his primary weapon. At the same time, Kenny and Bennie were armed with an M4 with suppressor, and M249 SAW.

The team brought two inflatable black F470 Combat Rubber Raiding Craft boats: one primary, one backup. Both had already been inflated to use for quick extraction if the surveillance mission became compromised. They were both outfitted with the maximum 55-horsepower pump-jet propulsor, which is essentially a shrouded impeller instead of the conventional exposed propeller.

For surveillance, the team used the latest in drone reconnaissance. Paulie and his team were equipped with the latest in insect spy drones. They had five fly-like drones at their disposal. Kenny advised them not to use the drones in real-time because their transmissions could be tracked with the right equipment. The team always had two drones on the station, one on stand-by with the other two plugged into their charging station. Once a drone's storage reached capacity, it would automatically return to its home base. It would land in its designated docking/charging station and begin the process of uploading its data. Once the data was uploaded, the system would initiate the automated process of encrypting and sending a micro-burst transmission to Kenny for Arabic to English translation. If anything of importance was found, Kenny would send the team a message with the critical dialog.

The recon team still employed traditional surveillance equipment to maintain eyes on the target. If anything important was found, the drones could quickly switch the drone's mode to real-time mode to get close eyes on the target.

As part of the team preparation, Paulie quickly beefed up on his archaeological knowledge. He wanted to ensure that his team was positioned at the most optimal point for observation. Paulie learned that one of the most imperative aspects of an archaeological dig site is pinpointing and recording the locations of objects found, particularly the horizontal relationships between artifacts. The most widely used system for doing this within a place is the grid system. To accurately accomplish this, a surveying team lays out a horizontal grid over the site, and stakes with reference numbers are put into the ground at regular intervals. Paulie was very familiar with this process because of the similarities to a grid on a military map.

Over the past couple of days, the activities at the site intensified. It appeared that the dig team had finally found something interesting. All other activities within the dig site ceased except for this one grid. The dig team brought in extra pumps to vacate the water from this area. Up to an hour ago, they had been pulling out vases of various shapes and small statues. In the past hour, the dig team pulled out a large crate, 4'x 6'x 3'. Based on this finding and increased activity, Paulie ordered the drone switched into real-time surveillance mode and for James to zoom in on the crate. The crate appeared to be made of some sort of shiny metal. Paulie was surprised at how well preserved the box was, considering how the vases and statues looked when they came out of the ground.

While the dig team cleaned the uncovered crate, Paulie and the rest of the team listened to the conversation. They asked Kenny to put priority on the latest translation. It seemed that the archaeologist believed they found the crate that contained the Ark of the Covenant. The inscriptions on the container indicated that the contents were the source of all knowledge. Only the worthy could receive and interpret the message without suffering the wrath of God.

Urgently, Paulie reached out to Joshua to issue a warning that things were about to get interesting. The Ark had been found!

BAGHDAD, Iraq

ISIS loaded the crate onto a Ford F-350 Super Duty pick-up truck. The truck with the crate was one of seven in the ISIS convoy. It was located dead center of the convoy. It was guarded by two men in the front and two in the bed of the truck. The first and last trucks in the convoy were technical vehicles with Soviet-mounted machine guns. One was equipped with an NSVT 12.7×108mm heavy machine gun. The other is a PK(M)S 7.62×54mmR general-purpose machine gun. Each truck also had four men. Two in front, one on the machine gun and one ammo bearer. The second and fifth vehicles were SUVs loaded with five soldiers each. The third and fourth trucks were loaded with improvised rocket launchers. These were stolen from the Iraqi police force during a raid a few weeks earlier. The improvised rocket launchers were classified as a Multiple Rocket Launch System with a range exceeding 3,500 miles. There are two missiles loaded on each launcher. There was a total of twenty-eight men guarding the convoy, including the six men with the rocket launchers.

Wayne and his team of Night Stalkers had been following the convoy at a distance far enough away that they couldn't be spotted. They were using drones to confirm the convoys location so they could follow at a discrete distance. After about 30 minutes, when Wayne was sure of the convoy's direction, Wayne called in the strike team to set the trap. Jessie's Night Stalkers had been dropped off about 10 kilometers in front of the ISIS convoy, roughly giving his team 15 minutes to set up the ambush. The Apache had been given a new priority target based on the HUMINT from Wayne. The pilot was now three mikes out, lining his laser guidance targeting system up with the two vehicles around the center truck. The pilot switched on his NVGs because the sun was starting to set. While not quite dark, at this distance, NVGs were necessary. Based on the updated intelligence, while the lead and trail trucks had machine guns capable of taking out his Apache, the rocket launchers were his immediate threat. Flying NAP of the earth, the Apache was doing its best to fly under the radar system of the rocket launchers. At less than fifty feet off the ground, it took all the skills the pilot could muster to stay locked on target and avoid hitting anything on the ground. The pilot armed two AGM-114 Hellfire anti-tank missiles as he received a target lock indication. Unfortunately, he would have to come up to an altitude of at least 100 feet to properly fire the rockets. As soon as the Apache was at 100 feet, the pilot fired both Hellfire missiles. The pilot immediately dropped back to 50 feet and turned North to Northwest to circle the convoy setting up another shot at the technical vehicles.

The Night Stalker snipers Patrick and John had their scopes for the .50 caliber Barrett M107 rifles trained on the front and rear vehicles. When they saw the flash of the missiles launching, both fired their weapons, hitting the engine blocks without fail.

Both rocket launchers exploded into twin balls of flames. The heat emanating from the burning wreckage was beyond intense. The rocket fuel added to the already burning truck fuel. The F-350 carrying the Ark swerved around the burning truck directly in front of them. It stopped almost as quickly when the driver realized the lead technical vehicle was disabled and smoking. The ISIS soldiers in the convoy immediately reacted and launched into action. The driver of the lead troop SUV immediately rammed his SUV into the lead vehicle. They had to put some distance between themselves and the burning vehicles before the missiles exploded. After moving the disabled lead vehicle about 200 hundred yards farther down the road, the burning vehicle exploded in a shower of dirt and rock. The F350 carrying the Ark had immediately followed the SUV and put enough distance between itself and the burning vehicle that the explosion caused no damage. The rear troop SUV had executed the same maneuver on the disabled technical vehicle. The troops in the SUVs fanned out. The leader of the convoy had to admire the attackers. The ambush location was perfect. There was a steep hill flanking one side of the convoy and a deep wadi on the other. With the lead two vehicles and the rear two vehicles disabled, they had no choice but to fight their way out. Half the team deployed to the front, and the other team to the rear, preparing for the attack they knew was coming.

The Apache circled around as per his initial mission orders targeted the lead technical vehicle. Right as the pilot was locking in on the vehicle, the technical fired on the Apache. In evading the machine-gun fire, the hellfire missiles missed the vehicle. They created a crater in front of the lead vehicle instead of blowing it up. Jessie's team advanced, moving from one position of concealment to another. Just as one of Jessie's men popped up from camouflage, he was immediately cut in half by a burst from the lead technical PK(M)S 7.62×54mmR machine gun. The rest of the team quickly ducked back undercover, and the technical continued to open fire. Jessie immediately got on the radio and cursed the pilot to get back on station and destroy that vehicle. Without prompting, Patrick, one of the Night Stalker snipers, zeroed his crosshairs on the machine gunner and squeezed the trigger. Unlike being hit by a 7.62 sniper rifle which creates an entry and exit wound, a .50 caliber sniper rifle was entirely different. The machine gunner literally was ripped in half, with his torso being utterly separated from the lower half of his body. A few seconds later, the Apache circled around in response to Jessie's call for air support. The pilot opened with his 30mm M230 chain gun, taking the driver and the ammo loader, who jumped on the now vacant machine gun, out of the fight. Just as the pilot finished off his target, he spotted a streak from a shoulder-fired RPG quickly closing in on his Apache. He knew there was no chance to deploy countermeasure from this distance, so he turned his cockpit away from the RPG and banked hard to the right. Hoping he could minimize the impact of the strike. A few seconds later, the Apache was thrown forward from the effects of the blast. Alerts went off, indicating his engines were on fire. Being so low to the ground, trying to employ fire suppression systems was of no use. Crashlanding was his only option. As the Apache hit the desert floor, it immediately exploded into flames. Jessie could only watch as the Apache burned. He knew there was no hope for the pilot, but now his team could advance. On signal, two canisters of CS gas were launched from M203s, followed by two more CS grenades, then white smoke grenades. As the team continued to close in on the enemy, two Flashbang grenades were launched, which signaled the rest of the team to engage and destroy the remaining enemy.

Paulie and his team watched with a professional eye as the other team dispatched the ISIS soldiers. It was a perfect pincher ambush. While the ISIS soldiers were good, it didn't matter. They were still systemically picked off, one by one. Ten minutes and it was all over. All the ISIS soldiers were dead. The Ark was secure, and the team was preparing to move it out of the ambush zone. They collected their wounded and dead on the way out. It was a successful mission, even though over one-third of the team's men were no longer mission capable.

The Night Stalkers were all loaded in their Humvees and heading to their extraction location. Wayne tasked two of his men to drive the truck carrying the Ark vs. moving it to one of their vehicles to save time.

* *

"Delta-One, this is Delta-Three. We are on station and hunting for targets." Tom had just radioed Joshua. He and Dan were looking for the enemy sniper team. They were armed with a .50-caliber sniper rifle vs. their 7.62mm sniper rifle. When the counter-ambush happened, they would get one shot at eliminating the enemy snipers before stopping Delta-One and Delta-Two. Tom knew his team did not have the manpower to survive a lengthy firefight. He and Dan were the combat multiplier. Surprise was the other. As Tom scanned for the enemy sniper team, he smiled, thinking only Joshua would have the balls to initiate an ambush on the ambushers. In truth, it was their only play if they wanted a shot at recovering the Ark. He would not let his team down.

"Delta-Two, this is Delta-One. We are set and ready to initiate the ambush. The claymore mines are in place, ready to take out the lead Humvee."

"Roger that Delta-Two. We are trailing the convoy transporting the Ark. ETA to your location five mikes. We can confirm there are seven able body tangos with two possible still able to fire a weapon."

"Acknowledged," said Joshua. "Delta-One Actual out."

"Delta-Four, Delta-Five, confirm your locations over," said Joshua.

"Delta-One, this is Delta-Four. We are half a click to your northeast. The blocking position is now secure."

"Delta-One, this is Delta-Five. We have the southern road secure."

"Roger. All teams, this is Delta-One actual, stay alert. Things are about to get hot." Then Joshua repeated a phrase he always said right before each battle, "Expect nothing, be prepared for everything." With that, the net went dead as the team prepared to engage.

The Night Stalkers yet again had accomplished the mission, thought Jessie. Jessie was riding shotgun with his M4 pointed outward. While the mission was a success, he never underestimated Murphy. Murphy was the master of fucking up anyone's day just when they thought the mission was over. Mike was driving with Sean in the gun turret operating the M60 machine gun. Blane was in the back, serving as the team medic working on the two wounded men. Just as Mike rounded the next bend in the road, the earth exploded around their Humvee. The M18A1 claymore mine delivers spherical steel ball bearings over a sixty-degree fan-shaped pattern that is two meters high and fifty meters wide. The ball bearings can travel up to two hundred and fifty meters. Mac knew these vehicles would be armored, so the mines were placed about fifty meters on each side of the road to maximize the damage.

Jessie immediately ducked below the dashboard of the Humvee. The pain in his right arm told him he wasn't fast enough. The vehicle was thrown into the air about five feet before it settled back to earth. As in all combat situations, time seemed to slow down. The effect was explained to Jessie during one of his martial arts training sessions as a Team Seal Six member. His Bak Mei Sifu stated that all irrelevant thoughts are suppressed when the brain focuses on survival only. The brain is powerful beyond imagining. We only utilize a fraction of its potential. Your martial training will help you learn to focus that power through physical training. I will introduce you to the Tachy Psyche effect. While it will take you years to master, listen well because this will save your lives one day. For someone affected by tachypsychia, time perceived by the individual lengthens, making events appear to move in slow-motion. Tachypsychia is induced by a combination of high levels of dopamine and norepinephrine, usually during periods of great physical stress or in a violent confrontation. Based on your chosen profession, you will see many violent conflicts.

Jessie saw Mike trying to move the Humvee out of the kill zone to no effect. They were hit with multiple claymore denotations. A tactic he had employed numerous times in his career. This immediately told him a lot about his attackers. They were American or American trained. Based on Thornton's brief, this could only be Joshua's team of ex-military guys. Jessie mentally told Thornton *his mission was a bust because Joshua's team was still in the fight by virtue of this attack*. He knew his team was also in trouble if they didn't get immediate support. With the Apache down, that was unlikely. Through the haze of the explosion, Jessie saw that Blane was uninjured, but the same could not be said for Mike. The steel ball-bearings from the claymore had ripped through his body as if he was paper. What was left of Mike had slid down inside of the Humvee from the gun turret.

Just as Jessie finished taking an inventory of his men, he turned to see a soldier holding an AT4 aimed at his head. Knowing the armor integrity was compromised by the claymore detonations, Jessie knew the AT4 would be the end of his team. Jessie had time to say two words before the AT4 was fired. "Get Out!". The act of yelling and action were simultaneous. Both Mike and Blane didn't question their leader. They both jumped out just as the AT4 slammed into the front windshield of the Humvee. The explosion aided all three soldiers in their escape effort by throwing them several feet from the vehicle.

Jessie laid on the ground, trying to shake the effects of the explosive concussion from his brain and ringing ears. In a matter of seconds, the source of their protection could have turned into a casket. He could only hope that Blane and Mike listened to him and escaped.

Just as Jessie and his team were recovering, Joshua, Mac, and Trinity lobbed Flashbang grenades. Jessie's team, already dazed and confused from the AT4 explosion, covering their eyes and ears was next to impossible when they saw the grenades bounce next to each of them. Joshua, Mac, and Trinity were like angels of death.

Matthew 26:52 Those who use the sword will die by the sword. Then Jesus said to himself, *Put your sword back into its place*. Jessie always liked that bible verse. He was a warrior and would have like to have been there to tell Jesus, *I would rather die by the sword.* With that thought, Jessie looked up into the eyes of a warrior he could only admire. *A warrior with the conviction and skill to give him a warrior's death.* With that last thought in a 5.56mm, round entered his skull between his eyes.

"Trinity, are you alright?" For a moment, Trinity did not respond to Joshua. She just stared at the soldier she had just killed, who died with a smile on his face, as if

251

he welcomed the sweet release that only death could bring. She wondered what kind of life he had lived to smile at death's door. "Yes, Joshua. I'm fine." With that, she turned and followed Joshua and Mac as they approached the F350 carrying the Ark. Trinity thought again just how precious life was. In a matter of seconds, they had killed six soldiers. Trinity was severely shaken when she watched Mac put two rounds into the wounded soldiers. Joshua saw her reaction and hesitation.

Joshua quickly ran back to her. "Trinity, we don't have time for you to think about what happened just now. Those two men were the bad guys doing their job. Given an opportunity, they would gladly put a 5.56 mm round in the back of your skull. We must secure the Ark, and we don't have time, resources, or the luxury to ask if those men were a threat or not. If one of those men were me or any of my men, you could guarantee, we would keep fighting until our last breath. Now let's get moving." She only hoped that what they were doing was right and gave meaning to Robbie's death.

After engaging with ISIS, Wayne had told Thornton to stay with the Ark to help secure it. When he saw Jessie's vehicle hit, he immediately radioed Thornton asking for a status update on their ETA.

"Wayne, hang tight. We just ran into a little trouble. It shouldn't take long to deal with, ETA 10 minutes to your location." With that, the line went dead. He hoped his support would arrive in time. He could hear the firefight around the bend in the road.

"Hey Boss," called Joey. "We have a vehicle closing in on us rapidly from the rear. Is it friend or foe?"

"It's foe," said Wayne. "You are free to engage." With that, Joey opened up with a heavy machine gun he acquired from the destroyed ISIS vehicle.

Patrick, seeing the predicament his team was in, opened fire on the approaching vehicle. Just like any good sniper. One shot, one kill. In this case, the vehicle chasing Wayne immediately came to a dead stop as his .50 caliber round tore through the engine block. Patrick then centered this sniper rifle on the vehicle occupants.

Knowing what just happened, Paulie didn't waste any time. He ordered everyone out of the Humvee and continued to close the distance to the F350 carrying the Ark using Individual movement techniques or IMTs. He knew there was a sniper out there trying to engage. His team could do nothing about the sniper, but the enemy approaching them from the back of the F350 was their immediate threat. Paulie had briefed his team to only engage if they had a clear shot. Damage to the Ark had to be avoided at all costs. As his squad ducked behind cover, he knew it was just a matter of time before the enemy sniper acquired his men.

Tom saw the muzzle flash from the enemy sniper rifle that had taken out Paulie's vehicle and directed Dan to that position. They both trained their weapon's scope on that site to eliminate the snipers. Tom knew based on sniper doctrine that the enemy snipers would be operating in pairs just like they were. Tom also knew time was running out for his team. Mac just reported he was hit in his body armor by a large caliber weapon. Tom was grateful that Omran was able to upgrade the team's body armor to Level IV. Giving them the ability to stop AP (Armor Piercing) rounds that typically blow right through level III plates. Level IV will stop M2AP (black tip) .30-06 rounds, containing a VERY hard steel penetrator. These rounds were often found undamaged after punching through up to a 1/2 inch of steel. The level IV ceramics erode and yaw this round, increasing its frontal area and making it easy for the backing material to catch it. If not for the upgrade and Mac moving, he would now be dead. As it stood, he would still need medical attention. Tom knew his team's luck wouldn't last much longer. Shots to the head rendered any type of body armor useless. Mac had been lucky. He wouldn't get a second chance.

"Second target acquired Tom," said Dan.

"Roger, Dan. Target acquired. Fire in three."

In three seconds, both Tom and Dan fired, sending twin 7.62mm rounds downrange. They were at the limits of their effective range at 900 meters, but they had no choice. However, it did not matter as both rounds were true, and both enemy snipers were neutralized.

"Delta-One, this is Delta-Three, enemy snipers neutralized," said Tom. Now to see if they could do anything about the machine gunner pinning Paulie's team down.

Thornton was cursing himself. They had lost precious time eliminating the two blocking positions. Still, they were now only three minutes from engaging the enemy attacking Paulie. He was not happy with the sitreps coming in. Wayne reported that Jessie's entire team had been eliminated. Patrick and John both dropped off the net, which could only mean one thing. The Blackhawks were inbound. ETA 8 minutes. One way or another, this would all be settled in ten minutes.

Paulie was grateful for his snipers, Tom and Dan. They just eliminated the machine gunner allowing his team to advance. He could now see Delta-One approaching as planned. Paulie's relief was quickly replaced with curses to Murphy. A heavily armored Humvee had just come over the ridgeline and started to engage with a mounted M60 machine gun. The soldiers in the vehicle dismounted and used the cover of the mounted M60 machine gun to engage his team.

Seeing Paulie's predicament, Joshua knew the task of neutralizing the soldiers in the F350 now fell entirely on his shoulders. With Mac wounded, that would be difficult, but difficult was the middle name of all special operators. Just as he was relaying instructions to Trinity and Mac, weapons opened up on their position from their flank. They were forced to take cover on the opposite side of the burning Humvee.

Seeing his opportunity, Wayne ordered the driver to floor it. If they were going to reach the extract point, they had to act now. The birds were five mikes out.

Joshua was screaming into his mic for Tom to take out the vehicle, but he received no answer in response. Tom and Dan were now running for their lives. One of the approaching Blackhawks had veered toward their location. Before Tom and Dan started their E&E maneuvers, he managed to get off one shot at the escaping F350. Unfortunately, his 7.62mm round did not have the same stopping power as the counter sniper's .50 caliber weapons. His round was true, but the vehicle kept rolling which meant, it was armored reinforced. The Blackhawk engaging them was equipped with ESSS (External Stores Support System), which consists of two external wing-like assemblies attached to the airframe above the cargo compartment doors. Sixteen Hellfire missiles were mounted on the ESSS. Four had just been fired at their previous location. Luckily, Tom and Dan picked a position that was surrounded by large rocks. Even so, they were effectively out of the fight. It would take at least two to five minutes to dig themselves out from the rocks that now covered them.

Joshua called their Blackhawk in to provide air support. It took out the armored Humvee that engaged his position, but the F350 was now out of range. Their

Blackhawk managed to get off another three Hellfire missiles to support Paulie's team before it was damaged and forced to leave the area of operation trailing smoke. It was enough because a few minutes later, Paulie reported that his sector was all clear.

"All nets, sitrep over.", stated Joshua.

"This is Delta-Two, KIA - James."

"This is Delta-Three, currently digging out from the debris, but all okay."

"This is Delta-Four, two KIA's, three WIA's." Hearing Omran's voice brought relief to Joshua, but it also meant they broke through the roadblocks.

After a few seconds, Delta-One repeated this call to Delta-Five. "Delta-Five, sitrep over." Not hearing anything meant one of two things: either their comms were down or more casualties. "Delta-Two, investigate Delta-Five and report back."

"This is Delta-One. We still have to secure our location with one more sweep but will join Delta-Four once finished."

Joshua, Mac, and Trinity advanced towards the remains of the enemy position in a classic wedge formation. Trinity looked over at Mac to see if he was alright. She knew he was in pain, but he kept going as if nothing had happened. When they checked each body, all were still minus one. Joshua moved towards the one left alive. Mac and Trinity approached the others to confirm they were dead. Joshua kicked the weapon out of reach of the injured soldier as he tried to aim his weapon. Joshua could see his injuries were fatal, but that did not mean this soldier was any less dangerous. After relieving the soldier of his weapons, Joshua knelt to see if the soldier might give him anything in his last dying breath.

"You think you have won, don't you?" said the dying soldier.

"No, I don't," said Joshua. "We both have lost a lot of good men here, and for what?"

"We still won. The Ark is in our possession now, and in case you haven't figured it out yet. We took out your men in San Diego. Soldiers like you are pathetic. You fight for a cause, ignorant of why you are even fighting. Just like your men here today. Their blood is on your hands."

Joshua did all he could not to take out his Glock and end the existence of this miserable excuse of a life. Joshua watched as he coughed up more blood.

"I might not know what's going on here, but my team died saving a lot of lives. In that, you failed. Even if we don't understand the bigger picture, we save lives, and that's what matters to us.", said Joshua.

Looking up at Joshua, the soldier weakly laughed. "Ignorant to the very end. Our lives were worth the Ark. If you only …." Thornton never completed his last thought as the light faded from his eyes.

Directorate Headquarters - Undisclosed Location Outside of Roanoke, Virginia

Colonel Myers stared at the sixty-inch flat-screen TV scanning between the various national news outlets displayed in the PiP (Picture-in-picture) mode. They all were reporting on the assassination of the President of the United States. It occurred at 14:08 EST while the President was giving a commencement speech at the University of Maryland. The agencies reported it was a single bullet to the head, decapitating the President. So far, there have been no leads. Col. Myers could only shake his head. He and the men and women under his command knew exactly what happened. When the Night Stalkers reported the successful recovery of the Ark, the Committee gave Myers the go-ahead to assassinate the President. Myers personally took the headset from his communication officer and released the restraints holding "Death" back with that command. With each mission, Myers was growing more and more concerned with Daniels losing his humanity. All Special Forces Operators walked a thin line between humanity and the monster within. It was the camaraderie between the team that kept the beast at bay. That's why so many soldiers could not cope with society when they returned home from war. No one understood their pain. It was even worse for the spouse of those soldiers watching their partner, who used to be the most loving and caring, now walk through life unfeeling. A powder keg of emotional feeling just waiting to explode. When Myers was stationed at Fort Bragg, orders were issued that all returning Special Operators undergo transitional therapy before returning to their families. While Myers did not know current statistics, the statistics back in 2002 were bad enough. In one six-week spree, four Army wives were murdered by their husbands or ex-husbands. There were 832 victims of non-fatal domestic violence between 2002 and 2004 at Fort Bragg alone. The unit, the friendships forged in blood, were the only people that understood the living Hell that occupied every waking and sleeping moment of their lives. Daniels refused to work with anyone. All his missions were solo. Since the Trinity mission failure, Daniels came closer and closer to becoming a monster on every assignment. The Melina Chávez mission only underscored that point. It was only a matter of time before Daniels, a homicidal maniac, would need to be put down, but for now, that day hadn't come.

Grimm went radio silent as per SOP after the successful execution of his mission. The President's security detail had no chance against someone like Grimm. The Secret Service Snipers used the M24 Sniper Rifles with an effective range of 800 meters. They just didn't plan on dealing with a sniper that could hit a target from a mile away. That's one of the reasons Grimm loved his .50

caliber sniper rifle. Not only was it effective, but it also gave him a chance to escape the area of operation. The authorities were always too slow in expanding their search corridor.

Grimm had been on MD 295 for the past hour heading to Linthicum Heights, MD. Traffic was always a nightmare in the greater Washington, DC area. He had a self-storage locker there, in which to store his tactical gear and sniper weapon. Once secured, Grimm started down the scenic route along the coast back to Chesapeake Beach. If stopped, which he knew would eventually happen, he had a valid excuse for choosing his path back home. While this route would add an additional one and a half hours, going the most direct route would add four hours. Roadblocks and vehicle inspections were a definite with the death of the President. His cover story was intact with hotel receipts from a hotel in Delaware. The vehicle he was driving had been driven to and from Delaware then dropped off in Linthicum Heights just in case someone decided to dig deeper into his story. A suitcase was packed with dirty clothes to also create a plausible background cover.

Colonel Myers was not happy, not one bit. Giving the order to assassinate the President of the United States was not something he thought he would be signing up for when he agreed to take command of the Directorate. With the assassination of the President, Vice-President Bill Sartingson would be sworn in as the forty-fifth President of the United States. The artifact recovered in Iraq had triggered a new phase in how the Committee operated. Their past actions were subtle manipulations. Things were changing, and he needed to understand why.

Myers resolved to himself; the new world order would be better. It just had to be. His many years serving in the U.S. Military and countless soldiers and friends dying proved democracy wasn't the answer. While being a soldier who follows orders, Col. Myers also questioned orders that endangered and/or killed his men. While the mission to retrieve the Ark was a success, he had lost two-thirds of his Night Stalkers. That kind of causality rate was unacceptable. Replacing the team members would not be easy, but the recruiting process has already started. Training the new Night Stalkers would be another story entirely.

Myers needed to meet with the Committee. He asked for an unprecedented face-to-face meeting with the Committee. To his surprise, they agreed. He would be picked up for the meeting in two days. The Committee had its own security detail, arrangements needed to be made.

Chesapeake Beach, MD

Trinity was tucked in the shadows waiting on Daniels to arrive. She had been preparing for this moment for two years. To Trinity, her life had been on hold, waiting for this moment. Her training with Joshua, honing herself into a lethal weapon. She had been following Daniels for the past week, making sure she understood his movements, patterns and making sure no one was with him. She was now confident that Daniels was alone, living in this two-bedroom flat on the edge of town off Old Colony Cove Rd. There is complete visibility to potential combatants, easy regress routes, and two nondescript vehicles: one in front of the flat and one in the rear.

As Daniels walked from his driveway to the house, he paused as if sensing something was amiss. When he didn't see any danger, he finally moved on with one last glance in the dark alleyway. Joshua had said, "Never underestimate special forces/covert operatives. The most experienced means they have developed a sort of sixth sense that alerts them of impending danger. It is how they survive. Those who do not develop this skill die young." Trinity recognized that that is what caused Daniels to pause. As Daniels resumed his walk toward the flat, Trinity slowly moved out of the shadows behind the old tree and eased into a steady pace following Daniels.

Daniels immediately spotted Trinity. Instead of going to his flat, he led Trinity to an area beside his flat, recognizing another professional. This wasn't a chance meeting. He wanted to have plenty of space to deal with whomever it was. Listening to the person's cadence, he quickly discerned two things:

1) this professional was a woman

2) this woman flowed with a grace that denoted this person has martial arts training.

Daniels learned a long time ago the folly of believing a woman can't be as dangerous as a man. Many men have been killed making that foolish assumption.

As Daniels entered the clearing, he immediately scanned the area looking to see if this woman had any other partners in hiding. Not spotting any, Daniels turned around to confront the mysterious person.

"So, who do I have the honor of meeting? Do you think you're good enough to put me down where so many others have failed finally?" Trinity didn't respond. Instead, she pulled back her hood and removed her hat. Daniels just stared at Trinity, not believing that the gods had finally answered his prayers. The only person he had failed to eliminate was standing before him. Daniels smiled, knowing that his name and reputation as the Grimm Reaper would be intact again. Trinity inwardly smiled. Joshua had told her, let the other person be overly confident. Don't let them taunt you into making a mistake. Look through them as if they don't matter. Keep an expansive view. Take everything in.

"Finally, you bitch! It's time for you to join your dead son. For this honor, I will not even use a weapon. I want to watch the life slip out of you while I strangle you with my bare hands." With that, Daniels removed his shoulder holster, which contained his Glock and two knives hidden in sheaths behind his back, then promptly launched himself at Trinity.

Not having time to think, Trinity did what Joshua trained her to do. Don't try and fight force with force. Bend like the reed in the wind. Flow with the opponent's strength. The fist intended for Trinity's face met only air. Trinity lifted her right arm and made contact with Grimm's right cross punch while stepping to the left to move off the direct line of attack. Using his momentum, Trinity moved to her left, delivering a palm strike to Grimm's ribcage.

Stepping back to gain a slight separation, Grimm quickly reevaluated Trinity. While not permanently damaged, Grimm knew his side would be sporting a nasty bruise for a few weeks. Not waiting to help her get overly confident, Grimm launched into a series of roundhouse kicks, spinning back kicks. While the kicks did not land, they served their purpose of distracting her. With the last roundhouse kick with his right leg, Grimm sank low and delivered a back sweep with his left leg that caught Trinity's lead leg. The force of the sweep took Trinity down. As Trinity went down, she instinctively tucked her chin and slammed her right arm down with the palm flat to absorb the impact of the fall. Grimm sensing an advantage, quickly got up from the sweep and reached down to trap Trinity and end this. Instead, he received a series of kicks to the face as Trinity performed a perfectly executed windmill maneuver.

Trinity was now in a crouched fighting stance. With Grimm shaking his head, Trinity used this opportunity to attack. Using her right foot, she stepped on Grimm's left thigh and pushed off. She then flipped over Grimm placing her hand on his back for support, scissored her left leg around Grimm's throat. With the momentum of the flip, Grimm had no choice but to go down as he was flipped backward, landing on his back.

Not giving Trinity a chance to continue the attack, Grimm rolled two times to his left trading space to provide him with the time once again to recover and regroup. This time Grimm moved in with measured steps, knowing he could no longer make any mistakes. As he closed the distance, he launched into a series of strikes. Trinity effectively blocked them all. Joshua had promised Trinity he would not interfere as he watched from the tree line. A promise he would keep as long as Trinity's life was not in mortal danger. He trained her too well to let his ego get her killed; however, as Joshua watched her moving, he relaxed. She was magnificent. Everything that Grimm threw at her she countered then gave it right back to him three-fold. It didn't matter if it was a hand or knee. Trinity was a feather quietly smothering the energy of a raging bull. Joshua settled back into his watch position. Trusting in the warrior he had trained but prepared to take Grimm out if Trinity went down. He would deal with the consequences of intervention if necessary.

Trinity was locked into a battle for her life, and she knew it. She was calm in the center of the storm. Time slowed for Trinity, like the first time she experienced this sparring with Joshua. She chased it in subsequent sparring sessions but never quite achieved it. Joshua told her to be patient. In time, learning to control Tachypsychia would be like breathing. While breathing happens automatically, you can increase or decrease your breathing at will. In Tachypsychia, just let it happen. In time you will learn to increase its effects to your advantage.

Being in a Tachypsychia state puts a lot of stress on one's body. At this point, Trinity's adrenal medulla was automatically producing large quantities of the hormone epinephrine (aka adrenaline) directly into her bloodstream. Her heart rate increased by two hundred forty beats per minute. Her bronchial passages dilated, permitting higher absorption of oxygen. Her body was dumping huge quantities of glucose into her bloodstream, allowing the body to generate extra energy. Her pupils also dilated, allowing more light to enter, creating visual exclusion. In essence, allowing greater focus, but unfortunately, resulting in the loss of peripheral vision.

Every punch that Grimm threw. Every kick, knee, or elbow was met with a block as if Trinity had seen each move a thousand times. When Grimm came hard at her, she redirected his energy. Use it against him. She was relaxed, calm. Then it became obvious, Grimm was slowing down, losing energy. His moves became desperate. He then made the last mistake of his life. Grimm had just returned to his feet after having been thrown. He knew he had to end this fast because he was losing the fight. Daniels cursed himself for discarding his knives. So, without shame, he picked up a nearby tree branch. Grimm resolved to himself that this would end in the next few seconds with her skull being smashed in.

He came at Trinity and swung with everything he had. Time was barely moving; Trinity could count the sweat beads rolling down Grimm's forehead. She quickly ducked the swing as if the club wasn't moving at all. As Grimm came back with his counter swing, Trinity came back up from her duck and struck Grimm with a right palm strike to the heart. Daniels stopped in mid-swing and dropped the branch. He blinked several times and stared blankly ahead. Finally, his vision settled onto Trinity. He tried to say something but only managed to cough up blood. Trinity's strike cracked one of the ribs pushing both broken ends into this beating heart. The blood immediately started pumping out of his heart into his chest. Daniels collapsed onto both his knees. Each beat bringing him closer to death.

Trinity looked down at Daniels and said, "my son Robbie sends his regards." With that, Trinity turned and left Daniels there to spend his last moments of life reflecting on who just killed him.

When Trinity turned around, she saw Joshua walking toward her. Without saying a word, they embraced, then turned and walked away.

Hill Flats - Washington, DC|Bellinzona, Switzerland

Senator Ryles sent a secure courier to Joshua's residency. The message was an invitation to meet with Senator Graham at this house in Washington, DC. He wanted to discuss their role in foiling the recent terrorist attacks. Even though those operations weren't sanctioned, he wants to compensate the families of the soldiers who perished defending this country. The message laid out the logistical details of meeting a private helicopter to transport them to Reagan International Airport. From there, a limo would take them to his residency. Both Joshua and Trinity were invited to attend this meeting.

Col. Myers had flown for the past ten hours, finally landing in Zurich, Switzerland. After another two hours driving, he arrived in Bellinzona, Switzerland. The final destination was Sasso Corbaro Castle on the other end of town. Myers was impressed with the location for its defensible position. The castle had 360 degree visibility. The only possible attack vector would be by air. To counter that, Myers spotted a mobile air defense unit located on the castle's east side. There was also a helicopter sitting in the space next to the mobile air defense unit crew nearby. Probably for quick evacuation of the Committee. In addition to the air defense mobile unit, armed security teams were guarding the castle walls. The teams included snipers and US-made Stringers or Man-Portable Air-Defense missiles. There were also roving teams on the ground walking in teams of three. One of the three men handled the reins of a K9. This place was secure with only one road leading to the castle, which was blocked by two Humvees with mounted M60 machine guns.

"Take a seat, Joshua and Trinity. There's a lot to talk about, and time is short. I know this meeting is unorthodox, but you and your team have proven resourceful despite the odds against you. You have stumbled onto a global war that spans centuries."

Col. Myers was escorted to a heavily guarded room. Once inside, the man sitting at the head of the table told him to take a seat. "Col. Myers, for the benefit of all that is here, we will not use names. Arrayed before you are some of the most influential people in the world. On our command, we topple governments. Global stock market increases and decreases with a push of a button. All the wealth in the world is immaterial to what we are about to discuss with you today. Col. Myers, you have joined an organization that has been fighting a global war that spans centuries."

"I don't understand, Senator Ryles. How can this war span centuries?" said Trinity.

"Please be patient Trinity, I have a story to tell you, and most of it, you will probably not believe. So much has happened over the years that I've lost faith in this world. Your team has shown me that maybe I need to re-evaluate my views. First, and most scandalous, I am an alien from another galaxy. My race is known as the Sanarians." When Kelsey saw the look of disbelief on their faces, he quickly added. "This body is a clone. Over the centuries, my team has adopted our clone bodies to blend in with the current evolution of humanity. My consciousness is transferred from my host body, hidden for protection, to my new clone body. My spaceship, the Alpheratz, crash-landed on Earth over 350,000 years ago."

"We have received our charter from ancient prophecies describing an alien race that needed our help to return to the stars. In exchange, we would be elevated and given powers beyond imagination, including our return to the stars with our creators."

"Wait a second, Sir. You mean these aliens created us?" said Col. Myers.

"Yes, you heard me correctly, Joshua. Our technology evolved the original chimpanzee during the "Miocene" period into what you have now evolved to, Homo Sapiens. While my team fought to prevent this evolution of man, other members of the crew felt differently. We wanted to give this planet time to evolve naturally and never experience the eon-long war with our ancient enemy. In truth, what you have evolved into are hybrid-Sanarians."

The next Committee member picked up the narrative. "By evolving mankind, it was their hope, we would eventually be able to help the aliens repair their technology to go back home. Unfortunately, the captain of our ship stole certain technology that would have allowed this to have happened tens of thousands of years ago. They were forced to evolve mankind without the help of their advanced technology. We are, in fact, their children hybrid-Sanarians."

"That's impossible, Ma'am.", said Col. Myers.

"If fact, it makes a lot of sense, Trinity. Think about it," Kelsey continued. "The human genome contains around twenty thousand genes. The DNA that encodes proteins accounts for only about 1.2 percent of the total genome. The other 98.8 percent is known as non-coding DNA. Over the centuries, we tracked the work of our ship's doctor. This non-coding DNA is mainly Sanarian. When they turned on this DNA in the past, it led to monsters that had to be put down. The great flood that is referred to in the bible was our efforts to destroy these monstrosities."

"We have been fighting our renegade crew over the centuries to keep mankind from evolving to the point where your technology could assist them in repairing our ship.

"The alien's captain that fought mankind's evolution has been responsible for some of the worst so-called natural disasters in our history. They created Smallpox, which killed over 300 million people in the 20th century. The Spanish Flu killed between 50 and 100 million people in two years. The Bubonic plague eliminated 75 million people. Malaria still kills about 2 million people every year. The list keeps going on. Col. Myers, you might find the Committee's orders hard to fathom at times, but the nature of our enemy requires us to be just as ruthless. No matter how many people we kill in the achievement of our goals. Those deaths pale in comparison to what they will do to keep us from helping our creators."

"You're a monster, Kelsey.", said Trinity. How can you believe, after listening to your confessions of mass genocide, that we could possibly ever help you?"

"I'm not proud of our actions. I truly believed that the end justified the means. At first, before humans evolved, it was easy. When mankind lived in filth, it was easy to think of you as a subspecies. AIDS was our last attempt at stopping mankind from evolving. As of late, I have come to think that our strategy was in error. I am not asking for your forgiveness for my actions. The global threat was just too great from our ancient enemy. You might think me a monster. I pray you never have to experience the Xandurans. My efforts culled the human population at critical points of your evolution. Meeting the Xandurans will be nothing short of total annihilation for this planet."

"Col., with the recovery of the Ark, our mission has moved to a new phase. Based on what we have read, the Ark is the ship's Artificial Intelligence for their computer system. With the AI, we now have the means to locate their spaceship, wake our creators, and fulfill the purpose we were originally created for."

"Trinity and Joshua, you might not like me or my methods, but they have kept this planet safe for the past 350,000 years. We have been mankind's protectors or guardians. Concepts like Good vs. Evil, Light vs. Dark, God vs. Satan, and Heaven vs. Hell evolved from what started as mutiny with my crew. They wanted to return home without regard for what would befall this planet. Over the centuries, our efforts to keep mankind safe have been associated with all things negative in religion. The Committee's goal has been to enlighten mankind. Their efforts have been associated with all things good. Now, I must make a choice. Either unleash the next plague, which will be a global pandemic of the Avian Flu, or seek help for the first time from mankind."

"The be truthful, the Committee, also known as the Illuminati, has been manipulating mankind for centuries. They are the tools of my renegade crew. Moving mankind to this point in mankind's history. They will be protected from any plague we unleash. They will safely secure themselves in their bunkers with their armies and scientists and be in a better position to implement their objectives without interference from a decimated world population. Without any knowledge of what's at stake and without the backing of your government's resources, your team has done more to hinder the Committee than our efforts. I polled my fellow crew members, and we agreed, we would like your help. Natural evolution has truly created a new species unknown to our galaxy. You might be the answer to helping us defeat our ancient enemy."

"Col., while we have the means to locate the spaceship, without recovering other key ship components, we will not accomplish our goal. You, Col., are now tasked with recovering three additional components. Over time, these components became the things of myth and central to religions throughout the world. The Holy Grail, which is the access key to the ship's navigational system. The Spear of Destiny, which is the decipher key for the communication's array. Finally, Pandora's Box is the matter/anti-matter energy source that powers the star-drive."

"I need your help to stop the Committee from recovering these ship components. While we tried to prevent mankind from evolving to this point, the fact is, you have. Now the question is, do you willingly join us in the intergalactic war or get used by my crew to simply repair our ship. We will leave your planet to be destroyed by our enemy. To influence the behavior of my old crewmates, I must have leverage. We need to recover these components before they do. I control the black ops budget for the United States. I will provide you with unlimited funding, plus any additional resources you might need. Unfortunately, until we reach a certain point, I can't bring the world governments in at this point. This world is not unified, and a discovery of this magnitude will only lead to global conflict."

Trinity and Joshua wouldn't have believed Senator Kelsey Ryles if not for the fact they were standing in the sanctuary staring at the bodies of several aliens in hibernation chambers.

Col. Myers might not have believed the Committee if not for the Ark he was presently staring at. Removed from the container, it was apparent the Ark was not of this world. Especially when one of the Committee members approached the Ark, used a keypad with alien symbols, and punched in a sequence. Suddenly, the AI. Came to life and started speaking in a language that could only be described as not of this world.

The end

Join the Trinity fan club to receive samples chapters from the upcoming book, "Trinity - The Search."